Saint Augustine Sisterhood

Eleanor Tremayne

Scotoma Books Publishing—Saint Augustine, FL
Paperback ISBN: 978-1-7323245-6-5
Hardcover ISBN: 978-1-7323245-5-8
Library of Congress Control Number:
Title: *Saint Augustine Sisterhood*
Author: Eleanor Tremayne
Digital distribution | 2024
Paperback | 2024
Hardcover | 2024

Cover Art by Tarn Ellis

Dedication

Marlene Joslin and Flo

Several years ago, during one of our early morning walks, my good friend Marlene Joslin suggested that I meet a friend of hers, Sunshine Dzierzynski Wilson, a Gypsy dancer that she suggested would be the perfect model for my latest novel *Saint Augustine Sisterhood*. Marlene was absolutely spot on.

Sunshine was exactly what I needed to include in this novel to express the eternal bond that exists between a group of incredibly talented ladies.

I dedicate Saint Augustine Sisterhood to Marlene Joslin for always being there when I truly needed a soul sister.

Gypsy Pirate Players of Saint Augustine
Photo credit: Sunshine Dzierzynski Wilson

Acknowledgment

Without an editor the aspirations of most writers would never be fulfilled. Dr. Mary Sisney, a retired English Professor from California State Polytechnic University, Pomona, my graduate advisor and author of *A Redlight Woman Who Knows How to Sing the Blues,* graciously agreed to be my editor for *The Agape Journey,* and once again for *Sisterhood.* It is with great appreciation that I thank Dr. Mary Sisney for continuing to support my creative writing.

Introduction

At a time when women should be soaring through glass ceilings, there are still too many that are standing on sticky floors unable to escape a stereotype existence.

Pirates and Gypsies throughout history are associated with negative connotations, mostly because of their nomadic lifestyle that many people associate with being dirty, deceitful, lazy, and prone to steal.

Why then would anyone want to become associated with a social group that promotes the Pirate Gypsy lifestyle? That was what I was determined to learn. Once I met groups of talented men and women who chose to participate in a variety of different Pirate "Krews," the commitment to enhancing their community became apparent. Their dedication to preserving historical accuracy that is used during reenactment activities and educational programs is essential to assuring that history is preserved. In addition, it is an opportunity for a group of men and women who share a passion for antiquity and maritime traditions to socialize while also working on events that raise money for student scholarships, as well as focusing on the needs of local community charities.

Many people do not realize that the original Pirate crews maintained a very strict social discipline during the time they ruled the seas. In the 18th century Captain Bartholomew Roberts illustrates how social issues are regulated.

*Every man has a vote in the affairs of the moment; They have equal Title to the fresh provisions, or strong *liquors, at any time seized, and may use them at pleasure, unless a scarcity makes it necessary, for the good of all, to vote a retrenchment.*

It is worth noting that even early eighteenth-century pirates required a strict social code. The cultural assumptions that pirates and gypsies are associated with, including drunken brawls, hoarded treasures, stealing, plundering, etc. has distracted from the reality of what their daily lives were like.

In all Pirate and Gypsy communities there was a highly organized, inherently disciplined, and successful mini society.

Economist Peter Leeson writes in his article, *Public Choice:*

Pirates' constitutional democracy is the holy grail of social contract theory.

Understanding how the free spirit of the modern Gypsy dancers and Pirates has evolved is the objective portrayed in *Saint Augustine Sisterhood.* It is this humanistic, loving, and spiritual nature that the dancers are dedicated to sharing with others.

My sincere appreciation to Sunshine Dzierzynski Wilson and *The Gypsy Pirate Players* for including me in their circle of life.

Although I have written six previous novels, *Saint Augustine Sisterhood* has been one of the most enjoyable and challenging. Huzzah fellow sisters! Huzzah!

Chapter One

The world needs strong women—women who will lift and build others, who will love and be loved. Women who live bravely, both tender and fierce. Women of indomitable will.

Amy Tenney
Music Therapist

Mandana Morrison, 2022
Saint Augustine, Florida

There is this reoccurring dream where I am wandering into a chapel, sit down in an empty sanctuary among freshly cut sunflowers covering the altar. Directly in front of me is a wooden coffin strategically placed on an ornate bier surrounded by lit candlesticks in the center of the nave.

Although the chapel is very dark, my eyes eventually focus on a picture frame mounted on the center of the casket. Moving closer to see the image on the coffin, my face is reflected in a nearby mirror that appears from nowhere.

Every time I recall this moment, I am breathless. It leaves me with suspended anticipation. Can this be a subconscious obsession with life? Or is it a result of some obsession with death?

This morning it is neither. I am actually seated alone in a designated alcove for grieving family members at *The Cyprian Episcopal Church* in Saint Augustine, Florida. It is difficult for me to appear mournful. You see, my relative in the casket near the altar today is Aunt Caroline Marie Brigid O'Sullivan Callahan to be precise. Most likely I am the only person attending this solemn service that has no recollection of the deceased.

Both my parents passed away several years ago. They were the only living relatives that I am aware of. Since my parents immigrated to America from Persia, now known as Iran, fifty years earlier, I presume that it is possible that I may have living relatives in Iran, but even that seems unlikely.

I do have a slight recollection of being briefly introduced to a lady named Caroline many years ago, although I certainly do not recall her ever being referred to as my aunt. Yet here I am attending a memorial service as her only living relative.

Who are all of these people paying homage and how do all of them know Caroline? What are their stories and memories? Are they silently reminiscing about fond moments while I sit here with none.

This introspection is temporarily interrupted as I notice a woman wearing a floor length caftan glide elegantly from the front pew to the podium. I am fixated by the bold, chic Salvador Dali peacock print on her gown flowing majestically; gracefully.

There is a brief moment when I imagine that I am at the New York Fashion Week, and the host is narrating.

Argus in Color is the title of this 1963 etching by Dali worn superbly by Paloma, our stunning model.

The peacock, I now recall, has always been interpreted as an ancient symbol of spirituality and royalty. The tail feather circles appear as eyes following your every movement. But it is the way that Dali selects to interlock this image that projects a strong energy field.

It was once pointed out to me at a Dali symposium that in this painting the peacock feathers radiate like stars with male and female nudes adding an interesting mix to this vision. If one looks carefully, it can also be noted that Dali has added a woman stepping out of a vulva next to a man who has completely collapsed.

The Spanish use the word "polvo" to describe Dali's effect as a warm afterglow, as in an enjoyable love making tryst.

No one else, I am certain, is as easily distracted as I am at this very moment when I should be reverent.

Seriously I am now trying to focus on the podium realizing that the "peacock" lady has introduced herself as Pamela Harrison, a close friend of Aunt Caroline.

Could she have been Caroline's lover? Not that I would have minded or have been surprised.

Maybe I will learn more about their relationship later.

As Pamela shares with us Aunt Caroline's obsession with lighthouses and photography, it is her matching peacock earrings sparkling when the sunlight reflects through the stained-glass windows that captures my attention.

Is this an image Caroline might have appreciated as a photographer?

Pamela begins her speech.

"Caroline" is what I refer to as a photographer "junkie." She would capture images of everything from landscapes to dilapidated buildings, wandering animals, birds, and especially strangers.

Meeting people was Caroline's gift and passion. Whenever we would walk on St. George Street or places like Mount Dora, Caroline would begin conversations with everyone and anyone willing to talk with her. And, by the time we were ready to leave, Caroline was inviting them to Saint Augustine for a visit. Many actually did show up at her doorstep, and they were always greeted with Caroline's warm southern hospitality."

When the "Peacock Lady" finally concluded and stepped down from the pulpit, I was beginning to understand why so many people were here celebrating my "aunt's" life. It was a shame that I had nothing to share or to remember.

But it was the last gentleman's story regarding Caroline's playful personality that I enjoyed the most.

Adam Brown is an African American who has volunteered at The Lincolnville Museum for the past forty years. He introduced Caroline to Dr. Martin Luther King Jr. when he visited St. Augustine in 1964, fifty-eight years ago.

But it is not that event that Adam chose to share this morning. He spoke today of how Caroline enjoyed wearing silly costumes on Halloween, walking down St. George Street, mingling with tourists from around the country, and especially international visitors.

Adam shared with us how one Halloween season Caroline decided to dress as a jellyfish with sparkles and sunbeams that changed colors whenever she moved. The Saint Augustine Record, in the Lifestyle section, featured Caroline as wearing the *Most Original Costume* in St. Augustine.

Adam said that Aunt Caroline was so proud of this recognition that she clipped the article, framed it, and proudly displayed it in her living room.

This memorial service for Aunt Caroline is the final chapter in my aunt's journey, but the beginning of mine. What I share with you now is my awakening.

Death is inevitable. We will all experience Death. We all react differently to Death. And we all recall how we felt the first time we had to confront Death.

It may be a close friend or a relative. It could be a celebrity that we never even knew but admired. Sometimes it is a beloved pet that leaves this world too soon. Whatever our encounter is with Death, most of us will agree that when it slips into our lives, there is an awakening that we prefer to avoid.

DEATH travels with us through our life like an uninvited companion. Writers, artists, musicians, actors, and clergy attempt to enlighten us about the power of Death. Yet, until it is at our front door lingering like a stray cat, we turn away from its presence.

We are told from our earliest recollections that Death regardless of how wealthy, famous, or kind we are, it is our fate. Perhaps this may be why the audience in the popular musical *Cats,* by Andrew Lloyd Webber, is so delighted when Grizabella, the suffering cat, is granted a new life.

Don't we all want the gift of a new or extended life?

It is because of this desire that *The Saint Augustine Sisterhood* originated in the late fourteenth century, many years before anyone realized how exclusive the membership would become. Most people today still have no idea what "the quality of being sisterly" means. For many the suggestion of sisterhood connotes images associated with members of a clan or a cult. Often it has even been implied that we are contemporary witches.

Others claim that *Sisterhood* is nothing more than a radical breed of feminist elitists. Unfortunately, these critics have no idea how the innate circle supports a constantly evolving unity that expands and encourages others to self-actualize.

The chronology of our existence is often the result of an extensive metamorphosis necessary to achieve a final evolution that is both biological and emotionally difficult to obtain. This often results in various forms of exclusion.

Without proper support, isolation may lead to numerous abnormalities, even suicide. It is because of these challenges that the *Sisterhood* has evolved into its current esteemed reputation among scholars.

Nevertheless, skeptics continue to claim that *we* do not exist. Let me assure you that *we* are very much alive. *The Sisterhood* may seem to be unbelievable but do not be misled by that which appears improbable. The ability to transform imagination into manifestation is a powerful force that can alter our world for either the better or the worst.

Envision inspires action; action builds momentum for ingenuity. Is it not during these original moments when incredible revelations emanate, and innovation is born? Once fantasy emerges into reality, life becomes worth exploring.

Rabindranath Tagore, considered the most prolific modern Indian poet of the twentieth century, describes the immortality of love as "…in numberless forms, numberless times…in life after life, in age after age, forever."

Once I met Dr. Dante Griffith at the Extension Life Institute (ELI), my reoccurring déjà vu moments no longer frightened me. But I am now moving too far ahead of my real purpose.

To truly share the significance of *The Saint Augustine Sisterhood,* you must meet the other five ladies, hear their stories, and learn how we all came together.

Saint Augustine, Florida, is a melting cauldron where people from many different paths congregate naturally, not always knowing why or how they chose this ancient city as their final destination. There is a variety of theories associated with a gravitational pull that draws many people like a magnet to this ancient metropolis.

Otttis Castle, located on Vilano Beach, across the bridge from St. Augustine, may offer some answers to these questions. It is a structure over fifty feet high and weighs more than seven million pounds, completed in 1988 by two men, Ottis Sadler and Rusty Ickes.

Sadler and Ickes intended for their structure to invoke the spirit of an old Irish Abby. The entire masonry was completed by these two men with no additional assistance.

The interior of this castle, which includes all cypress wood and southern heart pine, was created by one man, Lee Carpenter. It took him three years to complete his part of the project between 1988 and 1991.

During this time, Mr. Carpenter built eight elaborate staircases, a pulpit, altar, choir loft, bishop chair, and several pews. When finished this magnificent stone castle became a reflection of the men's strong belief in their Christian faith.

After Ottis's death, Rusty added the additional 't' to *Otttis Castle,* symbolizing God's one entity. But it is the location of the castle on the same latitude as the Egyptian Great Pyramids that creates a supernatural connection worth noting.

Ancient Egyptians regarded death as a temporary interruption, simply a pause in their eternal life. This critical link is essential to understanding why *Saint Augustine Sisterhood* originated in this setting.

Dr. Griffith claims this phenomenon is also the reason ELI chose to conduct their research in St. Augustine. It is the cornerstone where the extended life theory thrives.

When Aunt Caroline passed away, this resulted in my relocating to St. Augustine. At the time I had no idea how ELI would alter my life.

As the executor of Caroline's modest three-bedroom colonial home located in Lincolnville, a historical district in St. Augustine, my original plan was to assess the value of her property, locate a reputable real estate agent, and sell the house for a nice profit as soon as possible. Remaining in Florida was never even a serious consideration.

Once I arrived here, it soon became evident that Aunt Caroline's estate included much more than what I initially imagined. The first revelation was learning that my aunt's home is located in the center of the most prominent historical black neighborhood, founded by formerly enslaved people in 1866.

By the twentieth century, this area was a significant subdivision where the residents became notably vocal in political policies. Later I learned through old newspaper clippings and letters found in Caroline's basement that she was one of those residents that marched with Dr. Martin Luther King Jr. on June 9, 1964. She also spent a night in jail after that protest march to the Plaza de la Constitution.

This demonstration resulted in a violent confrontation. Many people were brutally beaten while others, like my aunt, were arrested. This was only one in a series of exciting events surrounding Caroline's life. I was slowly discovering just how thrilling my own journey would become.

Included in Caroline's will, was a 1999 BMW M3 convertible, a substantial life insurance policy, and a fourteen-year-old Weimaraner named Lancelot. But it was the moment when I met Lancelot that I knew destiny had changed the course of my life forever.

In New York I was familiar with William Wegman's whimsical

photographs that capture the unique personality of this elegant mysterious breed. There were even a few occasions when I saw Wegman leaving his Chelsea loft studio apartment with *Man Ray,* the Weimaraner he named after a Dada artist that he admired.

Yet not even Wegman could have captured my unexpected first meeting with Sir Lancelot. The moment the dog handler, Julie, walked into the reception hall where I was to take possession of this regal, silver-grey coated animal, there was an immediate spiritual connection between the two of us. Julie felt it as well.

"There is no doubt that Caroline knew that you and Lancelot would share a special bond, Miss Morrison," Julie said, watching how the dog immediately nuzzled his nose into my chest.

"Have you two ever met before?" Julie asked, handing me the leash.

"No. Never. I only met my aunt Caroline once or maybe twice when I was a child living in California. And I am sure that must have been many years before she ever had Lancelot," I said, feeling a strong sense of serenity in this dog's presence.

"Well, then, the two of you must be soulmates from another life cycle. I have rarely seen any dog, especially a Weimaraner, react this way with a human they have never met before. It is a reunion that I hope will bring you both many years of profound happiness," Julie said.

Lancelot raised his head like the royal knight he was named after, looked into my eyes with a strong sense of confidence, and led me to the exit door.

Soon we were on our way back to the house he once shared with Aunt Caroline. I had to admit that this dog did not look or act fourteen years old. Lancelot was a model of perfection. At this moment, he had more energy than I did. Maybe Caroline tapped into that fountain of youth water line that Ponce de Leon discovered nearby.

When we arrived at the house, I was worried that Lancelot might be depressed without Caroline greeting him as entered his familiar habitat. But he adapted immediately, moving to a large green recliner where he jumped into naturally watching attentively what my next move might be.

"So, here we are, Lancelot, just you and I. What do you think we should do about this situation?" I asked, waiting for a response.

Lancelot cocked his head to an angle with one ear pulled to the side thoughtfully.

This was my first time returning to the house since Aunt Caroline's attorney gave me the keys. The last few days, I stayed at *The Cozy Inn* downtown, sorting through various documents and making arrangements to pick up Lancelot from his temporary kennel.

After all the details were in order, I determined that returning to the familiar house where Lancelot lived with Caroline would be a much better option for both of us, temporarily.

Mr. Arnold, Aunt Caroline's attorney, also provided me with a portfolio of papers that I was told Aunt Caroline insisted I receive immediately.

Since this was the first opportunity to review the contents, I moved to the kitchen table to begin reviewing the documents.

Lancelot followed me as I presumed, he once instinctively did when Caroline was still alive. There was a comfortable dog bed in the corner of the kitchen for him to settle into whenever he chose to.

"Okay, Lance, let us begin to examine what your mom left us among all of these formal-looking papers," I said, starting to separate what appeared to be bank statements, stock commodities, tax returns, and primarily financial statements.

But then I noticed a collection of handwritten papers folded neatly together and tied with purple ribbon. On the outer surface was a giant Christmas tag with my name.

To Mandana
Love, Aunt Caroline

It had been many years since I had seen my given name so eloquently displayed. Although on legal documents I have used *Mandana* for over twenty-five years, people have known me as Mandy. Even my mother and father eventually respected my decision and accepted my name, although they never truly approved of that change.

For some unusual reason I now distinctly remember the day my mother learned that I had changed my name.

"What would ever make you decide to change your beautiful name, Mandana?" she asked me one day after returning home from a meeting with my sixth-grade teacher about this issue.

"What would make me want to change my name, Mama? Well, maybe when all the boys started calling me 'Mandana Bandana Banana'? Or maybe when the girls always make fun of the *tahdig,* you insist on packing in my lunch box every day. Do you know how many of my friends eat a crispy layer of rice every day for lunch, Mama? NOBODY!" I said, both screaming and crying at the same time.

Rather than reprimand me for being disrespectful, my mother cradled me in her arms, rocking me back and forth, trying her best to calm me down.

Once I was no longer trembling, she began to speak in her most gentle voice.

"You, my darling, must never be embarrassed by who you are. *Mandana* was a Median Princess, mother of *Cyrus the Great* of Persia, writer of the first declaration of human rights. Women in Persia were greatly honored, often holding prestigious positions of power such as Courthouse Magistrates, Treasurers, and Ministries. Our women held more power in their world than history has given them credit. The civilized modern world that we live in today has a long way to go in gender equality. If your generation does not continue to plant their feet in the future, we will always remain slaves to our sexual roles. Your name, Mandana, means Eternal. Perhaps one day you will understand the significance and earn the respect that your name deserves," my mother said, drying my tearful eyes.

Although she could not convince me to be proud of my name that day, there was a seed planted in my mind by my mother. We never had that discussion again, and I continued to be known as Mandy throughout my early life.

It was not until several years after my mother's death that I realized she was right. But would I ever be strong enough to fight the battles that she expected me to fight? Would Mandana eventually emerge with dignity? It is a question that I ponder even more frequently now.

Before living in Manhattan, I spent six years studying theatre and film production at UCLA in California, transferring to Berkeley after graduating. At Berkeley, a talented group of artists, musicians, and actors that I roomed with were hired by a traveling Renaissance Faire troop. It did not take much to convince me to join them. After a few months being cast as a "washing woman wench," I was moved to the stage as an understudy for several minor roles in *Midsummer Night's Dream*.

Being a part of the rude mechanicals, the skilled laborers, or artisans in the play offered me many opportunities to improve my acting techniques. Nick Bottom became my favorite role since he is the only mechanical who interacts extensively with other cast members outside of the group.

This entire experience reminded me of a large circus family or a group of gypsies. I thrived traveling throughout the country together with these free spirits, spreading laughter and happiness, adding a little "fairy dust" here and there to communities that welcomed our medieval entertainment.

Although this was a profound learning experience offering me a unique opportunity to tour the country after three years, I was still spinning my wheels in soft sand.

Several of us decided to remain in Ashland when offered the opportunity to work permanently, performing at The Oregon Shakespeare Festival. I discovered a new sense of confidence. It was my passion for live theatre that led me to use my given name Mandana once again, this time as my stage name.

I was not yet ready to conquer the world like my namesake, but it was the first step.

Then as the directors began to offer me accolades for my performances, the internal voices residing inside began tempting me.

Move to the City, Mandy... If you can make it in New York, you can make it anywhere, people say.

That may be true for some actors, but the harsh reality is that without a credible agent and some real connections in the theatre business, you are going to spend most of your time acting as a fairy tale character at Birthday parties and working at the local coffee shop to stay alive.

I was luckier than most. Somehow my agent did manage to get me some off-Broadway gigs that paid for my rent most of the time. Extra side jobs took care of the food. But it was pretty clear that I was still on that treadmill moving nowhere.

When the letter first arrived about Aunt Caroline's passing, I was finishing a traveling tour with *Cats*. My role was an understudy for Victoria the White Cat, and I was also in the chorus.

The company allowed me to take a few days off in Florida since they were also going to be on hiatus for a few weeks. I had no idea where St. Augustine was, but it had to be better than staying on the tour bus.

The original plan was to meet with the tour group in Ohio once all the documents had been signed. From previous real estate transactions when my parents passed away, I knew it was not necessary for me to remain in Florida while the house was for sale.

All those documents could be sent online for signatures. That was now almost a year ago and before I met Lancelot. Since then, I decided to give my notice to the theatre group, keep the Lincolnville house, enjoy my semi-early retirement, and spend some quality time discovering who this Mandana Morrison, aka Mandy, is.

My first week residing in this new house felt like a vacation. I was initially uncomfortable about rearranging anything. This was still Aunt Caroline's house in my mind. It was when I decided to take Lancelot on his morning walks that I met Jocelyn and Floe and everything started to feel natural.

Some may say it was very unexpected, yet it is exactly what I would expect in such phenomenal surroundings. The streets are steeped in ancient history. People sitting on their porches resemble those black and white photographs of old days displayed in The Lincolnville Museum that I pass nearly every day.

"If you don't mind, Flo sees the two of you coming each morning around the corner, and when you turn away she gets so disappointed. She would appreciate it greatly if you would maybe pat her head?" I heard someone saying a short distance behind me.

Since Lancelot and I were the only ones nearby, I assumed she was directing those remarks to me. As I approached the polite dog sitting patiently waiting for us, the first thing I noticed was her chocolate almond shaped eyes watching every move Lancelot and I made. Her tail was wagging with utter delight.

Once I was close enough to avoid shouting at the dog's companion, I noticed that the lady was wearing an apron around her waist and a *Salty Dog* souvenir hat from the famous Hilton Head bar and restaurant in North Carolina.

"Good morning! My name is Mandy, and I have a hat that matches yours. I also have some good memories of visiting *The Salty Dog* a few years ago," I said, feeling an instant bond with this stranger.

"Nice to meet you, Mandy. We are so happy to see Lancelot. I wasn't sure who would take him after hearing of Caroline's passing. We were all worried that he might be placed in a foster home or worse. I apologize for not introducing myself; I am Jocelyn, and this is Flo. She is the ambassador of Lincolnville," Jocelyn said proudly while offering a dog treat to Lancelot, who was occupied sniffing his friend.

"Discovering Lancelot was a surprise for me as well. I had not seen

Aunt Caroline for many years. When I was contacted about her estate, I must confess that it was truly a surprise. Lancelot is trying to convince me to remain here in St. Augustine. At least for a while," I said, leaving my options open.

"Well, I should warn you, many of us had the same reservations about this place but have never left. There is just something quite extraordinary about this town, like a magnet. Once here, nobody ever wants to leave. Anyway, you may be the exception, Mandy, but I hope while you are here, we can be good friends," Jocelyn said as we continued our walk together.

That was the beginning of my introduction to Lincolnville and my first real friendship.

When I returned home, I remembered that it was my birthday. What I couldn't explain was the basket of flowers and fresh vegetables that I found on my doorstep with my name on the envelope and the words,

"HAPPY BIRTHDAY"

Chapter Two

There shall be no more death. Because we have already seen all that, it's old, and we are tired of it. And now we need something new. And this new thing is Eternal Life.

Boris Pasternak
Russian Poet and Novelist

Mandana Morrison

Deciding to remain in St Augustine was much easier than anticipated. Perhaps Jocelyn was right. It seemed that everywhere I went and everyone that I met made me feel welcome. It was an unexpected natural transition.

New York never really felt like home. Most of the time, my apartment was merely a temporary residence between performances. It was the typical lifestyle of a gypsy actor, but until now, there was no other lifestyle to compare it to.

Lancelot is more grounded than I am. How long it might take before the urge to revert to a vagabond lifestyle is uncertain, but for now, there is a lot to explore right here in Aunt Caroline's backyard, both literally and figuratively.

To begin with, there are these mysterious flowers and a basket of fruit. There did not seem to be any logical answer. Maybe it is time to visit my next-door neighbor. Someone may have noticed a delivery truck or perhaps even recognized the person who left these clandestine gifts on my porch.

I began with the house on the right side of Aunt Caroline's. Every evening, the sweet, sultry jazz sound can be heard at about 8:00 PM. Anyone who enjoys the sensual sounds of Miles Davis, Ella Fitzgerald, and John Coltrane certainly must be friendly.

Since there was no doorbell, I tapped gently on the metal screen door, waiting patiently for a response. After a few more taps with no answer, I started walking down the brick steps back to Aunt Caroline's house.

"Can I help you?" I heard from behind once I reached the sidewalk.

When I turned around, I saw a young girl, possibly in her twenties, with dark-colored dreads wrapped around her head in the shape of a basket.

"Yes…I live next door, at my Aunt Caroline's house," I said, turning around hesitantly.

"I'm Mandy Morrison. I wondered if you happened to know who left the flowers and fruit on my front porch this afternoon?" I asked, extending my hand politely.

The girl took my hand gracefully. I couldn't help but notice how smooth her skin felt next to mine. Her fingers were like a pianist, long, slim, yet strong.

"Yes. I know who you are, Ms. Morrison. We wondered how long it would take before you would step outside of your gilded cage," the girl said surlily.

Rather than respond with an equally cantankerous remark, for some odd reason, the image of Maya Angelou reading an excerpt from her 1969 autobiography, *I Know Why the Caged Bird Sings,* flashed in my head (or before my eyes).

In March 2011, after receiving the news that she was to be honored with *The Presidential Medal of Freedom*, Dr. Angelou needed to postpone her visit to UCLA. But then, one month later, she was sharing her memories and the *Presidential Medal of Freedom* with all of us.

It was the African American poet Paul Laurence Dunbar's poem *Sympathy* that inspired Maya to write I *Know Why the Caged Bird Sings*. The caged bird, an image Angelou continued to use throughout her writings, symbolized chained, enslaved people throughout history.

Although I am neither black nor an enslaved person, this feeling of being "caged" resonated throughout my entire life. These words from Maya Angelou's poem became etched in my mind.

Caged Bird
By
Maya Angelou

A free bird leaps
on the back of a wind

and floats downstream
till the current ends
and dips his wings
in the orange sun rays
and dares to claim the sky.

But a bird that stalks
down his narrow cage
can seldom see through
his bars of rage
his wings are clipped and
his feet are tied
so he opens his throat to sing.

The caged bird sings
with a fearful trill
of things unknown
but longed for still
and his tune is heard
on a distant hill
for the caged bird
sings of freedom.

The free bird thinks of another breeze
And the trade winds soft through the sighing trees
and the fat worms waiting on a bright dawn lawn
and he names the sky his own.

But the caged bird stands on the grave of dreams
his shadow shouts in a nightmare scream
his wings are clipped, and his feet are tied
so he opens his throat to sing.

The caged bird sings
with a fearful trill
of things unknown
but longed for still
and his tune is heard
on a distant hill

for the caged bird
sings of freedom.

"Ms. Morrison? Are you alright?"

It took me a few seconds to remember where I was and why.

"Yes…I am fine. It was just… never mind. I am so sorry to have disturbed you," I said, turning back toward the path leading me home.

"No, please don't leave. I am sorry if I came across as rude. It's just my sarcastic attitude at times. Your aunt spoke of you often. She was an extraordinary lady, loved by the entire community, including myself. I am sorry that she is no longer here. I miss her every day.

"People sometimes mistake the tone of my voice as being condescending. I apologize once again. My name is Kiara King Jackson. I hope that we can be friends?"

I was initially taken aback by this about-face reaction. It was not like me to be so sensitive. Wasn't it I who wanted to learn more about Aunt Caroline? How did I expect complete strangers to respond?

"Yes, of course. I, too, hope we can become friends. I should be apologizing for some of my annoying quirks," I said, trying to recover.

I also wanted to clarify that Caroline was not my aunt, but that might be too much information to include without knowing all the details myself.

"For the time being, it is just Lancelot and me. I haven't decided yet if this will be a permanent move. But, since I don't know anyone else in the city, I was hoping that you might know where these flowers and fruit basket came from that were left on the porch?" I asked once again.

"Oh, you must mean the gifts Caroline's boyfriend leaves for her. He never forgets her birthday and their anniversary. Always sunflowers for her birthday and red tulips for their anniversary," Kiara said.

"But didn't anyone tell him that Caroline passed a few days ago? And, the card had my name, not Caroline's," I said, confused.

"Nobody needs to tell Liam about Caroline. Liam has been dead for hundreds of years. That doesn't seem to matter. The gifts keep getting delivered."

Now I was thoroughly confused. Caroline is receiving gifts from a deceased sweetheart, and nobody seems to think this odd?

"Do you mean that in all of these years, Aunt Caroline never questioned where her gifts were coming from? Certainly, someone should have the answer? It is a loving gesture, but now that Caroline is no longer here to enjoy these gifts, I would assume they will stop?" I asked, sounding perplexed.

"I wouldn't count on it. After a while, you will learn that there is nothing normal in St. Augustine. We all learn to adapt. I have some sweet potato pie in the oven. Why don't you come back inside and have some pie and a cup of tea?" Kiara asked, taking my hand and leading me back up the stairs even before I had the opportunity to decline her kind offer.

I was extremely pleased that I accepted the invitation to return to Kiara's cottage. It was a fantastic afternoon. What Kiara shared with me about her heritage, Aunt Caroline, and Lincolnville was only the beginning of my journey. Still, it was sufficient for me to decide that I had to learn more about this mysterious city and its diverse citizens.

I never expected to be included as one of the *Sisters* that continue to enrich this city with living historical spirits. But apparently Aunt Caroline did.

My first introduction to ELI (Extended Living Institute) was when Kiara spoke of her distant relative, Anna Madgigine Jai Kingsley. Her story about being captured at the age of thirteen years old in West Africa by slave traders in 1806 is not a unique tale.

It was common to find young African girls that plantation owners in America would pay top dollar to use in their households. Anna was one of those girls sent to Cuba, where plantation owner Zephaniah Kingsley, also a slave trader, not only purchased and impregnated her but also married Anna before returning to Florida.

"That information about my great, great, great grandmother can be found in historical archives. But it is the details that your Aunt Caroline discovered about Anna, whose birth name is Anta Majigueen Ndiaye, that convinced me to become a member of the *Sisterhood*," Kiara said, waiting for my reaction.

"I am not sure I understand. Isn't a *Sisterhood* a sorority club that one joins in college? When I was at UCLA many years ago, I considered joining a sorority because several alumni advised me that a sorority would provide me with the social opportunities to meet influential people.

Unfortunately, or maybe for the best, my theatrical interests led me to an entirely different group, a group that gravitated toward a counterculture with a gypsy mentality.

"I could never envision myself a *Sister* in any social movement," I said, trying not to insult my hostess.

Kiara could no longer hold back her laughter.

"Are you suggesting that I am a member of a sorority, Mandy Morrison? That is hysterical. Wait until I share this with the others. They will get a definite hoot from that comment," Kiara said, sipping her tea and shaking her head in disbelief at my comment.

"Well then, what other *Sisterhood* are you referring to?" I asked cautiously.

"Oh, my darling, there is so much you still need to learn before we can even consider crossing that bridge," Kiara said, offering me another slice of sweet potato pie.

I glanced down at my watch and realized that it was three hours since I left the house, and I still had no idea why Liam's gifts to Caroline were still being delivered to me or who else might be sending them.

Although *Sisterhood* sounded interesting, many other matters required my attention, for example, sorting through Aunt Caroline's personal belongings, examining her monthly financial liabilities, and determining what to do with her house. And now, of course, there is always Lancelot to consider in any of my decisions.

"As tempting as I find spending the afternoon with you reminiscing about my family, it is time for me to start planning how all of these loose tiles from this complex mosaic will eventually form a picture that I can appreciate," I said, standing up before Kiara could object.

"Another time then? You know your way back here now. Don't let anything stop you from coming back. There is so much you will soon learn about the ELI and Caroline's contribution. When you are ready to hear more about the *Sisterhood,* I am right here," Kiara said, waving goodbye.

Waiting anxiously for me to return was Lancelot at the front door. I was curious how long he must have been sitting there attentively. As soon as I entered, I kneeled next to him. His eyes were shining like precious polished amber.

He inhaled a deep breath and lay down with his belly up, ready for some loving hands to comfort him.

"Were you afraid that I would not return, Lance?" I whispered, continuing to stroke his sleek fur gently.

"No worries. I need you as much as you need me, my special knight," I said, for the first time acknowledging that this might be a permanent life change.

Lancelot also seemed to understand this as well. He stood up gracefully and moved to the basement door, where he took a sitting position until I realized he wanted me to follow him.

"Is there something that you want to show me downstairs?" I asked, not knowing really what to expect as a response.

But, when he opened his mouth and put his teeth around the doorknob, there was no doubt what Lancelot wanted me to do.

"Okay…okay. But, the first rat I see down there, I'm going to board up this basement permanently," I said, hesitantly opening the door and searching for a light switch.

Aunt Caroline's Colonial house even had a basement. This is quite unusual since Lincolnville is known to have such terrible drainage issues. Most of the historical homes were not built with basements.

One hundred and fifty years ago, the newly freed slaves chose this area to establish their colony in the center of Maria Sanchez Creek. Anytime there is a severe rainstorm, Kiara told me that the entire downtown vicinity, including right here this street floods.

If this is true, why would Aunt Caroline ever choose her basement as a storage place for any valuable documents?

Kiara did not know why, but everyone in the neighborhood knew that Aunt Caroline's home was the only one in the city that stayed dry. Many neighbors would ask Caroline if they could use her basement temporarily to store essential items. They would even offer to pay her for any inconvenience, but Aunt Caroline never accepted money for helping her neighbors.

During the now-famous 1964 Dr. Martin Luther King Jr. visit and sit-in, Kiara said it was in this basement at Aunt Caroline's home where many of the secret preparations were organized.

Although this information is all fascinating, as I am standing at the top of the entrance to the dank basement still not convinced that I want to proceed any further.

Not until Lancelot starts barking do I realize that it is no longer my choice. To make it appear safe, Lancelot takes the lead running down the stairs to show me that there is no imminent danger.

"Alright, I am coming," I say, following obediently behind my leader.

Once downstairs, I find it is fairly pleasant. There are several chairs, a table, lamps, and even a tiny kitchen.

Because it is already dark outside, I cannot determine how much natural light might come in during the day from the small windows, but even with the artificial light, it is comfortable.

Lancelot is seated in front of a solid wood roll top desk that I assume is where Caroline keeps her documents. When I push the roll-top up, it reveals a large vanilla folder with my name.

Why wasn't this included with the other estate documents?

I hesitate to open the envelope, even though it is addressed to me.

Perhaps I should take it to the lawyer's office first and have them advise me on what it might contain?

What would Alice do?

Yes, of course now it is all becomes quite clear. One day when Alice comes to a fork in the road she sees a Cheshire cat in a tree, and asks him what the best route is to take.

His response is, "Where do you want to go?"

"I don't know," is Alice's response.

"Then it doesn't matter what road you choose," the cat says.

Oh, what a clever cat he is. I always find forks on my roads, and I keep returning to this advice from the Cheshire Cat.

I now sit at the desk chair and use the lovely Fleur De Lis envelope opener.

Inside is a tiny envelope with tulips and sunflowers hand painted with the following instructions:

To be opened only after my passing, by Mandela Morrison.

I take a deep breath and exhale. On the desk is a bottle of *Ardbeg Uigeadail, Glenmorangie Vintage 1997,* a sealed whiskey decanter, and two whiskey tumblers.

I carefully break the seal and pour two glasses, one for me and one for Lancelot, who is eyeing my every movement.

"You do understand, Lance, that this glass of whiskey is only a symbolic gesture in your honor, not to be consumed by you," I say aloud.

He yawns but refuses to take his eyes off me.

"To you, Aunt Caroline, may your journey be safe and your spirit joyful," I say drinking both glasses of whiskey.

Chapter Three

By clearing your mind, you cleanse the karma of this lifetime, all the memories, biases, and conditioning that prevent you from experiencing and seeing the truth. When you free your mind, you simultaneously set your spirit free from the karma of all your lifetimes. That is the moment of Mukti, salvation, liberation, enlightenment, born again freedom.

Zen Everest
The Extended Living Institute

Dr. Dante Griffith

Who Wants to Live Forever? Brian May, the lead guitarist for the band Queen, wrote that song in a taxi after viewing the film *Highlander* in 1986. The scene where Connor McCloud holds his dying wife in his arms inspired May's lyrics. That song would be included in the final cut of *Highlander*.

My mother was obsessed with SCI-FI. On my tenth birthday, we celebrated with fish and chips at her favorite pub, *Sherlock Holmes*, in London, followed by the newly released film *Highlander*. The lyrics from that opening song haunted me for many weeks, possibly years later.

There's no time for us
There's no place for us

After my dad decided he no longer wanted a wife and child, Mum and I became a team. She was my anchor. Whenever I felt that life was too difficult, my mum assured me that I could accomplish anything. In turn, I was her main purpose for living. Neither of us disappointed each other. Not ever.

Unfortunately, she was unable to benefit from my research achievements at ELI. When we learned about her cancer, I was living in the Silicon Valley, a region in Northern California known for high technology and innovative scientific studies.

For years Mum's cancer went undetected. Even after I relocated her from London to the United States, we had no idea her condition was terminal. Thankfully, the suffering was brief and her passing almost immediate.

After her death, I must have watched *Highlander* ten times. *Who Wants to Live Forever?* played in my head for months.

Of course, I wanted her to live forever. Without her, away from fond memories on the other side of the pond, life was meaningless. She had become my obsession. Although I could not bring her back to life, I could prevent anyone else from losing those they loved. At the very least, I was determined to extend their time together.

When I was offered a position with a private company known as ELI, located in Chicago, I accepted although this was still a new and challenging technological endeavor.

What I did know was that these studies were moving extremely fast. By the twenty-first century ELI was ready to begin clinical trials on humans. It was an exciting time, but because of the nature of these studies, they were also extremely confidential.

None of the subjects had any idea what the trials were really testing. It was hidden by more acceptable studies like cholesterol or cell reproduction.

During early trials, we solicited both genders. The results began to reveal that females benefited more from the longevity procedure than do men. We learned that women who were of childbearing age could produce the next generation of life with a potential extended life expectancy of perhaps two hundred years. That possibility was especially exciting to all of us.

As the trial studies continued, those working on the research and development phase began to exceed our expectations.

Would it be possible to extract DNA from a certain group and reincarnate their ancestors while maintaining their own original thumbprint?

Just imagine Ruth Bader Ginsberg sharing harmoniously the same body as her great great granddaughter. Sounds ludicrous? Well, not exactly.

Do you recall the 1993 the sci-fi blockbuster movie *Jurassic Park?* Michael Crichton wrote *Jurassic Park* in 1990 using his genetic studies and DNA research *to* restore living dinosaurs.

In his novel, scientists needed to first find dinosaur blood to clone their species. This was achieved by discovering fossilized mosquitoes preserved in amber. Once this blood was successfully collected, the scientists sequenced the dinosaur's genome and supplemented missing parts from frogs.

With this completed hybrid code, it was possible to inject an egg to be fertilized.

As scientists we, of course, wanted to take this rather crude interpretation of scientific fantasy and apply it practically to our own study of extended life theory.

It may sound quite bizarre to a layperson, but to us the hypothesis appeared quite convincing. What was not easy to decide and agree upon was whose DNA pool we would begin with.

There were twelve of us selected by the *ELI* to research various ethnic groups, as well as genders, to begin our pilot testing program. We were often referred to as the ELI disciples. Unlike the original Jesus disciples, in this group there were more female scientists than men.

The male scientists with tenure didn't want to be associated with an ineffective, futile study that would be a blemish on their careers. To me it was an opportunity to change the cosmos. I refused to leave the future to a group of self-centered, egotistical neophytes.

Since I was the scientist with the most seniority, the ELI trustees allowed me to select my team. I was also convinced that my female colleagues would offer a vastly diverse opportunity for the type of discussion required in this environment. I was not disappointed.

"Dr. Griffith, is there any significance in the name *ELI?* I, of course, understand the anagram represents Extended Life Institute. However, is there any additional rationale for its Biblical title?"

Amara was one of my brilliant female interns who studied anthropology at Harvard as an exchange student from Africa. After graduating with honors, she applied to medical school at Johns Hopkins, where she majored in genetics.

"That is an insightful question, Amara. I would be interested in hearing the reason for that inquiry," I said, volleying the question back to her court.

"Well, as I am certain everyone here knows, Eli was a Jewish priest who, according to the Book of Samuel, served God at the tabernacle in Shiloh. Without going into too much Biblical history, it was Eli's sons that went to battle and brought back *The Arc of the Covenant.*"

Amara paused, waiting for me to respond. I looked pensively around the table for any reactions from the other members of my team. Most of them were either doodling on their notepads, scrolling through their cell phones, or watching the snow begin to fall outside on the courtyard. It was reminiscent of my lecturing years at Stanford University, minus the snow.

"Doctor Wilding, what are your thoughts on Amara's observations?" I asked, watching delightfully how everyone else began to nervously react to not knowing if they too were also going to be asked to respond.

Wilding's eyes were as shallow as a deer about to realize that those headlights were aimed directly at his head.

"I'm sorry, Dr. Griffith, could you repeat your question?" Wilding finally responded.

"No. Dr. Wilding, I will not repeat my question. What I will state quite emphatically is that our meeting requires all of you to stay focused. There are no questions or discussions that are frivolous."

We are a team. I have selected each one of you to contribute your expertise to making this project successful. If for any reason you do not feel that you are capable of performing those duties, please let me know immediately to prevent me from asking you to resign," I said, standing up to emphasize my disgust with the lack of attention.

The room remained silent. It was that genuinely unnerving silence that one experiences when something quite serious but unknown is about to occur.

It was Amara that decided to move ahead. This time all of the members were staring directly toward her.

"I would like to add that although currently I am Agnostic, the Bible does offer some quite fascinating perspectives on universal human behavior. That is initially why I asked about a possible connection."

I was now determined to add more to the discussion.

"Your observations are quite insightful. As scientists some of us do not thoroughly investigate all the information available. This often results in false assumptions in our studies. Those of us who were on the original framework for the program chose *ELI* as our title because of the numerous possibilities. We all desire to maintain the breadth needed to expand our horizons. So, Bravo, Dr. Amara Anderson for providing us with more ideas to cultivate during this extensive journey," I announced before leaving the room.

It was not the time to expand on any of the theological assumptions associated with extending life. I, myself was struggling with the idea of playing with God-like powers.

Who am I to provide individuals an opportunity to live beyond their projected life cycle? And, even more questionable is who determines those that will have the opportunity to extend their lives?

Amara introduced a fascinating, thought-provoking idea. What was Eli's relationship with God? As scientists we frequently face moral questions that may defy our scientific inquiries.

Does that mean we abandon our mission? Absolutely not. If ethical standards prevailed, we may never have discovered fire!

Therefore, I would suggest that Eli's role in the Bible is to provide us with lessons; even pitfalls to avoid when new opportunities are introduced.

The Extended Life Institute is an opportunity to do more than provide people with additional years to live on planet Earth. It is an opportunity to harvest the best talents from those who have passed on and restore new life that will improve our universe, hopefully before we destroy it.

To achieve this goal will require much more than the efforts of brilliant scientists. It will depend on perfect timing and God's Blessings.

Chapter Four

Whatever life you have lived so far, all the stages of your past life have come together to make you who you are now.

Llchi Lee

The Ancient Secret to Longevity, Vitality, and Life Transformation

Mandana

The letters that I discovered, written by my Aunt Caroline, read like a romantic novel, but not like any contemporary one that Amazon offers.

This story was in true romantic literary form; Elizabeth Barrett Browning class of superiority.

You remember, those great writers that filled our imagination with endless questions, confusion, and inspiration? The novels that challenged readers to extend beyond their normal breadth of reasoning?

Four hours later I was still trying to comprehend but it was quite exhausting. There were just too many questions to examine in one afternoon. So, I chose the most obvious one.

My aunt was born Caroline Marie O'Sullivan on New Year's Day, 1768, in Black Burton, a village parish about two miles south of Oxfordshire, England. The village is located on a tributary of the river Thames.

What? 1768? That must be a typo error. Maybe 1968? But, no, that would have made her only eleven years older than me. But then what was the answer?

I could only conclude that yes, the year of her birth is correct. That would have made my auntie two hundred and forty-six years old at her death.

Naturally that fact alone is enough to challenge the validity of anything else that I was about to discover. But Aunt Caroline already knew that she would need to offer me much more than a collection of these letters to validate such a presumption.

These letters were only the beginning of a bizarre legacy I was inheriting. Nevertheless, the letters should not be ignored. It is essential to study them carefully before moving on to any theories realistic or bizarre related to this conundrum.

"Are you also 246 years old, Lancelot?" I asked, almost expecting him to respond.

Lancelot stretched his long legs like a sprinter toward the sunshine reflecting through the kitchen window, took a long yawn, and lay down as if he had heard that question many times before.

Although Caroline's age was definitely a mysterious surprise, there were so many other aspects to her life that were just as intriguing.

One of the first that drew my attention was why she added Caroline to the front of her name, and when did she do this? The answer to that question was in the next letter.

The wax stamp was what first caught my attention. The intent of a wax stamp during the Middle Ages was to assure that an official document would only be opened by the person it was intended for.

The seal on this stamp was *CEA,* embedded inside of an infinity emblem, a figure eight on its side that represents limitlessness, or better known as eternity. I could only conclude then that Aunt Caroline's final wish was for this document to be seen only by me.

Once the seal was broken I, removed several cream-colored sheets of stationary. Each page included the same infinity symbol but now with the initials *CMOC* embossed in gold. The first line of the letter, as I suspected, was addressed directly to me.

My dearest Mandana,

The last time that I saw you was on an Easter holiday vacation at Carmel by the sea in Northern California. It was a joyous occasion that I would often reflect on years later. But now that you have arrived in St. Augustine, participated in my Celebration of Life Ceremony, started to bond with Lancelot, met my dearest friends Jocelyn and lovely Kiara, it is time that you learn about the true mission of Sisterhood.

This will require you to open your mind to many new ideas that may appear radical or even impossible. Let me assure you Mandana everything is real; everything is universal.

My goal is to provide you with all of the answers about my role in

ELI. Dr. Dante will then acquaint you with any scientific explanations needed to understand the next stages of your participation.

I paused for a moment. *My participation? What was it that Aunt Caroline was suggesting? My only commitment was to ensure that my aunt's final wishes be fulfilled and that Lancelot be cared for.*

I glanced over at the regal dog to assure myself that he was still on his dog bed in the corner napping.

He moved slightly but appeared quite content to allow me to continue reading as long as I was not planning on leaving the cottage without him.

I returned to the letter, hoping to find more concrete details.

I certainly understand that discovering my true age might be both perplexing and disturbing. But for the moment please focus on who I am not what you thought I was.

Many people have no idea who I once was, or perhaps they simply no longer care about my contribution to literature. Even Jane Austen was gracious enough to acknowledge my novels. But most have forgotten that I was one of the first realist writers of children's literature as well as having a significant influence on the novel's evolution.

Due to my Irish background, it was impossible for me to ignore the inherent problems my people were enduring through religious and social injustices, gender bias, and poverty. I chose to be their voices in my novels,

<u>*Castle Nowhere*</u> *and* <u>*Beyond Below*</u> *were both quite controversial.*

I was especially pleased when fellow novelist Seamus Dean wrote the following about me, "she was not the first novelist to have chosen Ireland as "her scene"; but she was the first to recognize that there was within it, a missionary opportunity to invert it to Enlightenment faith and rescue it from its romantic conditions."

You see, Mandana, I have always been a trailblazer. One who continues to pursue whatever is needed until change occurs. In my century, the one that I was born into, it was very difficult. But it was my determination that encouraged me to look beyond the limits known as reality, and that attitude led me to infinity.

But that is another discussion for the future. What I do need to share with you is Liam Callahan.

There it was. The mysterious man who I have been searching for. I continued reading now with even more interest.

Our relationship is far too complicated to explain in this letter. I will say, however, that Liam Callahan is certainly a fine gentleman, and Death cannot even change that.

Was that it? I scanned through the remaining letter searching for something more. Anything that would suggest a clue to what my real role is in this odd situation could possibly be.

Instead, it appears that any further questions that require answers need to be addressed directly to Dr. Dante at the *ELI. It now seems obvious that I* can no longer avoid meeting Dr. Dante.

Tomorrow after my morning walk with Lancelot, I will make an appointment to do just that. It seems to be the only reasonable solution at this point.

As I am about to return the cedar box to the cabinet, I notice a small velvet pouch with my name written on a gift tag. It is signed by Aunt Caroline.

I untie the ribbon, revealing a rose gold chain with a dragonfly preserved in an exquisite Lalique crystal bubble, completely intact.

It is as if the dragonfly is being protected until it is safe to be released once again into the world.

This gift is quite extraordinary and no doubt fascinating, but it was not anything that I would personally wear.

Jewelry has never really appealed to me, and certainly not anything that preserves an insect, regardless how exquisite it may appear. I own one pair of golden hoop earrings and an Apple watch that I bought myself last year for Christmas, primarily for use while exercising.

Even the heirloom jewelry left to me by my mother when she passed away is in a safety deposit box because I don't know what to do with it.

"I wonder if I could make this dragonfly necklace into an elegant collar for you Lancelot?" I directed my question to the one who must have known Caroline the best.

Until I could decide what to do with the dragonfly, I returned it to its velvet pouch. It was just then that I decided to take one more look at the necklace.

Removing it this time, I examined the back. The dragonfly was surrounded by a sterling silver framed case. Engraved in the center was the date 10/25/2022. Today's date!

How did Aunt Caroline know that I would be here today on my birthday opening this gift? And why was the deceased Liam Callahan leaving me flowers and fruit when it wasn't Aunt Caroline's Birthday at all?

These questions and many more would result in future sleepless nights. There were just too many loose pieces surrounding my life at this moment. But Lancelot's behavior was the real mystery.

He always appeared to stay quite content. At no time does he ever seem disturbed. He never even expresses any sorrow about missing Caroline.

Was this not odd? After all, everything indicates that Lancelot and Caroline were lifelong partners, yet he has accepted me without any hesitation as his new mistress. I imagine that even dogs experience a period of mourning when they lose someone they love.

Once the sun rises the next morning, Lancelot and I are out the door walking at daybreak. At a distance, near the St. Francis Park entrance, I can barely make out the shadows.

Finally I see it is Jocelyn and Flo. Flo, is sitting patiently as always waiting for us to meet with them under the lamp post.

"Well, good morning, stranger. We haven't seen the two of you for a few days. Did you forget about us already?" Jocelyn asks, offering Lancelot a beef stick before I can respond.

"No, we didn't forget, but there have been some strange happenings lately that I am trying to make sense of," I said, moving away from the park toward *The Blue Hen,* a neighborhood breakfast café.

"Can I buy you a cup of coffee and maybe a scone?" I ask.

"This must be serious. Okay, but Flo won't sit around quietly for too long. Maybe we can get it to go and head back toward the park?" Jocelyn suggests.

Once we are settled down, I share with Jocelyn what I have learned about Aunt Caroline, Liam, and my visit with Kiara, hoping that she can offer some additional insight.

"This is definitely a lot to digest early in the morning. If you are looking to me for answers all I can suggest is that you follow what Caroline has outlined... Your aunt is a very wise woman. There is nobody that ever met Caroline that didn't admire her. You must have inherited some of her qualities, or she would have never appointed you as her successor," Jocelyn says, sipping her coffee.

"Successor? Successor to what? Maybe her executor, but that certainly is not a permanent position," I say more confused now than ever.

"I do believe that it is time for you to talk to the experts at ELI. All that is happening at this point is that you are trying to unscramble pieces of a puzzle with missing parts. Dr. Dante is your best source to explain your role in the future," Jocelyn says quite reasonably.

Perhaps Jocelyn is right. I may be avoiding my meeting with Dante primarily because of the anticipation that my obligation here might be permanent. Quite frankly it is scaring the hell out of me.

If this is all about some strange ploy to convince me to stay in St. Augustine for some social club, I intend to stand my ground firmly, reminding everyone that my obligation to Caroline ends once the estate is finally resolved.

After all, I am free to leave whenever I decide to. All of this nonsense of kindred spirits and a ghostly environment is nothing but part of this charming ancient city.

Once Lancelot and I are finished with our morning routine, my first priority on returning home will be to call the ELI Institute for an appointment with Dr. Dante.

However, once I check my phone messages, there is already a request from his office to return their call.

Why is the ELI Institute calling me anyhow? Well, it must be one of those odd coincidences. You know, like when you start thinking of someone you haven't seen for many years and suddenly out of nowhere, they call you.

My appointment is scheduled for Wednesday afternoon, at 2:00 PM. I am both relieved and annoyed; anxious perhaps is a better assessment.

What is it that Dante will reveal about Caroline that I don't already know? It could be anything. After all, what do I know about my eccentric aunt?

Rather than dwell on the numerous possibilities, I decide to take a stroll downtown to clear the cobwebs that are spinning in my mind.

Saint Augustine in October is quite a contrast from any other time of the year. At least that is what I have been told by the few local residents who enjoy taking back their city from the millions of tourists that visit from as near as Jacksonville as well as those who visit internationally.

Walking has always been an excellent method to overcome my anxieties. While living in New York whenever I had moments of insecurity, and they were quite frequent, walking through Central

Park, or streets like Fifth Avenue would bring me a sense of relief.

All the magnificent window front displays, inviting wealthy women in six-inch heels, carrying Louis Vuitton bags to spend money in their shops was fascinating.

Especially when a few feet away street vendors are selling tourists the same knock off items in Saks or Macys on every corner. All this is extremely therapeutic. Here in St. Augustine, there is a different vibe, but the result is as effective.

Early mornings during the week, the heartbeat of this ancient city can be felt entering St. George Avenue. Even the delivery trucks, parked on the narrow side streets, remind me how near the commercial world is to this secluded paradise.

It may be merely a momentary distraction, but it is enough to return me to reality.

This is where I first saw people strolling through the cobblestone walkways in Pirate garb, colonial attire, Gypsy skirts; dancing, chatting, and greeting everyone with a welcoming, "Ahoy, Matey," and robust laughter.

It is also where I met Emerald. Emerald deserves much more than a footnote in this chapter. She is the Sisterhood matriarch.

But for now, I have achieved my purpose. My patience has been restored. Whatever new information Dante shares with me about Caroline will be accepted and appreciated. At least that is what I am striving for.

Chapter Five

I believe we all have a Gypsy spirit, filled with desire, passion, life, vibrancy, energy, confidence, and flow. Your gypsy spirit is the embodiment of your essence, and what makes you, YOU!

Andrea B Riggs,
Gypsy Living

Mandana

*M*eeting Emerald was a life-changing event, literally. It didn't happen naturally or even mysteriously.

Reflecting now on that moment that I first saw Emerald it is actually quite apropos how we met. But, then again, nothing involving Emerald is ever predictable.

That is what makes everything about her so irresistible. The serendipitous spirit that attracts everyone who knows Emerald or who wants to know more of her is contagious.

It was almost a year after I arrived in St. Augustine when my first unexpected encounter with Emerald occurred.

Daylight savings time had just started, so it must have been early November. Lancelot and I were taking our evening stroll toward Castillo de San Marcos, built by the Spanish in 1672.

The fort is walking distance from downtown on the bay front, but it always takes a little longer to reach my destination with Lancelot since he is now competing with Flo as the designated official greeter to every visitor, jogger, or child that takes time to stop for a few moments to give him a friendly pat on his head.

By the time we reached the entrance to the fort, it was closed for the evening. The parking lot was beginning to fill up with the dinner crowd who were taking advantage of the warm November Florida weather to stroll through the ancient city after stopping in for a pleasant meal at one of the many popular restaurants nearby.

This is also an ideal time for a few of us locals to enjoy a tranquil walk on the perimeter of the fort at night.

The lights reflecting off the water on a variety of small craft boats, peppered among exclusive yachts, some with specks of movement on the deck, spark the imagination.

Who were these nomads drifting at a distance? Why were they here? How long would they stay?

But soon it is the sky above that changes my direction. Ribbons laced in chartreuse with a purple haze streaming randomly like wild kites leaving a trail of magenta, coral, fuchsia, and wild orchid in their path.

The spectacular painted sky is soon replaced by a giant, shining silver sea moon, exposing an ethereal glow beneath.

In only a few weeks, these same streets will be filled with new visitors, some from as close as Jacksonville, others as far away as Beijing.

Everyone will be here in this ancient town to celebrate "The Nights of Lights," a spectacular display of millions of white lights throughout the historic city.

But what I am witnessing now as I walk behind the fort is almost as spectacular. At a distance there are some lights dancing on the nearby walls.

I approach cautiously, so as not to disturb anyone. It is Lancelot that suddenly stops first, his head cocked to one side as if to ask, "What are these strange creatures projected on the wall doing jumping around quite randomly?" I actually have the same question.

After a few minutes observing and speculating at a distance, I am able to convince Lance to move forward slowly, with a bacon dog treat. Thankfully I am learning that bacon treats never fail when I need to resort to bribes.

Not to disturb what I am witnessing, I move slowly past the stone wall and take a seat on the grassy hillside, by now in awe of what is being performed at a short distance. It is almost like a private show.

The fort wall is reflecting a variety of dancing images from butterflies to long neck ospreys, to dolphins, to iguanas. Each new movement begins to transform into a creature gracefully gliding through purple, green, blue and even yellow hues of flowers sprouting through cracks formed in the walls.

At the conclusion, I lead Lancelot down the hill where I notice a small group of ladies in elaborate costumes packing away their screens and special lighting effects.

"Excuse me. I just wanted to express to you how lovely I found your show to be it is quite impressive, even quite remarkable I must say, out here in this setting."

No one responds.

A few seconds pass before anyone even notices that I am standing next to them. But then what follows is surreal.

"My darling Mandana, why has it taken you so long to seek us out?" said the rather tall slender lady, her hands filled with paper lanterns, umbrellas, and origami butterflies in various sizes and shapes.

"Have we met before?" I ask taken aback by the question.

"Well, of course, we have met before. Perhaps it will take you some time to recall. Most people who arrive here first sense a familiarity before they are able to fully reconnect to the memory. Déjà vu I believe is what some say this is," the lovely mysterious woman replied.

Just as I was about to request more details, a bearded gentleman wearing a patch over his right eye dressed in traditional pirate garb joined the group of ladies who by this time are discussing their next rendezvous across the street at *Ann O'Malley's* pub.

"Good evening, lovely ladies of the night! Conjuring up the ancient spirits once again I see? The Hallow evenings are past us now. What is the purpose of your shadow dancing on this moonlit evening, pray tell?" asked the friendly Pirate.

"Oh, you scurvy old mate. Who conjured you from the graveyard tonight? It certainly is good to see you in all your wickedness," answered the same lady I was speaking to earlier.

"Oh, my lovely Emerald! You must know that I would travel across the deadly sea just to get a glimpse of that special smile. Let me buy the first round of drinks for all your Gypsy dancers, and even your newest admirer standing over there in awe with her grey ghost companion," the Pirate says, nodding my direction.

Before I can reject his kind offer, I am being led by two other Gypsies across the street, arms laced together, dancing our way to *Ann O'Malley's* with Lancelot prancing in front.

Once inside the pub, everyone moves to different directions greeting other fellow Pirates and Gypsies at the bar leading to the patio. Emerald, who is embracing the scurvy Pirate with a friendly demeanor must have suddenly remembered that I am alone, and close by.

Within a few seconds, she reaches for my hand and leads me to a corner booth. Someone from the kitchen brings Lance a bowl of water and what appears to be a giant ribeye bone with plenty of beef. That will definitely keep him occupied for most of the evening.

"I hope you don't mind joining us for a little evening of merriment. We adopted your aunt many years ago. She is an honorary Gypsy dancer. Caroline always enjoyed making others happy. That is why she is a natural. I hope that you have inherited some of that same sparkle my dear?" Emerald says her comment sounding more like a question than a statement.

"There is so much that I am still learning about Aunt Caroline and so many new details that are filled with mystery. Maybe you can help me unravel some of the perplexing cobwebs that I continue to find surrounding her life. And how, by the way, did you even know who I was? You implied that we have met before, but that would have been impossible," I say, more confused than ever.

Emerald reaches across the table, takes my hand in hers. I feel a strange, yet comforting force of energy pass from her to me. It is very subtle but powerful at the same time.

"Everything in proper order, my dear. You are in the perfect place, at the perfect time, surrounded by everyone that cares for you. This ancient city will fill your lungs with the same air that has enriched the lives of each person who has come before you, and each person that will follow in your footsteps. There is nothing for you to fear," Emerald says, releasing my hand just as the server places a mug of Irish Coffee in front of me. It is the perfect libation on a fall evening in an Irish pub.

"Can you explain to me what you were doing at the fort tonight? I have never seen anything quite so inspiring before," I say, curious to learn more.

"We belong to a group known as Gypsy dancers. It is much more complex than most people realize. We live our lives with a different code of ethics from other people. Yet we also must survive in this modern world that doesn't always accept our lifestyle. Nevertheless, we have taken an oath to always be accepting and inclusive. Anyone, and everyone is welcome to join us for an afternoon or a lifetime. Our dancing is only one piece of the mosaic tile that contributes to our totality," Emerald adds.

It may have been the alcohol or the atmosphere or both, but from that meeting on, I am less anxious and more eager to learn why I am here.

That first meeting with the Gypsies led me to research where they originated, why they have been outcasts, and who they are today.

The *Shadow Dancing* that I witnessed at the fort was more than an impromptu event. I was determined to learn more. Not only was I now committed to learning more about this group of modern Gypsies, but also what exactly motivates them to express such joyful emotions while surrounded throughout centuries by hostility.

Speaking directly to Emerald and her followers may seem like the obvious way to find the answers I was searching for, but before I approached them, I wanted to have some historical knowledge.

What role do these modern gypsies have in St. Augustine today? Are they related in any way to the original gypsies? And what do they want to accomplish by being gypsies?

Many people, myself included, have had a negative first impression of gypsies. This may be contributed in part to a slanted media, as well as how they are portrayed on the movie screen, or even in literature.

It was not until I started my own research that I learned that the first Gypsies originated from India. For centuries, because of their nomadic lifestyle and lack of written language, tracing their origin was nearly impossible. Gypsies didn't even know where they came from.

Many of the Gypsy communities were claiming that they emanate from Egypt. It was the European scholars, in fact, that discovered the Gypsy Romani language is a derivative of the Indian dialect, establishing their origin to be India.

Later this was collaborated in the year 430 when 12,000 Gypsy musicians from the tribe *Jat* were given as a gift to the Persian king, Bahram V. They performed in the royal court as jugglers, dancers, and acrobats, until the Byzantine army captured them in 855.

By the 12th century Constantinople notes that these nomadic groups were known as bear keepers, snake charmers, fortune tellers, and mostly sellers of magic.

Later, as the gypsies moved throughout Europe in large boisterous groups, communities began to fear them.

Women were particularly feared since they were seen as having mysterious powers when they sang and danced. Because of this presumed power, community leaders would often pay the gypsies substantial amounts of money, collected by the citizens, just to have them move outside city limits.

None of what I was learning about gypsies was very flattering. Why would anyone living in the twenty- first century be a gypsy if given a choice?

Emerald and the other dancers did not appear to be doing their dances to get free donations. There certainly are enough pan handlers and homeless people squatting on the streets of St. George and other nearby communities to know the difference.

What I witnessed at the fort the other night was an artistic expression being shared with whomever stopped by to appreciate it. Yet somehow, I know that this is much more than just a form of entertainment. There must be something related to the dancing that I have overlooked.

Just as I am about to turn off the computer in the research section of the public library, an older gentleman dressed in his Pirate garb takes a seat next to me.

"Do you mind?" the gentleman asks politely.

"Perhaps we can have a pleasant little chat on this lovely afternoon," he adds.

That is when I recognize it is the same pirate captain who invited Emerald and her crew to O'Malley's the other night at the fort.

"No, I don't mind at all. You are Emerald's friend, Captain Morgan, am I correct?" I ask, curious why he is at the historical library in the first place.

"Yes, most of my mates know me as such. Martha told me I could find you here searching the archives about St. Augustine gypsies. I thought I might be able to assist you," Captain Morgan says.

Although I really want to know how he got so much information from librarian Martha, I decide not to pursue that question. It really doesn't matter after all. If Captain Morgan actually has any helpful details, I certainly will appreciate knowing them.

"It is very friendly of you, Captain. Most of what I have learned thus far is about the gypsies from India. I am really trying to find some specific connection to my Aunt Caroline and the *ELI* institute," I say, trying to be honest, yet sounding elusive.

"Well, I can tell you that your auntie left her footprints on many different paths surrounding this city, including the gypsies," Morgan says, smiling.

"I know so little about my Aunt Caroline. Everyone that I meet seems to know more about her life than me. At times I feel that Caroline is many different people," I say, feeling rather confused.

"But aren't we all at times, Missy? Some of us simply absorb everything and everyone they meet, adding to our own many layers of life. Your Aunt Caroline was one of those, and we all loved her for that," Morgan said, reaching into his pocket and pulling out a small photo album.

"I think Caroline would like you to have these. It is a little collection of photos that I snapped whenever I wanted to capture some of that magic that she instinctively spread wherever she went. I don't think that she ever knew that I was keeping these. She might have thought that I was stalking her if she knew. I was just fascinated by the joy surrounding me in her presence," Morgan says.

"Oh, I can't possibly take this from you, Captain. They are your memories of special moments," I say, offering the photo album back.

"No...No... my dear! I don't need these photos to remember your precious Auntie. I have her here in my heart all the time," Morgan says, pushing the album back into my hands.

"Well, then, Morgan, I am forever in your debt. These photos will help me to know my aunt better. I will keep them close."

Captain Morgan salutes, bows, and walks away as quietly as he appeared. Once he is gone, I regret not talking to him more about Caroline.

There is something about their relationship that goes beyond what he shares I am certain. Perhaps a closer examination of the photos and meeting with Emerald might reveal more.

For now, it is time to go home, fetch Lancelot who I am certain is pacing the cottage floor wondering where I have been for most of the afternoon.

The first Friday of each month, downtown St. Augustine has an *Art Walk*. The galleries open their doors from 5:00 PM-9:00 PM, inviting the public to browse new art exhibits and enjoy lively receptions where the artists are all available. Since I arrived, the *Art Walk* has been one of my favorite events. Tonight would be the perfect time to take Lancelot with me.

Once I arrive home, I grab Lance's bacon treats, and we were on our way back to town. Before I get past the first block, Jocelyn and Flo are at the corner to meet us.

"Hey, stranger. I just had a premonition that you might be headed downtown to the *Art Walk*. Do you mind if we join you?" Jocelyn asks.

"Not at all. We would love the company. I apologize for not calling you. Everything has been moving so fast lately. I barely get Lancelot out for his walks," I say, knowing that this excuse sounds lame even to me.

"No reason to explain, Mandana. I totally understand. There is a new local artist that I have been following on Facebook. I am hoping that he will have some of his art on display," Jocelyn adds.

At the next corner near the park, she shows me the artwork she is describing on her cellphone It is quite impressive.

"You are definitely right. His art is amazing. Looks like the ones on Facebook are mostly of St. Augustine. Maybe they are priced reasonably. I would like a few prints just in case I decide to ever sell Caroline's house and move away," I say, for the first time realizing the possibility of that statement.

"Seriously, Mandana? I thought you were beginning to like it here," Jocelyn responds genuinely surprised.

"I don't know. There are days that I think I know what direction I am going, and then everything changes," I say, sounding frustrated.

Before we continue with this conversation, I realize we are downtown among a swarm of people.

"If we get separated, I will see you tomorrow morning," Jocelyn says, moving in the opposite direction from where Lance and I are headed.

An urgency more powerful than I have ever experienced before takes control. There is a sudden vision that makes me immediately stop directly where I am. Staring at me through the art gallery window is a painting of Emerald shadow dancing in front of Castillo de San Marcos.

She is wearing her mariposa butterfly costume. The artist has captured the vibrant colors perfectly, juxtaposed with the dark shadows reflected on the fort wall. An image that I could never erase from my mind.

The details are exquisite. The painting reflects precisely what I experienced that evening. A moment that I thought was mine exclusively, until now.

"Excuse me. Are you interested in this painting? You have been staring at it for several minutes. May I perhaps answer any questions you may have?" A young man with an Irish accent asks.

I turn toward him. When our eyes meet, we are both speechless.

Is this what it means by life interrupted? For a brief moment I feel ice running through my veins. A flash of lightning, like an eclipse, reveals a very young couple.

She, with crimson hair, cannot be more than fifteen years old. The boy, slightly older, is wearing a fisherman's cap. He glides toward her like a sleek bird on a frozen sleet of ice completely confident that he is not going to crash.

I have no idea how or why, but I know that I am that girl, and the stranger across from me is this young boy. Somehow, we are now blending together reunited.

It is at this very moment when I finally understand what Anais Nin means when she writes,

Each person represents a world in us, a world possibly not born until they arrive.

Chapter Six

The ghosts of all women you used to be are so proud of the woman you have become.

Nikita Gill
British Indian poet, playwright, writer and illustrator.

Brigid and Liam

"**I** have decided that I am going to live forever," stated the presumptuous young girl with hair the color of chocolate raspberry.

"Truly, Brigid? That will be a great accomplishment. Nothing less would ever be expected from someone named after a Saint, I imagine."

Almost immediately after I voiced that statement, I regretted it. But it was too late for a retraction.

"Are you mocking me, Boy? Because if you are, you know I will twist your ear from here to eternity," Brigid said, lunging towards me like a wild cat ready to rumble.

I knew well that wrath, expressed in her smoldering green eyes. Hastily, I scuttled to the far side of the room, kneeling down behind my grandmother's rocker.

It was known throughout Dingle, our small Irish fishing village, that when Brigid O' Malley gets angry nobody dare approach the tiny redhead tyrant. And that was quite often, by the way.

There were even times that I questioned returning to this house. The house where no one else would dare walk within fifty feet of the entrance.

It had been five years since my grandmother stoically marched over to the rat-infested shanty where Brigid was living alone. Her mother had mysteriously disappeared one day, and her father left for Killarney soon after, never to return.

Brigid was like an abandoned wild animal barely living off scraps that vultures wouldn't even eat. If it had not been for a small community vegetable garden a few kilometers away from Brigid's shack, she may not have survived at all.

My *Maimeo* (MAM o), the Irish name for grandmother, tried to convince the village elders that it was their civic responsibility to rescue the child from such terrible squalor. Mamo was ignored.

Nobody, not even the village parish, would dare take on that responsibility. So *Maimeo,* past seventy years old by this time and suffering from a variety of age-related ailments, knew that she had no other choice but to save the abandoned child.

It was only five years earlier that she found herself raising me when both my parents died from typhus. A small pension inherited from Mamo's deceased husband and whatever funds she was able to save from her meager teaching retirement were barely enough for the two of us.

If it had not been for old man Jacoby hiring me at his ranch a few days prior to Brigid moving in with Mamo, we all may have ended up on the streets of Dingo begging for food.

Three years later, Mamo was diagnosed with lymphoma. That was when she insisted that I promise to care for Brigid until she could care for herself.

What was I to do? It was a dying woman's last wish. *I could never deny anything that my Mamo requested, and especially not now.*

But what I would not do was move back into the cottage once Mamo passed away. It was too difficult to predict when or what might disturb Brigid. There would be days when everything appeared normal. That never lasted for long. Like a seemingly dormant volcano, without warning, the eruption would begin.

Sometimes it was over a very minor disagreement, like whether the lark or the nightingale produces the most melodic music. Brigid could never accept that there might be different opinions.

"Naturally I understand that everyone has their preferences. What I do not concede is when their preferences are not based on logic. Therefore, their assumptions, if not the same as mine, must be invalid," Brigid would argue whenever I attempted to point out the flaws in her arguments.

Because of this attitude, there was always a potential for serious consequences to my actions. Nevertheless, to keep my promise to

Mamo, I visited the cottage once a week, making certain that Brigid was still breathing, providing her with a weekly living allowance, and offering her a variety of poetry to read.

Surprisingly, it was the poetry, music, and plays that Brigid enjoyed the most. Over the next few months, I began to notice a positive change in the young girl's demeanor.

It was as if a transformation from a savage beast to a gentle doe was occurring each time, we started discussing Shakespeare, William Butler Yeats, and Oscar Wilde.

My visits now became more frequent and enjoyable. At times, I even added my own wages to Brigid's allowance to assure that her inheritance would not be depleted before she became independent.

"Are you scared of me, boy? There is nowhere to hide. Come out here and face me like a man," Brigid said, her voice softer, but her eyes still wild.

I stepped away from the rocking chair, noticing from the corner of my eye a wicker broom close enough to grab if I needed it to ward Brigid the "witch" off.

Timing was everything. I knew if I moved too fast Brigid would pounce like a Jaguar going directly for the jugular. Moving too slowly might catch her off guard, allowing me to retain my balance and tower over her petit frame.

What I did not expect was what happened next. Brigid was throwing her entire body at me with full force, like a missile launched without warning. Within a matter of seconds, her screaming stopped. In my arms I was embracing an innocent dove with her neck settled gently next to mine and her body wrapped around me as if we were one.

"What took you so long to get here, baby?" Brigid whispered in my ear, her tongue finding mine. She tasted salty and sweet, like chocolate covered pretzels.

"One day Brigid you are going to greet me like a proper lass does her lover, and not like a banshee, screaming, wailing, and shrieking," I said, both exasperated and excited to feel her femininity in my grasp.

"Now what fun would that be, darling? If I was as predictable as all the wenches at Donovan's Tavern you would tire of me tomorrow," Brigid said, her tongue now licking my inner ear.

What she was saying was true, although I refused to acknowledge it to her. It was the chase that kept me returning for more. How she knew what pleased me was a mystery. From the first moment that I penetrated her there was no doubt that Brigid was a virgin. Yet our love making was unmatched.

"Where did you ever learn to satisfy my hunger for your wanton body, my demon lover," I would ask, sometimes in jest and sometimes truly in awe.

"If I were to reveal to you my magic, what satisfaction will you offer me?" Brigid said, removing her panties, holding them like bait.

She spreads her legs apart, reaches for my fingers, places them in her mouth. I feel her moist tongue, sucking them like a sucker. With her eyes staring deep into mine, she is watching my every reaction until she has captured me. My eyes follow hers obediently. At this moment whatever Brigid wishes of me I will do. She is my master; I am here to please her.

Once she knows that she has me my eyes start to follow hers, she moves my fingers slowly, methodically, into the wet cleft between her legs, never releasing me from her gaze.

I already know how she feels inside. I have been there many times. Each time I am hungry for more. But now I lift Brigid up, legs spread wide, and gently lie her on the floor.

The same salty chocolate sensation that I tasted earlier fills my mouth. I hear Brigid groan with pleasure as she moves her hips in perfect rhythm with my mouth.

The game has shifted. I am now in complete control. Once our bodies are in perfect cadence with one another, we reach our climax together. Everything surrounding me explodes into a light show unlike any fireworks that I have ever experienced.

Liam stops talking, sips his coffee and waits for me to respond. I am not sure what to say or how to accept what I have just heard. It takes me a few moments to gather my thoughts.

What Liam is sharing with me at this moment is a relationship that he claims he had with his lover and wife, Brigid O'Donnell, in 1895. And I am that wife. I am sitting in front of the man I have loved my entire life, now reunited mysteriously at Meehan's this very moment, one hundred and twenty-six years later. But am I? This is not the man I once knew. Not the man I lost at Stonehenge.

"Are you really trying to convince me, Mr. Callahan, that you are in fact Liam?" I ask, reaching for Lancelot's leash. He is munching on a steak bone that one of the servers gave him when we came in.

"Wait a minute, please! I know that this is a lot for you to accept, but there is so much more. I just can't tell you everything right now, right here. You must trust me," Liam says, grabbing my hand gently.

I stand here awkwardly for a moment trying to rationalize a completely irrational situation.

What does this stranger have to gain by fabricating this wild story? Does he know anything about Caroline? Everyone that I have met seems to know more about my life recently than even I do, or at least they claim to.

Before I can ask any further questions, Liam looks directly at me and says, *"What we call the beginning is often the end, and to make an end is to make a beginning. The end is where we start from (Little Gidding, TS Eliot).*

Without even thinking about what I have just heard, these words came flowing from my mouth, *"We shall not cease from exploration, and the end of all our exploring will be to arrive where we started and know the place for the first time."*

What was it that I just said? And where did those words come from?

Liam and I look at one another, instinctively now knowing that we had finally reunited after a very long journey.

Chapter Seven

She saw the myriad gods, and beyond God his own effable eternity; she saw that there were ranges of life beyond our present life, ranges of mind beyond our present mind and above these she saw the splendors of the spirit.

Sri Aurobindo
Indian Philosopher and Spiritual Leader

Mandana

The most recent scientific research that has evolved regarding the study of immortality has actually existed since early Greek mythology.

When Tithonus was taken away by Eros from the royal house of Troy, it was her desire to make him immortal. Unfortunately, when Zeus agreed to grant Eros this gift of eternity, he failed to give Tithonus immortal youth.

Certainly, modern man and woman can immediately recognize this flaw. Without extending youthfulness, life becomes a curse rather than a gift.

During all of the studies and testing at the *ELI Institute,* Dr. Dante knew that living eternally must have a purpose beyond a self-centered, egotistical desire. Many of the candidates who volunteered to be studied did so for the sole purpose of vanity. Caroline was the exception.

During the initial interview for the program, Dante learned that Caroline was truly a philanthropist. Everything that she shared about her desire to contribute positively to the community was a refreshing testimony.

Later, when Dante learned that Caroline was already over a century old, while appearing no older than forty, he knew that she must be the initial prototype for his perfected component.

From Dante's first meeting with Caroline, he knew immediately that she was not from the twenty-first century. There were just too many idiosyncrasies in her mannerisms.

To begin with Caroline refused to own a cell phone, participate in any social media, and rarely watched television. It was not that she was computer illiterate, it was that she had no desire to be trapped in a cyber cycle that offered little human connection with no positive attributes.

Dante did find this attitude rather ironic since the only reason Caroline was still alive on this earth was due to someone, or something that extended her life through an advanced scientific anomaly.

It was that mysterious missing clue that Dante knew he must discover to make his thesis valid and possible.

Although the prospect of living forever is much more desirable than the alternative, death, there are many challenges when the possibility of achieving extended life is provided as an actual viable choice.

First, there are the physical and mental limits of the actual body. It does not appear practical to extend those important human attributes separately.

But, even if we are able to overcome these obstacles by offering extended life that assures people will retain youthful appearances and strong sharp intelligence, there are the philosophical possibilities to consider related to the mysterious soul and spirit.

Many questions regarding our harmony with the natural balance of life, religious implications, and of course moral responsibility all offer a variety of reasonable debates. Some have already been discussed.

Recently, a three-year Immortality Project, worth $5.1 million, headed by the University of Riverside, California research team was completed. This was followed by the Templeton Foundation funding Philosopher John Martin Fischer's project.

After reviewing thirty-four principles studying the current state of thought on Extended Life, the researchers agreed to continue experiments on non-human species.

One study that now seems quite primitive concluded that mice lived nearly five years (twice the normal mouse life span) when a gene for a normal growth hormone was removed. Can you imagine what those scientists would have done with Caroline once they established that she was 246 years old?

I have heard that the normal life span for a woman in the twenty-first century is eighty years old. But, if Caroline was born in 1774, the life span at that time was only thirty-four years, depending on your financial status.

That certainly is a much more impressive longevity result than what the lab mouse study indicates.

All of this information that Dr. Dante has provided me is randomly filtering through my mind.

As fascinating as all of this is, I have no idea how it relates to me.

After leaving Liam, also known as Brendon, on Monday at the art gallery, I stopped at a small courtyard behind one of the many shops on St. George Street.

Someone had left a bowl of fresh water near the shade tree where Lancelot was headed. I found a bench nearby and took a seat, trying to clear my mind of everything that was racing through it at the moment.

The first thing that I wanted to know was how Liam/ Brendon was able to capture the very same scene that I witnessed at the fort.

Then there was the letter that I read in the pile of notes that Caroline left me.

It was her emotional memory of meeting her husband unexpectedly after many years of separation. There were some lines from a poem that convinced her that he really was her husband.

How could those lines from an Eliot poem verify his identity? Why wouldn't she know who he was? And how long were Emerald and Caroline friends?

I was familiar with the Eliot lines that Caroline wrote, but I never memorized them.

Google verified what I expected. Both verses were from *Little Gidding,* the fourth and final poem from *Four Quartets,* a collection of poems by TS Eliot all about time, humanity, and salvation, published in 1942.

Little Gidding is a small village in Cambridgeshire, England where Eliot chose to write his poems after surviving air raids during World War II. The specific lines that Liam quoted and that Caroline replied to are Eliot's spiritual message of the unity in past, present, and future.

Eliot claims that without this unity there is no salvation. What I am perplexed about is why were those words chosen by Liam and Caroline.

Someone nearby was strumming an unfamiliar, but pleasant tune on a guitar. I briefly closed my eyes, feeling a gentle breeze blow past. When I opened my eyes, there was a shadow of a man standing in front of me.

The sun was glaring in my eyes, forbidding me to focus on anything but the stranger's fisherman's cap.

Startled, but not afraid, I reached for Lancelot's leash to stand up mostly so that I could see clearly. But, before I was on my feet, the stranger sat next to me on the bench. It was then that I recognized he was Brendon.

"Did you follow me here?" I asked, trying not to sound annoyed, although I was, slightly.

"Not exactly. It is a favorite place Caroline often stopped at on her way home from the art gallery. I sometimes come by and reminisced with her," Brendon said, quietly but not melancholy.

I waited a few seconds before responding. *Was he Liam or Brendon at this moment?*

"It is definitely a pleasant place to meditate," I said, realizing that my phone was still displaying the information in *Little Gidding*.

Brendon glanced briefly at the screen.

"Do you want to know why your aunt memorized those lines?" he asked, taking my hand in his.

I wasn't sure if I was ready to hear his explanation, but I did not pull my hand away. He looked directly into my eyes. It was as if he was looking deep into my soul.

After a few seconds, I nodded my head since I was speechless.

"There is nothing to fear, Mandana. You are exactly where you are supposed to be. Always with me."

Although I did not understand what Brendon meant at the moment, I believed him.

"When Caroline and Liam were wed, they pledged that nothing, not even time, would ever separate them. Dr. Dante will explain to you the scientific circumstances that made their pledge possible, but what I can share with you is the pact," Brendon said, without taking his eyes off me.

"I am not sure why, but I think I already know," I answered.

"Perfect. Then you tell me, Mandana," Brendon said, smiling.

"It was on their wedding anniversary. They were on a cruise. It was a transatlantic ship to New York. Liam gave Caroline a signed copy of poems by T.S. Eliot, her favorite poet. There was a bookmark on the page marked *Little Gidding*. She read it to him and said that when the time comes for them to leave this earth they must have a way to identify each other when they meet again in another life. They agreed on reciting the lines from the poem."

Once again, I felt as if my being was being melded with another. Tears were tracing my face. Brendon moved closer to me, kissing each tear away and holding me tightly in his arms.

"Welcome home, Mandana," he said, cradling my head.

When I felt his mouth on mine, there was a sense of both peace and panic!

Chapter Eight

She was beautiful, but not like those girls in the magazine. She was beautiful for the way she thought. She was beautiful for the sparkle in her eyes when she talked about something she loved. She was beautiful for the ability to smile even if she was sad. No, she wasn't beautiful for something as temporary as her looks. She was beautiful deep down to her soul.

F Scott Fitzgerald
The Beautiful and Damned

Brigid Caroline Marie O'Sullivan Callahan
January 1, 1768-February 28, 2017

Life did not begin until I met Liam. At least nothing significant in my life is worth recalling until the moment that we met. What might be more remarkable is how our relationship endured for two hundred and thirty-nine years when it was unlikely for us to have ever met in the first place.

Living at Oxfordshire, in South East England with my father nearby, there was a wealthy family with whom we shared surnames, but nothing more. At least it seemed that way until I met Marie.

Marie Murphy was born at Black Burton, Oxfordshire, on the same date that I was born. Since there was only one infirmary we must have been cared for in the same nursery, quite possibly even by the same wet nurse.

Marie was the second child of Richard Murphy, an Anglo-Irish politician, writer, and inventor, whereas I was the only child of a commoner and scullery maiden.

Many years later, I learned that Richard Murphy also fathered twenty-two additional children with four different wives. Perhaps that's why the villagers referred to him as the Sultan.

When Marie was thirteen years old, an eye infection nearly blinded her, requiring that she immediately be sent home from boarding school. Unfortunately for Marie, but quite beneficial to us, a tutor would be required for the remaining semester.

My father, who taught in London prior to marrying my mum, immediately applied for this position. I was included in the contractual arrangement.

Every day I would accompany my father to the estate, since by this time Mum had run off with the local butcher six months earlier.

Money was scarce now, and if father had not received this tutoring position, which eventually included housing, I am certain that we would have both been homeless in a very short time.

Immediately Marie and I became close friends. We shared a love for literature as well as all arts. Of course, my appreciation was limited to the few books I could find in the small village library, while Marie had read so many exciting stories that I never knew existed.

Perhaps that is why Marie was so determined to save the world. It was she who introduced me to the *Lunar Society of Birmingham,* a British Dinner Club of elite intellectuals, including the *West Midlands Enlightenment,* known for their astute legal manifestation of scientific, economic, political, and cultural issues.

It all sounded quite sophisticated to me, since my interest was in poetry, not equal rights.

The *Lunar Society* adopted their name from meetings held once a month during the full moon. Marie, although only a teenager, continued a bond with this group through written correspondence until her sudden disappearance.

The scientific nature of the society reports always sounded boring until Marie shared with me their studies on extended life research. That was when everything began to sound interesting. Philosophers and mathematicians were beginning to explore ways to increase the span of life from birth to death.

"Just listen to this, Caroline. Just imagine what it might be like to continue living into many different, future centuries."

"Nicolas de Condorcet wrote these words in his latest study, 'No doubt man will not become immortal, but cannot the span constantly increase between the moments he begins to live and the time when naturally without illness or accident, he finds life a burden.' (*Sketch for a Historical Picture of the Progress of the Human Mind*). I for one am not afraid of living longer than I am expected to. Are you,

Caroline?" Marie asked, sounding excited as if she had already mapped out her future.

I now recall, fifty years later, when Mary Shelley published, (on my Birthday, January 1) in 1818, her most famous work *Frankenstein,* how this earlier conversation made much more sense.

How I wished that I had taken more seriously Marie's letters to the *Lunar Society* then.

This extended life theory ultimately led Marie to learn more about how the Irish commoner survived through so much poverty and despair.

She was determined to accomplish this study by mingling with the Irish gentry, sneaking away from the house into the stables or farm fields for many days.

The workers would share with Marie their meager bowls of soup, fresh bread, but most importantly their tales about Cailleach, known as the *Veiled One* or the *Queen of Winter.*

These stories about fairies and supernatural beings not only fascinated Marie, but she was also obsessed by them. I am convinced that it finally led her to decide on living permanently with the farmers.

"Have you lost your mind, Marie? This plan of yours will never succeed. We will both be punished for life, and my father will certainly be fired," I said, once learning what Marie was suggesting.

"Since nobody, not even my own father most of the time, can tell us apart, it will be simple to switch identities," Marie argued.

"Playing simple pranks is not nearly the same as a permanent, daily, personality shifting," I argued vehemently, with little success.

"I have it all planned. We will take a few weeks learning each other's entire daily cycle. By the time we have finished neither of us will know who we are. Even now we are more like twin sisters than any other people that I have known," Marie said, guiding me to the looking glass to prove her point that it was simple to switch roles.

First, we did it simply as playful pranks with the servants. Then Marie started insisting that we do it more often. She would say that it allowed her to experience for herself what "the authentic people" were like.

This was the only way that she could truly portray them in the novels that she was determined to write.

"You see, Caroline, this is why I need to be 'you' as often as possible. The peasants won't trust me. They fear that I am spying on them. But you are no threat to their well-being. To truly understand what motivates the underprivileged, to understand how they continue to have hope, I must observe them, live with them, share with them. You do understand, now don't you, Caroline?" Marie would ask, almost sounding desperate.

I had to admit that looking in the mirror it was difficult to tell us apart. Regardless how unlikely it may seem that we could ever truly achieve this role reversal, I already knew that it would be even more impossible to convince Marie of the obstacles.

Marie's eyes grew wide with enthusiasm.

"Caroline! Just look at us! We are the same person! I will finally experience what I am destined to achieve, and you, my second soul, will live the life of luxury that you deserve," she said, gleaming with joy.

There wasn't any way that I was going to convince Marie that this was a bad idea. Besides, she was correct. I was looking forward to enjoying the rich lifestyle, even if it was going to be only a temporary situation. What I never expected was meeting Liam.

One afternoon while Marie was out mingling with the common folk, I was enjoying tea in the garden with a house cat that strongly resembled a Rubinque painting voluptuous and fluffy.

"An excellent morning to enjoy a bit of crotchet while admiring the blooming gardens," the unfamiliar voice said, as a tall man stood in front of me.

It was not clear where this stranger came from or who he was. His presence startled me.

Did he know Marie? If so, how was I to answer him without revealing who I was? This was definitely an awkward, disturbing set of circumstances. If the stranger suspected that I was impersonating Marie, it could be the end of our charade. It would also be extremely difficult to explain who I really am.

"This is one of my favorite times of the day to peacefully reflect on how I should move forward," I answered, with my face turned away from his, hoping that my evasive response was adequate.

What I never expected was the young man reaching toward my chin, lifting it up, and staring directly into my eyes.

Whoever this young man is there is no escaping his presence now.

"Then I am exactly where I should be," the young man said confidently.

Moving away, rather startled, I said, "Excuse me, sir, have we been introduced? You appear to be quite familiar, yet I do not recall our meeting."

Knowing that this might be a presumptuous, even dangerous response, I really felt trapped with no choice but to ask directly.

"Liam Callahan, a proud member of the Callahan Clan of Munster," the young man said proudly taking a graceful bow.

It was the first time that I noticed his flaxen blonde hair, and lean but muscular body. Staying focused was my only concern.

"It is a pleasure, Mr. Callahan," I said, now standing up, my head barely meeting his shoulders, extending my hand to meet his.

There was still no indication why Liam was here, or who he was visiting.

Do I dare ask?

"And who do I have the pleasure to be meeting with this morning?" Liam asked, his eyes sparkling with intense curiosity.

Before I could respond, thankfully I was interrupted.

"Liam, my darling! It is so gracious of you to stop in and visit with us. I will ask Sadie to fetch more tea and scones. Have you met my doppelgänger yet?" Marie asked, unexpectedly appearing from behind the rose bush trellis.

"I do believe that we were in that very process Marie, although I must say that although the two of you are quite similar in beauty, I knew immediately that Caroline was NOT you," Liam said, my hand still held in his.

Had I told him my name? I was quite sure I had not. How did he know it was Caroline?

Marie looked at the two of us, smiled, and said, "Well, my dear you never held my hand like that either."

I pulled my hand back at that remark, not sure if Marie was being playful or jealous.

"Well, Marie, I am quite sure that sometime during our childhood romps that I not only held your hand but tugged on your ponytail, kissed your cheek, and stuck out my tongue at you," Liam said, walking toward Marie wrapping his arms around her shoulders.

They both laughed, appearing happy to be reunited.

"Why has it been so long since our last visit? You must tell me about all of your adventures. You know how much I want to travel, but Papa refuses to allow it. He fears my health will be in jeopardy,"

Marie said, as Sadie started to pour the tea.

"I am much more interested in what has been happening here with you, Marie. And particularly with your houseguest. What are the two of you plotting? It must be great trickery. You have always found wild ways to have fun Marie," Liam said, looking at me for a response, although the question was directed toward Marie.

"Well, if you swear an oath not to breathe a word to anyone, I will tell you some exciting news," Marie said.

Liam placed his finger on his lips to take the oath of secrecy.

"Caroline and I are exchanging places. For a short time, I will be her, visiting the farm laborers daily. She will remain here on the estate with father and the tutors, living my daily, boring life. When I have finished my research, I will begin writing my novel. And it will be a best seller. Isn't this just the most exciting adventure that I have ever created?" Marie said, anxious to hear Liam's response.

"It is definitely challenging. How long do you think that you will be able to get away with this façade, Marie?" Liam asked, sounding concerned.

I was beginning to feel uneasy already. Not that Liam would reveal what Marie was doing, but if anyone else learned about this plan, we both would have plenty of explaining to do.

"Liam, you know how clever I am! Nobody will discover our little secret. And now that you are here it is perfect. Certainly, you won't mind taking Caroline out for afternoon carriage rides, evening dinners, and boat excursions. That will keep her, or in this case me, away from my father, her father, and the other tutors, making it less likely that anyone will discover the switch," Marie said, looking at us both.

Liam took a few minutes to consider the proposal.

"It will definitely give us a great opportunity to learn more about one another, Caroline. That is, if you don't mind spending that much time with a stranger?" Liam asked, looking amused.

Suddenly, becoming Marie was much more inviting knowing that Liam would be my escort.

"I am looking forward to hearing all about your travels, Mr. Callahan. Thank you for such a kind offer," I said, trying to be calm, when in fact the idea of spending so much time with this impressive gentleman made me extremely nervous.

That first meeting in the garden was to be the start of a journey that would lead us through many different lives, so extraordinary that neither of us knew what to expect.

Spending time with Liam was natural. It was as if we had known each other forever.

For privacy we would secretly escape from the estate to be alone, although our relationship was quite platonic at this stage. That would soon change without any forewarning. It all started once the *Banshee* arrived.

I had never actually seen a *Banshee,* although we all knew who they were and what they did. Then one day as I was returning from the village, it happened.

"Is that truly a *Banshee,* Liam?" I asked, noticing the old woman feebly walking on the dirt road toward the estate.

"It certainly resembles one. Although I could not clearly see her face. The grey cloak over her head is covering most of her head. But did you notice how small she is. Certainly, no taller than two feet," Liam noted, warning me not to look back at her.

"Do you think that she is coming to the estate? That certainly must be a bad omen, if she is," I said not sure what to do next.

"There is nothing that we can do but wait," Liam said, as we approached the gates to the entrance.

Three days later, there was still no sign of the *Banshee,* and yet I felt her presence everywhere. Marie was spending more evenings away from home without anyone noticing, or at least nobody, including Marie's father, seemed to care about her absence.

When my own father resigned from his tutoring obligations, Marie insisted that I remain as long as possible. She argued that I was her only true friend and that without my companionship she would experience serious depression.

This was obviously only a decoy. Marie had no need for me, or quite honestly, no need for anyone.

But now it seemed that all of our diabolical planning to deceive everyone was unnecessary. Nobody cared where Marie went or that Liam and I were spending hours alone together.

It was as if some strange veil had been placed like a tent over the entire community. Everyone appeared the same, but their actions were apathetic, lethargic, completely indifferent. I was convinced that this new attitude was a result of the *Banshee* arriving.

"Have you noticed, Liam, how everyone surrounding us appears to be detached from reality? It is as if they are moving about mechanically without any emotions ever since we saw the *Banshee* three days ago," I said, one afternoon while horseback riding near the ocean.

Without answering me, quite suddenly Liam grabbed the reins of my horse, jumped off his stallion, and led me silently into the surrounding wooded area. Once he found a secluded path, he stopped near a tree, secured both horses, reached his arms around my waist and lifted me down from my saddle.

"What are we doing here?" I asked, uncomfortable at how silent and secretive Liam appeared. This was definitely not like him.

Without answering me, Liam placed both his hands on my face gently, yet firmly, his eyes staring intensely into mine, refusing to acquiesce; refusing even to blink. I was frozen with unexpected anticipation.

What is happening? Why am I not shaking with fear? My body is quivering, but with excitement, not fright.

Without any forewarning, Liam suddenly placed his mouth over mine, pulled my skirt up, his fingers finding my wetness, plunging them inside me.

My eyes closed; I felt his stiff tongue and lips sucking my breath as the nipples on my breasts hardened.

In seconds we were on the ground, covered with a blanket of dry leaves. Liam's mouth ravaging my body with a gentle force that I never had experienced or imagined ever existed.

Yet it was happening at this very moment to me. My body was quivering, uncontrollably shaking, not with panic, but with an extreme desire that this intense intoxication would continue forever.

Not knowing how much more I could take, I began to feel a warm gushing flow from between my legs as Liam's hard member pushed relentlessly in and out, up and down, in perfect harmony, with my legs wrapped around his waist, and the sweet smell of honeysuckle making me dizzy with joy.

Then it stopped, as suddenly as it had started. Liam remained inside of me for moments without moving.

After what seemed like forever, I felt a release. Empty once again, alone once more, all I wanted and needed was more. More of Liam. Something wonderful was gone, and I wanted it back. Whatever it was that I lost, that I never had before, I now knew I needed.

It took Liam a few more moments to speak. He lifted my half naked body cradled in his arms, whispering gently, "My Niamh! Gra go Deo!" Repeating those words over and over.

It would be much later when I would realize the significance of those words and how Tir na nOg would affect our lives.

My head was spinning uncontrollably, my body filled with Liam, and my mind unable to focus on anything but these words. Nothing was real, but us.

The surrounding world was nothing but a melting wax candle that we must escape or be destroyed.

Chapter Nine

"She is the one in my heart and I'm zero without her. When the world tries to divide her from me that's where our love becomes infinite."

Nanruth Nanda

Whatever it was that led to Liam and I becoming intimate I attributed to the *Banshee*.

Naturally, Liam argued that there was no relevance at all to my conclusion. He claimed that his desire to be affectionate was a natural reaction to the many hours that we were spending together. There was nothing more to explain but that his physical needs had exceeded his patience.

Liam was and would always be, my only lover. Not the only man that I ever shared intimacy with, but absolutely the only man I ever truly loved. It was a distinction that I learned after many years of separation and reuniting.

Nevertheless, it was always the *Banshee* that made me self-conscious. What power did she have, and for how long would she remain in the village, hidden, yet present?

Throughout the Irish countryside, there are mounds that appear almost randomly, although these tumuli are actually stones raised over ancient graves. Barrows, or kurgan, as they are often called in other parts of the world, date back hundreds of years.

I once read that George Petrie, an Irish painter and musician in the nineteenth century, became interested in archeology. When he, surveyed a tumulus near Grianan of Aileach it was determined that the mound predates the Neolithic Age.

Banshees are also known as "women of the fairy mound," since they are female spirits called to herald death of a family member. Their tortuous screams of painful grief are known as keening, also referred to as Sean-nos singing.

A vocal music composition performed in the Gaelic language with such severe lament, including long melodic phrases, love songs, and intense lullabies that once heard nobody ever wants to hear it again. The pain is too intense.

This Sean-nos singing is at least seven centuries old. Many academic musicians believe Sean-nos to be the key that unlocks all the Irish mysteries hidden in the culture vault.

Whatever the *Banshee's* purpose in visiting the village may have been, it was not only I who was disturbed.

"Did it ever occur to you, Caroline, that it is *your* obsession with the *Banshee* that is causing you to predict ominous events? If we continue with our lives as normal, the *Banshee* will move on without us even realizing that she was ever here," Liam said, obviously frustrated with my attitude lately.

Shortly after our first intimate encounter, Liam rented a room in the village. It was very sparsely furnished with only a bed, table, one chair, and a modest half washroom. Nonetheless, it was all that we needed for some privacy a few evenings during the week.

Since Liam needed to return to Dublin every week, this was an ideal arrangement until we could decide what would be our next plan. As of now there was no real marriage commitment.

In truth neither of us ever mentioned marriage. What we were experiencing felt much more committed than a legal document. After all, that document did not prevent my mother from running away with the butcher or Marie's father from having many wives.

Sensing Liam's frustration this morning, I raised myself up from the small bed and walked naked toward the breakfast table where he was sitting, sipping his tea and reading the morning paper from Dublin.

Before Liam realized I was there, I dipped my finger into the honey pot, anointed my breasts, which were firmly ready with the sweet mixture, fondling the nipples in preparation for our early morning ritual.

Liam was not prepared when I removed the newspaper he was holding. My naked body was now straddled around his waist with my breasts inviting his mouth to take in the sweet aroma. As well orchestrated as an erotic symphony, Liam's hard, moist penis was inside me pulsating in perfect beat with my heart.

The natural movement between us intensifies with Liam's mouth sucking my nipples, our hands intertwined as he plunges deeper and deeper, harder and harder until a sensual inner explosion simultaneously creates a surreal sunburst sensation.

Liam and I are now one.

"Was it something that I said, or is this the way you start your morning every day?" Liam asked, smiling with delight, refusing to release me.

"Only on the mornings that you decide to have tea and honey with your crumpets, darling," I say, slowly releasing his penis from my possession.

"Then let me proclaim that this day forward each morning will be a tea and honey day!" Liam smiles, kissing me passionately.

What was to happen in the next forty-eight hours could never have been predicted. What was predictable came many years later.

After being with Liam intimately, waking up in my own bed without him never seemed the same again. Longing to feel Liam nearby in the middle of the night, realizing he was gone, was becoming more disturbing each night that we were apart.

Yet I knew that if anyone discovered our relationship was now far beyond platonic, both of our reputations would be ruined.

Being a young female during the eighteenth century involved sexually with a man ten years older would have insured me being sent to the nearest brothel.

And Liam? Because of the age difference, would surely be prosecuted for taking advantage of my innocence. Ironically, if I became pregnant, my "bastard" child would be taken care of financially.

There were many gentlemen that boasted about their illegitimate children almost as if it were an honor, rather than a disgrace.

Regardless, none of these scenarios were suitable for either of us. Following the expected societal protocol until we were at least financially independent to make our own choices appeared to be the only option.

It was because of these potential severe repercussions that I knew that I must spend a few weeks at the estate, allowing all the truth mongers to focus on some other poor victims.

Liam would return to the university in Dublin at the end of the week, and everything would resume as it was prior to our rendezvous until we could decide a safe way to meet again.

Being without Liam was torture. The letters never seemed enough. The first semester seemed endless. Keeping busy with all of Marie's projects made the days easier, but not the nights.

"That is exactly why, my dearest Caroline, I refuse to be enamored by any young man. They steal our hearts, go off to university or army, and here we are left heartbroken," Marie said, trying to advise me.

"Neither of us intended for this to happen, Marie. I am not even sure if I understand how all of this occurred even now," I replied, setting aside some manuscripts that we were researching together.

"Well, I could give you an abridged anatomy lesson if you like, Caroline? But I have a feeling that you may know more than I do at this point in your relationship with Liam," Marie said, snickering.

"Are you implying that Liam and I have had an inappropriate relationship?" I asked, defensively.

"Oh, my sweetest Caroline, nothing is ever inappropriate when you are in love. Just be very careful that you and Liam have taken the precautions necessary. I will not be able to protect you if this results in a scandal, although you know that I will try," Marie said, walking toward me with her arms outstretched.

Her embrace was loving and genuine. I also knew that she was right in her assessment of the relationship Liam and I were now involved in.

This was my last conversation with Marie. She had left the estate unexpectedly, I presumed to be with the laborers as in the fields.

By this time, her father had given up keeping track of his daughter. To be honest, I am not certain where he was most of the day. Although occasionally we would eat supper together.

I concluded that Marie's father continued to allow me to remain at the estate as his companion to avoid any further gossip in the town. Unfortunately, that was not to be enough to prevent tragedy from occurring.

One week after Marie departed the estate, in the early morning hours, just before sunrise, I was awakened by horrific screams. At first it sounded like a wounded animal, but as the loudness increased moving closer, the wailing became more melodic and intense.

Grabbing my robe immediately, I ran downstairs. The drapes were drawn open but there was still no sunrise. Rather candles were lit, people were rushing around randomly with no direction. It was as if I had entered onto a stage where deranged actors were stumbling frantically, not knowing their roles nor their lines.

After a few hysterical minutes observing this absurd play, I confronted one of the maids who was carrying an armful of loose towels.

"Stop! Please! Wait! What is happening in this household?" I asked, screaming above all the outside wailing.

"Oh, something horrible, my lady! Mistress Marie and Sir Liam have been found in the pastures, their bodies barely recognizable. Someone says their faces have been eaten," the maid said screaming.

Liam? Marie? Dead? How? Why?

Impossible! Liam is in Dublin. And, if this is true, why were Liam and Marie even together?

Chapter Ten

We are the ones with the messy hair
The dirty feet and that wild sparkle
In our eyes.
We belong amongst the wildflowers.
Listening to the wind,
Or with our toes dipped in the sea.
We embrace the arts.
Creativity is often our universal
Language
Yet even with fire in our blood
Unbridled spirit and wild heart
We do not all wander
Some have found freedom in one
Place.
Home

Sunflower and Mandana

There is a natural juxtaposition that exists between Gypsies, Pirates, Nomads, and Mermaids. Throughout history, artistic depiction, literature, and music, it is obvious that the connection between these groups originates from a society that rejects a romanticized lifestyle that differs from the norm.

Meeting Mandana for the first time was like a family reunion. There are some people that the moment you see their faces or hear their voices a connection clicks, turning on an internal spark that assures you that somehow you must be connected from another time or world. Mandana and I have that bond.

Honestly, there were many times that I would imagine that Mandana was Caroline. Certainly, this is not as impossible as it may sound, once all the facts are known about Eli.

Regardless how comfortable we were with each other, Mandana had a lot to learn about the *Sisterhood.* Inviting her to this speaking event tonight is the beginning of the process.

Historian Marilyn Manchester is speaking at the Lewis Auditorium about the historical origin of the Gypsy Pirate community and the transformation into cultural artistic influence in the twenty- first century.

On the screen in front of us is a black and white engraving titled *"Pirate and Gypsy"* 1807 by James Heath. It is an image of a young man, seated with a long rifle, a horn strung around his neck, and a brimmed hat.

In front of him stands a woman with a long skirt, dark cape, holding a staff, and pointing to an overcast sky. Both objects are surrounded by the coastal landscape with several birds.

We are told that this is the front cover of *Dissertation of the Gypsies; a study of life, death, marriage, burial, language, science, and art throughput Europe.*

Dr. Manchester emphasizes that in 1744 the Vagrancy Act mandated gypsies, beggars, strolling actors, peddlers, and anyone who refused to work in a wage-based system to be beaten and imprisoned.

The entire auditorium is silent.

"I have heard this before. Even today many people don't believe that our Krews are legitimate, even when our events raise needed money for the homeless in our community," I whisper to Mandana.

"It is a stigma that many people can't overlook. When I was traveling with the Renaissance actors a few years ago many of the cities treated us like vagrants," Mandana says in response.

"People simply cannot or do not want to recognize how much we do here. We enjoy each other's company. We enjoy dressing in our period attire, and entertaining. All we ask is to be respected," I say, quietly.

Mandana smiles, clutches my hand, and says, "I know that change is coming, Sunny!"

What I wanted to say was change has already happened, innocent Mandana. What you are about to learn will not only be somewhat disturbing but beyond anything that your mind can ever comprehend.

"What Dr. Manchester will be speaking about next is directly related to your Aunt Caroline's ancestry. It should be quite enlightening as well as fascinating," I whisper, hoping that Mandana is paying close attention.

On the large screen at the center stage is a projection of pages from *The Yellow Book of Lecan,* a book of tales known as *"The Feast of Mongfind,"* a legendary witch queen that married the King of Tara.

Tara is one of the most sacred sites in Ireland where the seats of High Kings and the Stone of Destiny are found. One hundred and forty-two kings are said to have reigned here. The Hill is also referred to often as *Temair,* a sacred place where the gods would enter another world.

Saint Patrick is known for coming here to convert the pagans to Christianity.

I lean closer to Mandana so that she can hear me.

"The Irish, especially the ancient Celtic people, strongly believe that fairies and other supernatural beings are visitors that came from another dimension. The myths and legends of *Tuatha De Danann* created a sense that air in Ireland is filled with magic," I say, waiting for a reaction.

Mandana turns her face toward me.

"I often feel that way when I walk downtown through George Street in the late evening and early morning," she says, obviously surprised.

"Exactly! You are now beginning to sense the connection. But this is only the beginning of so much more, Mandana."

We both listen attentively as Dr. Manchester continues to weave her historical research from Ireland into the Saint Augustine tapestry she is artistically creating.

These tales are not unfamiliar to me. Caroline would often share her favorites with all of us after an evening filled with dancing freely through the moonlit cobblestone narrow streets after the tourists had all left.

It was not uncommon for a group of us to return to Caroline's cottage with a variation of libations to be served in the lush garden where there were always plenty of lounge chairs with homemade colorful afghans, beckoning us to relax near the open fire pit.

Caroline was like a mother hen with her baby chicks, taking care that each of us was peacefully situated before starting to share her delightful tales, which each of us was eager to hear.

Listening to Dr. Manchester provide an historical perspective only reaffirmed how authentic Caroline was.

How was I going to convince Mandana that her aunt expected her to remain in Saint Augustine to continue her legacy?

"Did Dr. Manchester just say that there are traces of Caroline Marie Brigid Callahan's heritage here in St. Augustine?" Mandana whispered in my ear.

I have been so preoccupied with my own memories of Caroline that I was not focusing on what was being shared at this moment.

"Sorry, Mandana, my mind is drifting in another direction. What exactly is your question?" I asked, rather embarrassed to admit that I was not paying attention.

Mandana said nothing. She was intensely listening to the speaker, as was I now.

"As many of you know, Saint Augustine is a trove of mystery. Excavations throughout the ancient city have revealed some extraordinary discoveries. How many of you sitting here today are aware of the tunnels directly beneath you?"

Everyone sitting in the auditorium was awe-stricken, that is everyone but me. I, of course, have known this for decades. Most of us in the Gypsy Pirate community try to keep this information private.

There are actually a few exclusively owned clubs that are still operating underground. They are only accessible through member invitation. I was hoping that Dr. Manchester was not going to reveal this information.

Thankfully, she seemed to only be using the underground tunnels as a hook to keep her audience attentive.

"Well, let me just save those details for another speaking event. Today I hope that you are here to learn more about the historical connection, as well as the significance of the powerful stories of Irish immigrants that remain here in St. Augustine. As you listen to Caroline Marie Brigid Callahan's tale, I am certain that you will not only find it quite fascinating, but also very perplexing," Dr. Manchester added.

By this time, the entire audience was anxious to listen to what they were told was a rendition of an ancient Irish folk tale. What they were unprepared to witness was a dramatization of the story on stage.

Dr. Manchester stepped away from her podium. The theatre curtain began to rise, lights turned down, and the actors took the stage.

The entire production was performed with no dialogue. All the movements and expressions were so intense that after a few moments the audience realized that it was the passion manifested by the mimes that held our attention along with an orchestra in the pit playing classical Bach.

There were only four main characters. Brigid Marie, the daughter of a wealthy Irish widow; her companion, Caroline, the daughter of Brigid's tutor; Liam, a handsome young college student; and a ghastly, frail, old woman, with long, white, streaming hair, wearing a grey cloak over a green dress.

The remaining cast did not appear until the dramatic ending.

The first thirty minutes established the friendship between the three younger characters, while the ghastly older frail woman was always present like a dark cloud of doom waiting for the moment to strike.

Just as Caroline and Liam proclaim their eternal love for one another, and Liam leaves the stage, Brigid enters to hear the joyful news. It is the final scene, the most dramatic one; immediately following that is the most powerful and disturbing.

When the curtain rises, the stage reveals Marie and Liam on the ground, covered in blood with hollow masks on their faces, indicating that there is no trace of their image left to grieve.

Only the *Banshee* is standing above them holding her staff and making terrifying noises as the remaining cast members enter in fear, tragically dancing mournfully around the two lifeless bodies.

When Caroline enters, she is aghast at the sight of her lover, Liam, and closest confidant, Marie, unrecognizable on the ground.

From afar, blending with *Come Sweet Death,* Bach's funeral dirge, the following voice is heard saying:

What we call the beginning is often the end
And to make an end is to make a beginning
We shall not cease from exploration
And the end of all our exploring
Will be to arrive where we started
And know the place for the first time

"I know these lines! They are from *Little Gidding: Four Quartets,* by T.S. Eliot. A few days ago, I met an artist named Brendon at the art walk downtown. He said these words to me…I mean the first half. I then completed it," Mandana said, sounding confused.

I took her hand gently.

"You won't realize it yet, Mandana, but I do understand. Brendon will help you learn more. We are all here to help you. It is what we promised Caroline. We are the Saint Augustine Sisterhood! It is our mission to build relationships upon a foundation of trust, respect, and honesty. We support each other's dreams and desires. There is no fear, jealousy, or anger, only love through spiritual motivation," I say, hoping that this information) will be enough for now until Dante can provide Mandana with the scientific details.

Chapter Eleven

The woman of Yesterday introduced me to the woman I am today.
The woman Today is excited to meet the woman of Tomorrow.

Poetic Evolution

Caroline

Without Liam my life is over. The *Banshee's* wailing is now my own internal lament. Each day, every moment without him, is as if I am being punished; punished for loving, punished for trusting, punished for believing in forever.

Then one evening, several weeks after I witnessed the horrific scene of two faceless bodies saturated in blood, a beautiful, pale, woman with long, flowing red hair appears. As she approaches me, the contrast between her and the ancient hag that remained even after the corpses were removed is stunningly obvious.

This creature, wearing a black sable cape, floats like a cloud elegantly in a vapor, back and forth, as if she is orchestrated by some invisible maestro.

Her transparent, translucent hand with long boney thin fingers glides toward my face. Her touch is colder than ice.

Startled, I nearly collapse, stepping backward, anticipating my escape route. But her soft, melodic voice is so mesmerizing that it paralyzes any movement.

"Fear me not, bewitching Caroline Brigid. I have been summoned to share with you *Tir na n 'Og*. It will be your redemption, your forever faithful healing Mecca," this enchanting creature assures me.

Before I can determine what to do next, my feet are inches off the ground in midair, gliding through the mist into the nearby forest, where gently my body is placed on a wooden stump.

Directly across is a regal oak branch where the mysterious mentor creature is seated.

"The tale that you are about to hear Caroline Brigid is the preparation for your journey to *Tir na n 'Og.* Listen attentively to every word, do not assume anything that you do not hear, and most importantly always have faith in the power of *Dagda!"*

Every child learned about *Dagda* as soon as she was able to speak. Like most legendary gods, *Dagda* wore a hooded cloak, was large in stature, sometimes described as a giant, with a long white beard.

But it was his *lorg anfaid,* Magic staff with dual powers that made this god the most powerful of all. With one end of his, staff *Dagda* could kill, while with the other, he could restore life.

Dagda also has a cauldron, *coire ansic,* which never runs empty, as well as a *uaithne,* the magic harp that has the ability to control men's emotions, as well as change the seasons.

Believing in *Dagda* was much easier as a child. After my mother departed suddenly with the butcher, leaving father to raise me, my faith in *Dagda* disappeared.

Now, sitting in this glade, mourning the death of my best friend and lover, listening to a translucent creature that has mythical powers, is more than uncomfortable, it is excruciatingly painful.

"Do not allow your emotions to dictate your logic, Caroline Brigid.

Listen without prejudice to the tale of *Cliodhna and Ciabhan,* the ancient story of how supernatural creatures once populated all the corners of Ireland prior to the arrival of mortals.

Cliodhna, the original *Banshee,* was the epitome of all love and beauty. Her home was on the island of *Tir Tairngire,* known as 'The Land of Promise.'

On this island lived three birds that had the power to cure any imaginable illness as long as they ate the fruit provided for them from the magic tree.

When *Cliodhna* traveled across the water to Ireland and met *Ciabhan,* immediately they fell in love. Unfortunately, *Cliodhna* did not consider the fact that her immortality was only possible while living on her island.

The conundrum that *Cliodhna* was now facing is that without *Ciabhan,* there would never be any happiness. Relinquishing immortality for her beloved *Ciabhan* was worth the sacrifice. What *Cliodhna* did not expect was how the gods would sabotage her decision.

The ancient Irish deities were determined to prevent Cliodhna's departure from the island. They would prevent any clandestine meeting between the lovers.

On her way to meet *Ciabhan* for their romantic rendezvous, Cliodhna encountered a tsunami-like disaster. Her body was assumed to be drowned in the water and never recovered.

But it was *Dagda* that found *Cliodhna,* returning her to her Island.

Unfortunately, *Ciabhan* hearing the news of his lover's death plunged from the highest mountain peak, determined to join her in eternal peace.

Dagda, to ease Cliodhna's mourning, provided her with the power to save requited lovers who are doomed by tragic circumstances.

It is because of this gift that you, Caroline Brigid, have been chosen to be reunited with Liam."

How could this be true? Liam and Caroline were destroyed by some powerful evil beyond any conceivable imagination.

"It is true, Caroline Brigid. Liam also knew and believed in *Dagda.* Do you?"

Do I believe? I must believe. If this means being with Liam again, I will do anything. I shook my head in affirmation.

"Then I will begin the travel arrangements for us. We will be leaving in the morning, at the break of dawn for *Tir na n Og,*" the mythical creature says.

"Will I have time to say farewell to my father? What will I need to bring with me?" I ask, confused.

"You will need nothing. You may say goodbye to everyone, but you must not reveal where or when you are leaving or any other information," the creature says.

Before I can ask anything else, she is gone. There really is nothing that I can tell anyone. How can I explain that I am going to be leaving for a mythical island to be reunited with my obliterated lover? I am not even thoroughly convinced that this is truly happening.

Prior to returning home to the estate, I make my way toward the village where my father is now living with his new wife.

It is nearly dusk and since the death of Liam and Marie the villagers fear being outside during the evening hours. I am certain Father will be home.

Just as expected, my father's new wife, whom I never address by her name, answers the door. Similarly, she is never anxious to see me.

Many times, I am told Father is unavailable or not in when I come visiting. But tonight, I can smell the familiar pipe tobacco and see father's feet propped on the ottoman from the doorway.

Not waiting to be invited inside, I step in front of the stocky woman and proceeded toward father's chair.

"Caroline! My darlin'… how wonderful to see you. Margaret and I were hoping that you would pay a visit after that horrific incident at the estate," Father says, placing his pipe on a metal plate.

I ignore his remarks and take a seat on the sofa next to him, thankful that Margaret has left the room.

"I am leaving the estate tomorrow and wanted to let you know," I say, taking my father's hand in mine.

"But why, Caroline? Is it because of the deaths? You must not let this terrible tragedy drive you away! What will I do without my Caroline," father says tearfully.

It is tempting to point out the hypocrisy in his statement. After all, it is he who left me. It is he who married Margaret the wench.

But I control my anger, remembering that it is also he who cared for me when Mother deserted us both.

"It has nothing to do with the murders on the estate," I say, lying.

"I have an opportunity to be a governess in London. It will also allow me to move away from all the disturbing memories here. I hope that you will understand," I say, standing up preparing to depart.

Father rises from his chair slowly and embraces me gently. It is the first time that I realize how feeble he has become.

Perhaps it is a blessing that Margaret cares for him, regardless of my personal disgust with her.

I kiss Father's cheek knowing that this will be our last few moments together.

"Remember, Caroline, always be a good girl. I have always loved you, my darling. God speed!"

Those are the last words that I would remember of my life in Ireland. At least those were the last memories I have in this life sequence.

Occasionally flashes of my life prior to being here as Brigid will surface, but they never lasted long, which makes what is happening the next morning an entire mystery.

Sleeping is nearly impossible. All that I am told by a mythical creature is that by dawn I should be prepared to leave this earthly world and travel to a land only known through folklore. How I am to arrive and when is never explained.

Preparing for my departure is impossible since I am told to bring nothing. Adding to this confusion is that the entire estate is still in mourning from the recent deaths. This mourning period does allow me to easily remain away from the household staff. No visitors will be stopping by.

Marie's father left soon after the graveside ceremonies, and nobody knows where he can be found.

Dressed in a simple traveling outfit, I lay on the bed waiting for my next instructions, not knowing what else to do for the evening.

What seems like seconds after I close my eyes, there are flashes of lights whirling near the window. Bolting up from my reclining position, I see that the same creature from the night before is gliding into the room.

"Now we travel," is all I hear before everything turns dark.

"Welcome, Caroline Brigid, to *Tir na NaOng,*" I hear as my eyes are adjusting to these new surroundings.

"Have I arrived?" I ask, feeling as if this is an exceptional dream that will end at any moment.

"Actually, my dearest, you have been here for several days. We have all been waiting for your Awakening," the graceful young woman says.

This is definitely no longer Ireland, at least not the Ireland I know.

Looking around without moving from my reclined position on what seems to be a lush flowerbed surrounded by massive trees, I see there is a group of enchanting fairies that vary in size, as well as color.

Marie once shared with me a book written by the thirteenth century scholar Thomas of Cantimpre, a Flemish Catholic, medieval writer who was also a preacher and theologian.

Although Marie stated that he was well respected for his encyclopedia on nature, it was his classification of fairies that fascinated both of us more than anything else in his works.

Cantimpre separated fairies into categories based on water, the *neptuni; incubi,* those wandering the earth; and *spiritualia nequitie in celestibus,* those that inhabit the air.

Naturally, both Marie and I knew that there were many more varieties than those few mentioned by *Cantimpre.*

But not until this moment could I attest to the truth of our theory.

At this moment, I am surrounded by a variety of creatures different in size, from petit to quite tall. Some appear to have translucent skin, while others glow in iridescent shades from poppy orange to lemon drops. A few who wear nothing on their webbed feet have long gracious fingers.

Three features that they all shared are round faces, star-gleaming eyes, and sparkling smiles.

Although most are standing, some are seated underneath floral trees, while others fly though the sky curious to get a glimpse of the new visitor from the outside world.

"Is there anything that I can provide you with, Caroline Brigid? You must have many questions now that you have arrived and have *Awakened,*" said the creature that I recognize from my previous life.

"First, may I ask why you refer to me always as Caroline Brigid? And, also when you first came to me, I was told that I would be reunited with Liam. When will I be taken to him?" I asked anxiously.

Nothing else really mattered. There was no reason to remain on earth without Liam, regardless what name this creature wanted to call me.

What would happen next never occurred to me. But here I am in some enchanted land, with inhabitants that I know nothing about, totally unaware of what my future holds.

"The answer to your first question is quite simple. Caroline Brigid and s who you are now. In another life there were two now both lives will be shared with Liam. In the future there may be many more lives that you will continue to experience together.

And you will be reunited with Liam and Maria as promised. But there is still much that you need to learn to make this transition successful.

Knowing who we are and why you are here at *Tir na nOg,* a land that excludes humans is essential. Our mission is to improve the human race before they destroy themselves.

You may refer to me as *Niamh.* My father is the King of *Tir na nOg.* Like you, I fell hopelessly in love.

My lover, the young Irish warrior *Oisin,* and I lived here for three hundred years. Because *Oisin* was mortal, his desire to return to Ireland overcame his love for me.

Knowing that *Oisin* could never be truly happy without one final visit to his homeland, I agreed to provide him with my magical white mare, hoping that once his voyage was complete *Oisin* would return safely to me for eternity. Unfortunately, this was not to be my destiny.

After many pain-filled years, my father provided me with a gift. This gift allows me every one hundred years to grant eternal life to a mortal couple who has experienced an untimely tragedy," Niamh said.

"I am still not sure what this means. I don't want to sound ungrateful, but how are you able to do this? And does this gift require Liam and I to remain here in *Tir na nOg* forever? We are not mythical, spiritual creatures as all of you are. To adapt to eternal life here may not be possible," I say, regretting that I may sound ungrateful.

"I understand, Caroline Brigid. You are not the first human to have been selected. There is more that you will learn once Liam returns. The alternative may not be as appealing," Niamh says, taking my hand and leading me to a path into the nearby cave.

All that I can now recall is a poem by Robert Herrick that Marie handed me the last time I saw her alive.

Oh years! And age! Farewell:
Behold I go,
Where I do know
Infinity to dwell.
And there mine eyes shall see
All times how they
Are lost i' th' see
Of vase eternity:-
Where never moon shall sway
The stars; but she,
And night, shall be
Drown'd in one endless day.

Chapter Twelve

It is during our darkest moments that we must focus to see the light.

Aristotle

Sunflower

It is impossible to understand the significance of the Sisterhood without knowing how each of the Gypsy sisters came here.

Each of our stories, although unique, all share a similar fundamental role in Caroline's life and her contribution to the Sisterhood.

Sharing with you each of our personalities, stories, and talents will address why Dante chose us for his longevity project known as ELI.

Meet

Calypso, The Magnifique:

New York is the most diverse area on earth. There are entire Harlem communities where generations have lived their entire lives without ever leaving the forty-five-block stretch from Central Park to 155th street.

I was not one of those people. From the moment that I heard the soundstage music from the Apollo Theatre, located on west 125th street, only a few blocks from our apartment, I was attracted to the sounds like a moth to fire.

It was not until I met Bobby that I realized how deadly fire is to moths who fly recklessly without knowing their surroundings.

Bobby was the stage manager at the Apollo Theatre for more years than anyone can remember. Let's just say that Bobby's footprint was part of the history when Jimi Hendrix became an Amateur Night winner in 1964 and then later in 2006 when James Brown's body was laid to rest here so his fans could pay homage to the Godfather of Soul.

By the time that I started hanging out at the Apollo, Bobby was using a walker and hooked up to an oxygen machine, but nevertheless he was working full time.

Some people thought that eventually Bobby would simply fade into the mahogany walls, or we would find what was left of his body in ashes with only his false teeth left behind.

Thankfully, I left before that time and haven't been back since.

My first time on stage was as a backup singer for Bob Marley. It was a last minute gig where I was finally at the right place at the right time.

It was October 29, 1979, when Bob Marley and the Wailers introduced reggae to Harlem.

During one of the last numbers, the three female backup singers, one of them Bob's wife, Rita Marley, became ill during rehearsal.

Since I was familiar with all the songs, when it came time to find a last-minute substitute, immediately I stood up and bellowed out the tune perfectly on pitch Acapella. Bob Marley came right up to me and said, "Sister child, where did you ever learn to sing like that?"

"I guess it is just a gift God gave me, Mr. Marley," I said, not sure if he was impressed or mortified.

"Well, Hallelujah, sweet Jesus sent us a songbird. Someone get this Angel ready to perform!" Marley said, enthusiastically.

And that was my first and only time on the Apollo stage. Two weeks later, at the age of sixteen, I was asked to join Banging Molly, a newly created rock band as their female singer.

Since I was able to play the guitar and saxophone, the guys thought that I might attract attention.

After a few gigs locally, our agent/drummer was able to convince the Blues-breakers, a London touring band that Banging Molly would be the perfect warm up for their next concert at Whiskey a go-go in Hollywood, California.

Once they heard our sound and apparently my saxophone, we signed our first contract, which was barely enough to get us to California, but definitely enough to get me out of Harlem.

Blues-breakers had a talented guitarist named Peter Green, who recently replaced some other musician known as Eric Clapton.

By the time our show at the Whiskey was over, the Blues-breakers had hooked up with another female vocalist whose name was Stevie something.

All I know is that her band, the Fritz Rabyne Memorial Band, was playing after ours, and this Stevie girl was phenomenal.

Apparently, Peter Green was also impressed with her. It would not be until years later when I started my own band in Saint Augustine, Florida, that Stevie's influence on me would surface once again.

By that time the Blues-breakers would be known as Fleetwood Mac, and the song "Gypsy" released in 1980 would have special meaning in my life.

But it really was not until I met Caroline and the other Gypsy dancers that everything surrounding me would make sense.

Like so many other things that we experience early in life, it is not until later that we are able to appreciate how those moments dictate our other choices.

Like a two-edged sword, we dance through dangerous unknown territory hoping that our inner selves will lead us towards the next level of understanding.

Reflecting now on all my many past lives, relationships, positive and negative experiences, sharing some with you is a decision I have made to enlighten others who are traveling on a similar road with many different paths to explore.

By the time Caroline and my paths crossed, we knew that our goal was to preserve the Saint Augustine Sisterhood and to expand our message throughout the community.

The stories that we share is our way to create a loving tapestry meant to inspire others as well as to protect those who are struggling, suffering, or are orphaned either physically or emotionally.

I am a Gypsy Dancer! It is my life's philosophy. Each of us that is included in this manifesto will be sharing our contributions. We are all unique, just like the pieces of cloth used to create a tapestry, yet tied together that same thread unites each of us.

Arriving at St. Augustine was serendipitous. There was no logical explanation, no reasonable assessment that led me to this ancient city.

As you will learn from all of us, nobody came here with any preconceived purpose towards saving the world.

Knowing how each of my Sisters were able to find each other is a fascinating story on its own. When we also consider the relationship, we now have with Caroline, her amazing contribution, and of course Dr. Dante's dedication to assuring that our lifetime is extended as long as possible our story is truly worth sharing and appreciating.

By 2011, after many road trips with several different bands, it was clear that my time had come to at least begin acting like an adult.

The one intelligent decision I made while living in California was to complete my education, earn a BA degree in music, and a teaching degree. Teaching was never intended to be my profession. That choice along with several others made the difference in my life. Sometimes you are so sure you have all the right answers and then you realize you are clueless.

My roommate suggested that we take a road trip to Florida during spring break. For some crazy reason, the popular 60s movie, *Where the Boys Are,* made Janet's suggestion appealing.

Thankfully, after seriously reconsidering the driving distance, we decided to slightly change our road trip decision and fly into Clearwater. We were able to book a hotel and pack plenty of bikinis. This is really all we needed for a spring break holiday.

The unexpected detour was when our pilot announced that due to a threatening thunderstorm we were landing in Jacksonville, Florida.

That was when Janet and I decided that since the layover was going to be overnight, we may as well rent a car for twenty-four hours.

At the car rental, the agent suggested we visit Saint Augustine, which was only 45 minutes from the airport.

"What do you think, Caly?" Janet asked.

"Why not? I believe it is the oldest city in America," I said, remembering reading this in the travel magazine on the plane.

"That is correct," said the car agent, handing Janet the keys and adding,

"There are also great restaurants, shops, and even a fort. Definitely a great place to spend a few hours," the agent added.

We soon discovered he was right. Saint Augustine was something that both Janet and I imagined a European city would resemble. Since neither of us could afford to visit any international cities, this was certainly a nice consolation.

What we didn't expect was the tremendous gravity pull that both of us felt as we started walking through the cobblestone path leading to St. George Street.

"Are you getting the same vibe as I am, Cali?" Janet asked, as we stopped for a few minutes deciding where to get a cold glass of wine.

"Not sure," I replied. "There is definitely a sense of serenity. It almost feels familiar, like I have been here before," I said, slightly confused.

We decided on a quaint wine bar in a lovely courtyard covered by an ivy terrace. Although there were plenty of tourists, nothing felt crowded. Even here where we were sitting there were only a few people at the tables.

Janet and I decided on sharing a bottle of Chardonnay that the waitress suggested, ironically was from Sonoma, only a few hours away from where we flew in from.

Just as we began to relax, a lovely group of ladies dressed in elegant circular skirts started dancing to some lively flamenco music played by a guitarist on a small stage near a huge oak tree.

Immediately I recognized the characteristic music style associated with traditional folkloric instruments of the Roma people in the Spanish region of Anadalusia.

The women were moving gracefully, gliding in a pattern that made them appear to almost be suspended in the air. Each dancer was like a unique butterfly expressing her own individual style.

When the music ended, both Janet and I were handed a rolled-up message tied with a rainbow of ribbons. The ladies departed as quickly as they entered from the same portal.

"That was certainly special, and unexpected," I said, releasing my message from the ribbon.

"I am definitely impressed by the entertainment provided here in the early afternoon," Janet said, watching my reaction to what the mystery message included.

What I noticed immediately was that it was written in an elegant calligraphy print. Very impressive. But what was written was what caught my attention:

THE FOUR LAWS OF A SHAMAN

The First Says:

"The Person that comes into our life is the right person."

In other words, no one comes into our lives by chance, all the people around us who interact with us are there for a reason, to make us learn and advance in each situation.

The Second Law Says:

"What happens is the only thing that could have happened."

Nothing, but nothing, absolutely nothing that happens to us in our lives could have been otherwise.

Not even the most insignificant detail.

There is no: "If I had done such a thing, such another would have happened..."

Nope!

What happened was the only thing that could have happened, and it had to have been so for us to learn that lesson and move on.

Each and every one of the situations that happens to us in our lives is perfect, even if our mind and our ego resist and do not want to accept it.

The Third Law Says:

"Anytime it starts is the right time."

Everything starts at the right time, neither before or after.

When we are ready for something new to start in our lives, that is when it will begin.

The Fourth Law Says:

"When something ends, it ends."

Just like that.

If something ended in our lives, it is for our evolution; therefore it is better to leave it, move on and advance, already enriched by that experience.

I think it is not by chance that you are reading this; if these words came into our lives today, it's because we are prepared to understand that no snowflake ever falls in the wrong place.

Emerald

This was it! This is why we are here.

But why was the message handed just to me? And who is Emerald?

Did Janet receive the same message?

"Cali? Cali? Are you okay? What was on that paper?" I heard Janet's voice, but nothing was registering.

"I think you should open yours, Janet. Then we can share," I said, sounding mysteriously ominous.

Janet followed the same routine that I had; only she read hers aloud:

Whatever you're not changing, you're choosing. Create the best version of yourself, build the most mind-blowing experiences ever...refuse to settle for anything less than extraordinary.

"This is all beginning to remind me of an elaborate fortune cookie tournament. Maybe this is how St. Augustine welcomes tourists to their city," Janet said, less impressed than I am.

"I don't know about that Janet. It seems to me that these omens are especially designed for us. Your message is definitely spot on.

Ever since we met three years ago, it has been your goal to exceed everyone's expectations, especially your own.

And the four laws that I received are certainly something that I have ignored far too long. Maybe our detour here isn't merely an accident. Maybe we were meant to visit Saint Augustine today," I said, handing her my scroll to read.

Janet took another sip of her Chardonnay before reading the message that I received.

When she finished, I noticed the change in her expression. It was now more somber.

"I have never thought that snowflakes fell in the wrong place," Janet said seriously.

"Neither have I."

After a few moments of awkward silence, Janet said, "So I guess this means that I am going to need to start looking for a new roommate."

"Let's talk about this after we spend a great week enjoying the Florida beaches, like girls that just want to have fun," I said.

One month later, I was on I 40 E starting my 42 hour drive to Saint Augustine, Florida, singing with Stevie Nicks *Gypsy,* and feeling free for the first time in my life.

"And, you know that it all comes down to you
Well, you know that it does and
Lightning strikes maybe once, maybe twice
Oh and it lights up the night
And you see your gypsy
You see your gypsy."

Chapter Thirteen

When you know yourself you are empowered. When you accept yourself, you are invincible.

Tina Lifford,
American actress and playwright

Calypso's Tale

After returning home from spring break, I could not focus on anything but my brief visit to Saint Augustine and of course the message on my scroll delivered by the mysterious gypsy.

As crazy as it first sounded to leave my teaching job at Berkeley without knowing where in St. Augustine I would be living, or more importantly how I would be living, the desire to follow my instincts was preempting everything else.

"So, my Gypsy girlfriend, have you decided yet when you are going to give your notice?" Janet asked me directly one day.

Her question caught me by surprise since I hadn't talked to her or anyone else about my move since returning home.

"What makes you so sure that I'm leaving? Have you got some sexy guy on your mind that you want to replace me with?" I joked.

"Come on, Cali, tell the truth. Since we got back from Florida, all you have been doing is researching *Saint Augustine, playing flamenco music on your guitar, and watching the I Tube travel channel of this ancient city," Janet said.

"Did you ever think that maybe I was just curious? I don't move to every place that I visit."

"Maybe not, but not every place has the haunting vibe that St. Augustine does. We both felt it the moment we set foot on those ancient cobblestones. And that scroll you got from the Gypsies about the *Four Laws* of Shaman? You carry it with you everywhere," Janet replied.

Janet was right. I just had not taken the final step. The one thing that would make all of these images in my mind real was a definite commitment.

"Okay, already! I made the decision to move to Saint Augustine the moment I read that prophecy two months ago. I will be leaving the week after the school term ends. That is if you are able to find a roommate by then," I added.

"Not a problem. Lindsay…you know the new art teacher, she needs a roommate after she caught her boyfriend in bed with Jack, the boys' soccer coach. The timing couldn't be more perfect," Janet said.

There it was. The second law of Shaman exactly as stated in my scroll.

What happens is the only thing that could happen.

It didn't even matter that nothing else had been planned, or that it appeared like everything was moving along without any direction; all that I had to acknowledge was the first step. Once that had been accomplished, the rest would follow.

Born in Harlem, I was certainly aware of racial issues early in my life. That is one of the reasons why so many choose to never leave their neighborhoods.

But I was different. From the moment I heard my mama sing, I could identify any musical note she sang without ever hearing it before. I would then mimic her, making the exact same sound.

Later, one of her musician friends said that I had a rare gift known as perfect pitch.

One day when I was imitating my mama at the club where she was singing, the piano player told her that I had absolute pitch, a very rare ability that only 1% of all singers have. I was in the rare company with Amadeus Mozart, Ella Fitzgerald, and Michael Jackson.

None of this made any difference to me when I was six years old. Later, whenever one of the bands needed a last-minute replacement backup singer and I instantly knew all the songs, that is when everyone started noticing me.

That was also finally when I knew that staying in Harlem was like signing my own death certificate.

Even my mama, who was far more talented than I ever was, couldn't bring herself to leave the hood.

When I received the news of her passing from my uncle once he tracked me down in Belgium where I was touring with a small up and coming band known as *The Doors of Perception,* it may have been too late for me to share with her how much of the world she missed by never leaving Harlem, but her death was a constant reminder that I must never allow anything or anyone to prevent me from moving forward.

That band, *The Doors of Perception,* took their name from Aldous Huxley's book on mescaline.

But it was in William Blake's book, *The Marriage* of *Heaven and Hell,* published in 1790, where that famous line first originated.

"If the doors of perception were cleansed everything would appear to man as it is, Infinite. For man has closed himself up, till he sees things thro' narrow chunks of his cavern."

It was not until many years later in graduate school that I learned any of this. Something that obviously Jim Morrison of the *Doors* was aware of much earlier without attending college when he decided to drop the *Perception* title of his band and keep *The Doors* as his official label.

I was there with Morrison before and after the transformation, and yet quite honestly, I had no idea why he insisted on making the change until years later when I met him unexpectedly in Paris.

When I did learn what William Blake's poems meant it introduced me to a new philosophy in life.

I credit Blake, Huxley, and Morrison for my final decision to leave Berkeley and open my new "door of perception" in Saint Augustine.

You see, in Blake's poem he outlines the contradictions that all of us live with. For example, how much influence does society have on how we determine what is good and what is evil?

Blake explores the contradictions that he identifies as *The Door in the Wall.* He cautions us to beware against closing these doors in our mind. Once we close these doors, we cannot appreciate the variety of contradictions that influence our decision making.

But these ideas by Blake in the 18th century still continue to challenge authors, musicians and artists to express their own interpretations of opening the doors in our minds. The most neglected part of the universe.

Why does it take us so long to appreciate what the masters provide us with? Most of them have experienced what appears new to us.

The Doors of Perception that Jim Morrison walked through did not have thresholds in the physical world.

Through drugs perhaps, or maybe meditation he was able to express thresholds into new thoughts, new visions, new ways of comprehending our world while sharing many of the same thoughts of those that he admired:

Aldous Huxley shared with Morrison many of the same anxieties with a world that had difficulty with accepting great changes of perception while maintaining balance.

Years later I recall one afternoon in 1971 that a small group of us on a tour through Paris stopped overnight at a hostel near the apartment where Jim and his girlfriend, Pamela Courson, were staying.

It was a well-known fact that Pamela was a heroin addict, but it didn't matter to me. Living in Harlem, I saw drugs as natural.

I had mentioned to a few of my friends that I had once sung backup for Morrison. Not so much to impress them but more to remind them that I had experiences that many of them could never appreciate.

Anyway, we ended up at Café de Flore, located at Boulevard Saint Germain, one afternoon for a few drinks and any other indulgences that might be available.

I never really expected to see Jim there, although for many years, since 1888 actually, it has always been a popular hub for famous writers.

Philosophers such as Georges Albert Maurice Victor Bataille and Picasso frequented Flore often. But, when I saw Jim Morrison sitting in a booth away from all the other people, it was surrealistic.

I stood a few feet away staring in disbelief. Would he even remember who I was? Finally I decided to take the chance and approached his table.

Before I could say a word, Jim jumped up from the table, wrapped his arms around me as if I was a long lost relative, and said,

"Oh, my God, Clio, I can't believe it's you! Like a ghost from my past resurfacing after another lifetime."

We embraced for several seconds, much longer than felt comfortable. I was still in shock that Jim Morrison even remembered who I was.

"Sit down and tell me how and why you're here in Paris?" Morrison said, sounding sincere.

"I'm here with a group of traveling back-up performers. It was a great opportunity to tour Europe. I heard you were here, so I wanted to say hello and tell you how proud I am of your success," I said, honestly.

"You are far too talented to be still singing back up, Clio. Let me give you my agent's number. He is always looking for new talent," Jim said, searching for a card in one of his coat pockets.

"Don't worry about it, Jim. I was just wondering why you decided to change the name of the band to the *Doors.* You must have had something in mind," I said, curious.

Morrison, who I could tell was pretty much doped up on something, began to tell me quite coherently that when he read HG Wells short story, *The Door in the Wall,* he knew it was time to change the name of the band. He then continued to tell me about the story.

Published in 1911, the story relates to how Lionel Wallace discovers a door in a wall leading to an enchanted garden. What Morrison found fascinating is the difficulty of choosing between the different parts of the psyche that the door represents.

Many, if not most, of the songs that the *Doors* wrote focus on the metaphor of opening doors in the mind that offer new perspectives and insights into life.

In Morrison's most iconic song, *Break On Through to the Other Side,* he was sharing the frustration of being confined by traditional moral codes. If we are able to break through the barrier, we succeed.

This is what Emerald was telling me in St. Augustine. It was something that I had always known, but now it was finally time for me to break through to the other side and find the door that will shed the light.

Chapter Fourteen

Most lead lives at worst so painful, at best so monotonous, poor and limited, that the urge to escape, the longing to transcend themselves if only for a few moments, is and has always been one of the principal appetites of the soul.

Aldous Huxley,
The Doors of Perception.

CALYPSO

I refuse to be one of the lost souls that accept everything without questioning.

After driving 2,750 miles from Berkeley, California to Saint Augustine, Florida, only stopping when I could no longer keep my eyes open, the reality of what I had really done finally dawned on me.

There was no plan. There was only a temporary place to stay, no friends, no family. I did have some limited savings, but certainly not enough to sustain me for long. Yet, for the first time, I felt totally independent.

What I did not expect was some odd time warp. I left Berkeley, California, on Saturday, June 2,1997, and arrived at Saint Augustine, Florida, on June 5, 1964.

The ancient city seemed to be the only place where time-was suspended. This was a subtle transformation. What I mean by this is that since the entire architecture, roads, and even many of the people blend in with a town that reflects the sixteenth century it took me a few minutes to even realize that I was no longer in the 21st century.

My first thought that there is a time shift came when I noticed the car in front of me was a 1960 Ford T Bird. Now I do realize that many people purchase older cars, belong to car clubs, and enjoy restoring classic cars as a hobby, but this was different.

These cars were everywhere. I was beginning to wonder if my own car would be the only vehicle that everyone else would be pointing at. But, for some odd reason I seemed to blend in just fine.

It was my cellphone and GPS that went bonkers. I had to rely on my memory to get to the Lincolnville neighborhood, which thankfully was not far from Ponce de Leon, the street I was currently on.

Once I saw a street that I could turn on I recognized that a few months ago it was *King Street,* although now I had no idea what it was called since there were no street signs.

I also noticed that there was no park on the corner dedicated to Zora Neal Hurston. Previously the small memorial was located next to a pawn shop. As a matter of fact, there was no pawn shop either. All the buildings—Carmelo's pizza, gas station, and burger restaurant were gone. There was nothing but dirt lots now.

This was not the time or place to determine what was happening. I looked briefly at the address where I was going and let my instincts dictate the rest.

After circling a neighborhood with a church on the corner twice, I finally noticed a brown sugar-skinned young girl wearing a long dress and a multicolored kaftan waving at me.

Grateful to see anyone on these unfamiliar streets, I carefully parallel parked my car and anxiously got out.

"Welcome to St. Augustine, Calypso. I hope the drive from California wasn't too bad. I'm Kiara," she said, with a strong southern accent.

"Oh, thank God! Finally, a name I recognize," I replied, giving the stranger a warm embrace.

"What is going on here? It looks like I may have stepped into an old time traveler episode or maybe the *Twilight Zone,*" I said, realizing that I was beginning to sound a little frantic.

"Oh, you mean since everything around you appears to be antiquated? Well, you do know that St. Augustine is haunted, right? I don't mean merely during Halloween or whenever we have a full moon. I mean HAUNTED always!" Kiara said without hesitation.

"Well, I have heard that St. Augustine is known for a variety of different spirits that roam the city, but I am referring to how everything and everyone around me, including you, looks like you're from the sixties," I said, not convinced that Kiara understood my question.

"Oh, that. Well, it won't last too long. Nobody here in Lincolnville notices it when it happens. It is more like an eclipse.

"And not everyone experiences it. Those of us who have, determined that it usually occurs when someone from the exterior world has made the decision to become a part of our interior world," Kiara says, grabbing one of my backpacks and leading the way up the steps to the porch.

"After you get settled in your room, we will move your car to the back alleyway. Most of us walk around here since the parking downtown is horrendous. I imagine you might want to take a nap for a few hours after that long drive," Kiara suggested.

I really had no time to think about being tired. I am finally here, whatever that term really means.

Kiara King's name was provided to me when I contacted the Visitor Center about temporary housing until I could locate an apartment.

We had only spoken twice on the phone but texted several times. Kiara kindly offered to share her cottage with me until I found a suitable residence. After that I followed her on Facebook, learning as much as possible about what St. Augustine has to offer to those of us new to the city.

Since Saint Augustine is a fairly tight knit community, I was hoping that maybe Kiara would also know Emerald and where I could find the Gypsy dancers.

"After you have a chance to rest and catch your breath, I thought you might like to join me at a small coffee event tonight. We are meeting with Dr. King to discuss the Civil Rights strategies that he is proposing," Kiara said, quite nonchalantly.

"Do you mean **The Dr. KING**? But he has been dead for years! Assassinated in Memphis, Tennessee April 4, 1968. I marched in Washington DC several days later when that happened," I said, stunned at Kiara's invitation.

"Oh, my sweet Calypso, you have so much to learn. Lesson number one, no one ever dies in St. Augustine for very long," Kiara said, closing the curtains and the bedroom door.

I couldn't think about death or even life at this moment. All I could think of was closing my eyes for a few hours allowing whatever was happening around me to merely melt away as in Salvador Dali's *The Perception of Memory.*

For some very odd reason, as my eyes begin to close, I can clearly visualize. Yet, It is impossible for me to understand the unconscious symbol of the relativity of space and time, until perhaps now where apparently somehow, I am being placed into this Dali painting, meditating on the collapse of a fixed cosmic order.

As I fall into a deep sleep, the Dali clocks are now melting pocket watches, collected by a white rabbit that resembles the notorious white hare who must have escaped temporarily from the Alice chronicles.

It is not uncommon for me to imagine that I am Alice whenever I embark on a new adventure. Of course, in my version Alice has dark hair and dark skin like me. It is chasing this white rabbit character down my latest rabbit hole in St. Augustine that is the most challenging, bizarre, and complex situation thus far.

Several hours later when I finally realize that I am waking up in a new environment, it is slightly unexpected yet not totally foreign. My first thought is not only the time of day. Did I merely dream about the time shift? If not, are we still in the 60's?

Reaching for my cellphone, I recall that it was left in my car when I followed Kiara into the house. There is no other clock available in the room. But when I pull open the drapes, I see it is nighttime, although not totally dark yet.

Some might say it is twilight, but what I recall at this moment is what Jean Toomer identifies as *Georgia Dusk*.

During my early days in Harlem when I was in high school the only class that I would never miss was my English class. It was the literature, especially the black writers, that inspired me to keep my dreams alive.

Langston Hughes, Richard Wright, and James Baldwin were all well known in my community. And, of course, Lorraine Hansberry's *Raisin in the Sun* was an important influence in my life.

But it was a small book of poetry that my mama gave me days before her passing that meant the most to me.

Jean Toomer was one of those poets that I was unfamiliar with until my mother introduced me to his poems. Remembering him tonight makes me feel like mama is sitting on the bed next to me.

If Kiera is right about meeting with Dr. Martin Luther King Jr. later tonight, I find it quite fitting that I recall Toomer's life and poem as I watch the day pass into evening.

Like other Harlem Renaissance writers, Toomer witnessed incredible success amongst African Americans throughout the country, while at the same time he also could see the terrible effects that slavery still had on the American people, especially in the southern states.

My decision to leave Berkeley, California, where I felt for the first time some sense of equality and return to a state where the racial segregation pendulum continues to randomly swing without any significant changes, may seem like stepping backwards.

Then I remember Jean Toomer's poem, *Georgia Dusk*, my experience in Paris with Morrison, the research project on *Doors of Perception*, Blake, Huxley, H. G. Wells, and of course Emerald the Gypsy.

Without all of them, I would not be standing here at this moment reciting in my mind the following images. This is for you mama!

Georgia Dusk
By, Jean Toomer
The sky, lazily disdaining to pursue
The setting Sun too indolent to hold
A lengthened tournament for flashing gold.
Passively darkens for night's barbecue.
A feast of moon and men and barking hounds,
An orgy of some genius of the South
With blood-hot eyes and cane-lipped scented mouth,
Surprised in making folk-sounds from soul sounds.
The sawmill blows its whistle, buzz-saws stop,
And silence breaks the bud of knoll and hill.
Soft settling pollen where plowed lands fulfill
Their early promise of a bumper crop.
Smoke from the pyramidal sawdust pile
Curls up, blue ghosts of trees, tarrying low
Where only chips and stumps are left to show
The solid proof of former domicile.
Meanwhile, the men with vestiges of pomp,
Race memories of kings and caravan,
High-priests, an ostrich, and a juju-man.
Go singing through the foot paths of the swamp.
Their voices rise…the pine trees are guitars,
Strumming pine needles fall like sheets of rain.
Their voices rise…the chorus of the cane

Is caroling a vesper to the stars.
O' singers, resinous and soft your songs
Above the secret whisper of the pines,
Give virgin lips to cornfield concubines.
Bring dreams of Christ to dusky cane-lipped
throngs.

Chapter Fifteen

The man who comes back from the Door in the Wall, will never be quite the same as the man who went out. He will be wiser, yet less sure, happier but less self-satisfied, humbler in acknowledging his ignorance yet better equipped to understand the relationship of words to things, of systematic reasoning to the unfathomable mystery which it tries forever vainly to comprehend.

Aldous Huxley,
The Doors of Perception

CALYPSO

Meeting Dr. Martin Luther King Jr. was as surrealistic as any painting by Salvador Dali that I could ever imagine.

When Kiara and I arrived at Janie Price's small cottage house, there were cars parked for several blocks. It was a warm, humid evening but nearly everyone in the Lincolnville neighborhood was gathered in the backyard that expanded into a large empty lot nearby.

That area was where people gathered with their paper plates for barbecue spareribs, chicken, chitlins, black-eyed peas, candied yams, collard greens, cornbread, and more soul food than I have seen since leaving Harlem.

"There must be over a hundred people here tonight," I said, following close behind Kiara who was headed toward the tent where all the food was.

"This has been going on for the past four hours. Most people are here for the free food, but there are some that want to hear what the Reverend says about civil disobedience. We will eat first and then move inside," Kiara said, leading the way to a table with two empty seats.

"Do you really think that we can get close enough to Dr. King to hear him speak?" I asked, still doubting that any of this was real.

"Oh, we will not only hear Martin speak, we are going to be marching with him tomorrow morning. I have done this many times. You might say I am an expert protester by now. Whatever happens tonight and tomorrow, you need to remember has already occurred. It will be important for you to stay close. If not…I mean, if anything goes wrong, it could be difficult to unravel," Kiara sounded serious, but I wasn't convinced that I truly understood what she meant.

Before I could ask any questions, a good-looking man with the most spellbinding blue eyes took the empty seat next to Kiara.

"Where have you been, Jamal? I waited for you at the house, but we needed to get over here before it got too late," Kiara said, almost whispering.

Not responding directly to Kiara's question, the gentleman placed his hands around her face and kissed her passionately.

After a few moments, Kiara drew a long breath, turned her attention to me, and said, "Calypso, meet Jamal Jackson. My future husband."

Jamal stood up, reached for my hand, and kissed it gently. It was so unexpected I was not sure how to react.

"In the real world, wherever that is, we have been married for several years. Well, at least I think we have. Kiara keeps track better than I do. Nice to meet you, Calypso, and welcome to Saint Augustine. I assure you that everyday life here will not be this dramatic," Jamal said, expressing my feelings exactly.

"I must admit that even with all the chaos I am absolutely thrilled to be here," I said, hoping that my reaction was as natural as possible under the circumstances.

"All I can say, Sissta, is that you haven't seen anything yet; I hope that you have your seatbelt securely fastened," Jamal said, laughing.

"Knock it off, Jamal. You are going to terrify her before she even gets a chance to meet the Reverend," Kiara said, playfully poking his ribs.

"And that is where we are headed right now. You coming with us, Jamal?" Kiara asked, as we headed towards the main house.

"Naw, I think that I will hang out here with the boys for a while. I could smell this barbecue several blocks away, my mouth watering the entire way. Nice to meet you, Calypso. Hope I didn't trouble you too much. We will definitely meet again," Jamal said, tipping his baseball cap slightly.

Before I could respond, Kiara was leading me through the crowds to a back door where three men who were obviously bodyguards were seated.

At first, they reminded me of the bouncers that were at the backstage doors during my traveling days with the band. Groupies were always trying to find a way to sneak in at a concert to meet the players, even those that were not really famous.

It also is like that famous *Fleetwood Mac* song *"Players only love you when they're playing..."*

But these men were certainly better dressed, all in three-piece suits, and definitely much more intimidating than any bouncers I may have remembered.

"Hey, Bobby! How's everything going? The crowd tonight looks pretty mellow. Anyone offer you guys some ribs and chitlins yet?" Kiara asked, obviously knowing at least one of the men.

"Unfortunately, no eating during work. But it smells mighty tempting. Maybe once the Reverend retires for the evening and the new shift takes over, there will be some left," the man identified as Bobby answered.

"No worries, I will make sure you all have plates with plenty of food waiting for you in the kitchen," Kiara said.

The largest bodyguard standing by the door was smiling once he heard that, carefully letting us past him into the back parlor.

"You are an impressive negotiator, Kiara. I guess the way to any man is truly through his stomach," I said, half joking.

"Well, as much as I believe that old adage, in this case Bobby and I have known each other since we wore diapers. Trust me, not even food would let anyone else past him. He's been working for Reverend King for ten years. Loves him like a brother," Kiara whispered, as we started moving closer to the front room where there was only standing room.

"Dr. King? How are we supposed to live in this community peacefully like you keep wanting us to when we are watching our own children being beaten and spit at whenever we try to simply mind our own business?" An elderly man sitting in a rocking chair asked.

There was an uncomfortable silence for a few minutes while all the attention was now on the man sitting on a straight wooden chair. Everyone in the room was anxiously anticipating his response.

"My visit here to your lovely city is to address this exact issue. Therefore, sir, let me start by clarifying a few important points that you have introduced. The first being living peacefully while surrounded by turmoil, and the second is how to protect our next generation. I do believe that the answer is in the fact that there are two types of laws, and both have the same answer.

First, we must ask, 'how do we advocate breaking some laws, and obeying others?'

Since there are two types of laws—just laws and unjust ones. I would agree with St. Augustine that 'An unjust law is no law at all.'

I have picked your city as the focal point of my campaign this summer. We have decided after all of the examples of segregation witnessed in the past few months that your city is absolutely the most lawless one that we have ever encountered, and we have worked with many difficult ones.

Nonetheless, we are determined that this city will not celebrate its Quadra centennial celebration as a segregated community. If physical death is the price I must pay to free my white brothers and sisters from a permanent death of the spirit, then nothing can be more redemptive," Dr. King said, sitting back down, while everyone else in the room stood up, shouting with praise, including myself.

It was an overwhelming evening. Nothing in my life had ever moved me like this before.

Of course, I had heard the famous *I Have a Dream Speech* many times. You could not live in Harlem or anywhere else in the world as a young black child and not hear that speech. But what I just heard from the mouth of the man I had admired most was awe inspiring.

The knowledge that I had about his future assassination and the struggles that our people would continue to endure made it difficult for me to continue listening.

"I am so grateful to you, Kiara, for allowing me to witness this extraordinary moment, but I really need to leave as soon as possible," I said, whispering so as not to bring any unwanted attention toward me.

"We can leave the same way that we entered. Nobody will notice us. Everyone wants to hear more from the Reverend. And most of these people will be at the rally tomorrow, marching beside him, showing their support," Kiara said, as we found our way to the exit door.

Bobby and the other guards were now replaced with three other burly centurions. None of them looked friendly, but then I suspected that is exactly why they were chosen for this job.

It would take about fifteen minutes to return to Kiara's bungalow. Neither of us said anything the first five minutes, which seemed very awkward.

Then finally Kiara said, "I felt the same as you the first time I heard the Reverend speak. Especially knowing that he would not be with us for long. It all seemed like such a waste. But then as I continued to find myself sporadically in this strange time warp, the more often I heard Martin's words, the more meaningful they became.

Soon I realized that it was not the words themselves that were so powerful, it was the actions that led people to make changes that Martin could see happening.

This is the **DREAM** that he could see evolving and somehow I have become part of the team that will make it a reality," Kiara said with conviction.

I said nothing for a few minutes. Once what she was saying settled in my mind, in my heart, in my consciousness somehow it made sense in a very odd way.

After all, in retrospect three days ago I left Berkeley, California, to find a Gypsy dancer named Emerald, who handed me a scroll with life instructions. Today I am in St. Augustine, Florida, my final destination, only to discover that it is thirty-five years earlier, and I was just feet away from Dr. Martin Luther King Jr. a few minutes ago. I can't even imagine what day two will be like.

Chapter Sixteen

A sister is a gift to the heart, a friend to the spirit, a golden thread to
the meaning of life.

Isadora James

CALYPSO

Without Kiara King my new life in Saint Augustine would
have ended shortly after I arrived. She was the sister that I
had always longed for, the mentor that I absolutely needed.
Kiara created a lifeline that connected a group of women to an
unexpected past and future.

The day after I heard Dr. King speak, everything surrounding me
was back to normal. Well, as normal as I could expect. The decade
returned to 2017. It was once again the 21st century. I even recognized
hybrids on the roads.

But I was not the same. Hearing Dr. King's words directly from his
mouth, filled with so much life and enthusiasm, directly affected me.

"It is a shame that you could not participate in the Freedom March,
Calypso. But, then again, you avoided spending the evening in our
lovely jail," Kiara said, offering me a cup of coffee.

"How many days ago was that? It feels like only 24 hours ago that
it was the 60's. How do you live without knowing what to expect? I
guess I am confused as to how often these time warps happen and why
they even happen," I said.

"The answer to your first question is relatively simple. It has been
about ten hours since you went to sleep. But time is complicated. On
most days everything moves about as we all expect it to. You know,
twenty-four hours, reliable appointments, everything that we are
accustomed to in their places.

Then something sets off the norm. It may have been going on like
this forever in Saint Augustine, but I first encountered it when

Caroline arrived," Kiara said, nonchalantly.

"Caroline? Who is Caroline? And how was she able to control this time warp?" I asked, interested in knowing more details.

"Nobody really knows who Caroline is or for that matter where she came from. Most of the people who know her say she was always here. The most intriguing part of Caroline's life is how dedicated she is to the *Sisterhood.*

"Although when people remember Caroline, they focus on how ageless and beautiful she is. Many of the residents here are in their eighties or older, yet they all rave at how youthful Caroline has remained, especially when she is in her Gypsy attire, skirt dancing throughout the city during all hours of the night, and sometimes at the break of dawn," Kiara shared while pouring more coffee into my half empty cup.

As soon as I heard Kiara refer to Gypsy, it definitely perked up my interest.

Could Emerald be Caroline?

If not, she certainly must know how I can locate Emerald.

"The reason I decided to move to Saint Augustine from Berkeley so suddenly is because when my friend Janet and I were here a few months ago, quite by accident, a lovely Gypsy whose name is Emerald gave me a scroll with such inspiring advice that when I returned home it felt as if I was in limbo. Do you think that perhaps Caroline could introduce me to Emerald?" I asked, feeling hopeful at last that I might discover the mystery behind that scroll.

Kiara smiled, starting to laugh gently, "Oh, my dearest Calypso, you have so much still to learn about Saint Augustine, the *Sisterhood,* and especially your role in our world. What you experienced last night at Reverend King's informal gathering is an important foundation for the *Sisterhood* community. But, as essential as that message is, it is only a part of the entire tapestry that has been sewed into the lives of each individual that Caroline has touched.

"Later today, I am going to introduce you to some ladies that volunteer their time at the Lincolnville Museum and Cultural Center. It will provide you with another opportunity to understand what it is you are searching for," Kiara said.

I wasn't even certain that I was searching for anything, except perhaps Emerald, but Kiara did make some valid observations.

First, I had no idea what to expect once I met Emerald, and

whatever controls this time warp that I experienced yesterday is worth exploring.

"Is Caroline one of the ladies that volunteer at the Museum," I asked, still hoping that I might be able to meet the legendary goddess that Kiara admires.

"Oh, no, Caroline never worked at the museum, although she certainly supported it, using everything that it offers to promote the *Sisterhood* message. Caroline comes and goes sporadically like a Mariah wind or a serendipitous black hole. Trust me, she will appear when you least expect her to."

Although patience has never been one of my attributes, there really was not much choice but to trust Kiara and follow the plan she had set for me.

Visiting the Museum and Culture Center appeared to be next on my agenda. It was beginning to make me slightly nervous that I was being led around as a tourist when I still had no permanent housing arrangement, job, or any logical plan on how to proceed.

Trust and faith were the only words that my inner mind kept repeating.

Walking to the museum gave me an opportunity for the first time since arriving to appreciate how lovely this city is. There is a variety of trees, flowers, and even a community garden near a public park. And, although it is summer, the humidity is not yet overwhelming.

"That restaurant to your left, *The Blue Hen,* has the best biscuits and gravy in town. We will visit it one morning when there is more time to relax. Today is the beginning of your indoctrination process," Kiara said, making this sound like a military mission.

"I never did ask you, Kiara, who it was that referred me to you?"

"Flagler College. Whenever someone applies as a student or for any teaching position, the administration reaches out to a few of us in the community who have agreed to acquaint our fellow colleagues with their new environment. We are your mentoring committee. It makes your transition much smoother," Kiara was now sounding logical.

"That is an excellent program. When I started my residency at Berkeley, there was no support group. It was truly challenging," I said, thankful for any assistance offered.

"It just happens to be that in your case the teaching position is not the primary reason for your transfer, correct?" Kiara asked.

Knowing my real reason for coming here was shared in the first email I sent Kiara, reflecting on it now makes me feel I must have sounded like a real lunatic. But almost immediately I felt that I had found a soulmate, which is odd since I rarely make lasting friendships.

Sharing with Kiara my obsession with finding Emerald was almost natural. It wasn't until later that I discovered how much we had in common.

Kiara was an art professor at Flagler College who enjoyed traveling, hiking, yoga and occasionally playing her guitar in a local band.

We seemed to be perfectly matched. The coincidence of finding Kiara was almost too perfect.

"Here we are. *Lincolnville Museum and Cultural Center.* This site was once the Excelsior School Building where the Black high school started in 1925. My mother was part of the first graduating class. Later, she said that her experience here made her realize that the road to Black history runs directly through Lincolnville.

"I never truly understood what she meant by that until much later in my life, probably not until this museum opened as The Excelsior Museum in 2005. The name was changed to Lincolnville Museum and Culture Center in 2012." Kiara led me through the front entrance past the reception.

It was already mid-morning, but only a few people were in the building. Most of them were wearing name tags, indicating that they were either workers or volunteers.

Although Kiara obviously was leading me to a specific exhibit, I took the opportunity to stop a few times to read the comments on the exhibits. One in particular explained the role that runaway slaves had in building Fort Mose, as well as the influence that many of the prominent Black businessmen and women had in promoting churches, social movements, and cultural contributions.

But most of the exhibits seemed to center on the civil rights era in St. Augustine and the profound effect Dr. Martin Luther King Jr. had on this community.

When I finally caught up with Kiara, she was sitting on a bench in a room facing a portrait of a lovely Black woman wearing an oversized black feather hat and long beads.

"I wanted you to see this exhibit first, since it will help you understand how powerful the *Sisterhood* movement is in our community. Meet Mildred Parson Mason Larkins," Kiara said, moving slightly on the bench making room for me to sit next to her.

"Mildred is quite an elegant lady. What is her contribution?" I asked, anxious to learn more.

"Mildred raised three sons as a single mother around the turn of the 20th century. One of her sons, Otis Mason, became the first Black superintendent of schools in St. John's County. Another son was one *of the Tuskegee airmen. Larkin's (omit the apostrophe; is her name Larkin or Larkins?) also taught at the Excelsior prior to it being converted to this museum."

"And who are the other women honored in this room?" I asked, interested in how Kiara was making these relevant connections.

"To your right is Katherine Twine, a registered nurse who was arrested several times during civil rights marches right here in St. Augustine. The portrait to her left is Debbie McDade, a local musician like me, who became quite famous as a jazz singer performing with such great stars as Fats Domino and *Louis Armstrong. Then there is Barbie Vickers. She is our 'Rosie the Riviter mascot that contributed her skills during World War II and later again while protesting for civil rights through marches and sit-ins. She was also an advocate for the Saint Augustine Foot Soldier Memorial to be displayed in the Plaza de la Constitution. And, of course, there is Janet Price, who my mother was friends with. Janet was a nurse at Flagler Hospital who quit her job when she learned that people less qualified than her were being hired and paid more money. Eventually Janet was hired by St. Johns County Health Department where she advocated for prenatal and postnatal care for women who could not speak for themselves in migrant camps and in shelters. These are only a few of the women that were breaking ground for us to have a better chance for equality. The fight has not gotten any easier, but it has gotten stronger," Kiara said, standing up and moving toward the next room.

"I guess I had no idea so much of our Black heritage happened right here in Saint Augustine. Everyone seems to focus on the Spanish influence when referring to the significance of this city," I said, feeling thankful to learn about all the positive contributions by my people.

"This Museum is really only the beginning of your journey, Calypso. To understand and appreciate what the ELI Institute has accomplished, Dr. Dante's endeavors, Caroline's dedication and Emerald's role in advancing our mission is all Dr. King's vision. It is necessary for everyone who commits to our mission to understand the challenges they will face," Kiara said.

This was the very first time that I realized how intense everything here was. Up until now my decision to leave Berkeley, the time warp, including the surreal moment listening to Reverend King speaking, was all bizarre but seemed unconnected. Now Kiara was connecting the dots with a reality that was beginning to make sense.

The next room was filled with Civil Rights memorabilia, photographs, documents, even audio transcripts of famous speeches by King. Kiara was letting me roam around the room independently, absorbing the entire contents at my own pace without interruption. I was thankful for this. It gave me an opportunity to digest the information without any external distractions or comments that may have altered my initial reaction.

The three posters of Dr. King immediately drew my attention. He was wearing the exact same suit last night at the cottage we visited. The caption beneath the picture stated that:

"In 1964 Martin Luther King Jr. visited St. Augustine Lincolnville neighborhood, where he was the guest of Janice Price at 156 Central Avenue, St. Augustine.

"In the 1940's, Janice met Dr. King in Atlanta while at a dance attended by several Morehouse College students.

"When Dr. King announced that the campaigns, he was leading on Civil Rights would take him and Reverend Ralph Abernathy to Saint Augustine to address the Woolworth and the Hilton pool incident, Janice insisted that they stay at her home.

"Virgil F. Young, Janice's brother, had prepared for the guests a breakfast of fish, grits, biscuits, and gravy the morning before King's arrest at the Monson Motor Lodge."

Immediately I recognized the picture of the house that I had just visited the night before. And even now some of the people who were pictured and identified as Janice Price and Virgil Young I recognized.

Virgil was the barbecue chef that greeted Kiara and me as we entered from the empty lot next door.

What I was not familiar with was the Woolworth reference, the Hilton pool, or the arrest, although I did recall Kiara mentioning that it was lucky that this morning everything had returned to normal, or we would have been in jail.

"Are these stories related to our visit last night to Janice Price's house? I just made the connection after you pointed out to me that she is one of the recognized women of honor in the previous room," I said.

"I was hoping that you would recall most of this information on your own from last night. It is always so much more meaningful when you can actually experience the events rather than reading or hearing about them from other people.

"We are going to move on to the Woolworth exhibit next, and I will let you hear the audio explanation first. This was one of the reasons that Dr. King felt it necessary to visit Saint Augustine, along with the pool event that happened later," Kiara said, moving me along to the next display.

I recall reading about four African American students sitting down at the lunch counter in Greensboro, North Carolina, on February 1, 1960, and refusing to leave when they were informed that they would not be served.

A little old white lady was sitting a few seats away from the four protesters. I still remember today reading that one of the boys, I believe it was McCain, thought that she was glaring at him.

When finally, hours later, they got up on their own to leave, that older white-haired woman followed them out the door, put her hand on McCain's shoulder, and said, "Boys, I am so proud of you. I only regret that you didn't do this ten years ago when I could have helped you!"

"This isn't a replica of the North Carolina lunch counter, is it?" I turned to ask Kiara.

"Oh, no, it isn't. This one is the exact counter that resulted in four young boys from Saint Augustine being arrested. You see, after the Greensboro incident, similar protests were staged across the country. Ours took place in 1964, yes, the same year Dr. King was here, a few months later.

"I will let you listen to the audio version first. Are you now seeing a pattern of events threading its way into a great tapestry that will soon become your own vision that you can and will promote when the time arrives?" Kiara asked, adjusting the volume for me to hear clearly:

The Saint Augustine Four who chose to participate in a local civil rights protest at the Woolworth lunch counter were identified as JoAnne Anderson Ulmer, Samuel White, Audrey Nell Edwards, and Willie Carl Singelton. The group along with several other teenagers were arrested and taken to jail.

The group was advised that charges would only be dropped if all the defendants promised to no longer participate in further demonstrations and to acknowledge that the movement organizer, Dr. Robert Hayling, was guilty of contributing to the delinquency of minors.

None of the Saint Augustine Four, the original protesters, agreed to those terms. They were sent to reform school with the intention to rehabilitate them. Earl Johnson, an NAACP attorney, was unable to get them released because the judge claimed that they were beyond the jurisdiction of the legal system.

The teens were incarcerated until February of 1964 when the Florida Governor finally released them.

"Dr. King was so moved by the dedication and commitment that these students demonstrated that he referred to them as 'My warriors,' pledging that he would return to Saint Augustine to vindicate each one of them," Kiara added, after the sound system stopped.

"Dr. King knew that to make his Dream a reality he needed to convince the next generation that the Dream was worth fighting for," I said, always knowing that the future was in the hands of those born tomorrow.

"Well said, Calypso. As inspired as Dr. King was by the St. Augustine Four, it was the incident at the Mason Motor Lodge that made the greatest impact on his coming here for his Civil Rights movement. I will be interested to hear your reaction," Kiara said, leading me to the exhibit and a bench nearby to sit and listen.

It was June 18, 1964, at the Monson Motor Lodge in St. Augustine, Florida, that the owner of the hotel poured acid into the pool when a group of Black protesters decided to challenge the whites only rule.

The following day The Civil Rights Act was passed after an 83-day filibuster in the US Senate ended.

On June 11, 1964, only seven days earlier, Dr. Martin Luther King Jr. was arrested at that same motor lodge. While in jail, King wrote his very famous Letter from the St. Augustine Jail to his friend the Rabbi Israel Dressner in New Jersey -urging him to come to St. Augustine to support the cause. By June 18, 1964, seventeen rabbis arrived at the Manson Lodge. All were arrested, the largest number of rabbis arrested in American history.

"I had no idea that St. Augustine was the center of so many civil right disputes. You have lived here your entire life, Kiara, have you seen any significant changes since all of this turmoil," I asked, beginning to feel that maybe I had made the wrong decision to move here.

What Kiara was about to share with me changed all my earlier reservations.

"I have seen many different waves of change, some positive, a lot negative. About thirty years ago, Caroline Marie Brigid O'Sullivan Calhoun appeared in the house next door to me.

"Mama had passed away a few months earlier, and I was feeling extremely vulnerable. The house next door had been vacant for months, yet a few days after Marie moved in, the cottage style bungalow appeared as if she had lived there for years.

"The garden was miraculously blooming in June, where everywhere else gardens were wilting.

"The house that always appeared to be a dull gray was now a beautiful shade of Caribbean blue. There was even a lovely gingerbread trim surrounding the roof's eaves. In the backyard, I noticed twinkling lights and heard the pleasant sound of a relaxing water fountain.

"When I decided to stop by one evening to introduce myself, Caroline met me at the front door with a glass of wine and two candles for the front porch. It was the loveliest evening that I can ever remember.

"There really was not any specific reason for our immediate friendship; it was more like a spiritual connection. It was as if we were sharing an electric connection that both of us could feel running through our body and minds whenever we were together.

"This was the beginning of a friendship that lasted far beyond my imagination," Kiara paused, as if she wasn't sure that she wanted to reveal anymore.

"Will I have an opportunity to meet Caroline?" I asked.

Kiara looked up as if she was returning from a temporary daydream.

"Caroline is never far away. In time everything will become easier to understand, I assure you. At the moment, let's get you settled into your own abode. Once that happens, I promise that Emerald will be uniting everyone for a great reunion. Trust your instincts, Calypso, they will never fail you."

I can only hope that Kiara is right.

Chapter Seventeen

Once we believe in ourselves, we can risk curiosity, wonder, spontaneous delight, or any experience that reveals the human spirit.

EE Cummings

WHISPER

Emerald named me Whisper. It was because most of the time I would quietly observe everything and everyone around me barely ever speaking. It was just my way to avoid any confrontation from the time I was old enough to mingle with other children.

Someone once told me that it was quite normal for those children without siblings. That might have been reassuring if I was an only child. The truth is that I am the fourth child of a family of seven. I grew up with four sisters and two brothers.

To be perfectly accurate I have a transvestite sister, which makes the accurate count five sisters.

All of my siblings are gregarious, self-confident, successful, and talented with the exception of me.

Eventually, we all migrated to Florida from Cuba, a miracle in itself since many, if not most, immigrants find it very difficult to assimilate.

This is why there are pockets of neighborhoods where Cubans remain their entire lives without ever knowing any other cultures.

Sometimes I want to stand up and shout, "Why the hell did we fight so hard to come to America when all we are doing now is recreating a 'little' Cuba on foreign soil?"

But, of course, I never say this aloud.

My name is "Whisper" for a very good reason. When I whisper, I am able to express my frustrations without anyone hearing me.

Naturally nothing ever changes this way, but at least I am venting without being noticed.

That is until Emerald noticed me. Then everything started changing.

Before I reveal how my Whisper identity has evolved, it is necessary to understand who I was in my previous life.

When I arrived from Cuba to Miami with my transgender sister Jessica, I was known as Alejandra.

My "sister" was once named Pablo, that is before he realized that somehow there was a gender malfunction that must have happened somewhere between conception and birth.

When Pablo made the decision to begin the transgender transformation in Cuba, changing his name was the easy part.

Pablo started working at the age of thirteen at a local hospital as an orderly, which was really a hyped-up title for janitor because this hospital performed various transgender procedures.

Every paycheck that Pablo earned he deposited ninety percent in a savings account for his own gender transformation.

Of course, nobody, especially my parents, ever knew that this was his ultimate goal. I was the only one Pablo shared his secret with.

"I have worked out all the details, Alejandra. By the time you graduate from high school, I will have saved enough money for my facial feminization surgery, breast augmentation, and vaginaplasty. Those are the most essential ones I will need before moving to America," he said.

"What is vaginaplasty?" I asked, almost afraid to know.

"For me, it is the most important enhancement. It is creating a vagina along with all the other critical parts by using my existing genital tissue. Once all of this is completed, I will finally become the woman that I should have been at birth," Pablo said, excitedly.

"All of this sounds quite daring, Pablo, but have you ever considered how Mama and Papa are going to react when you finally tell them your plans? Or are you just going to disappear for a few months, return when all the surgeries are completed, and tell them that you were kidnapped by an evil sorceress who forced you to become a female?" I asked, trying to be lighthearted, although fully aware that my parents would be outraged once they discovered what Pablo was doing.

"I cannot control how Mama and Papa will react. I have been living in someone else's body for fourteen years. It is time for me to escape this curse and find out who I really am," Pablo said, determined.

Seven years later he had achieved his dream. Pablo was twenty-one years old when he started his first transgender operation.

My parents' reaction was totally unexpected. When Pablo first told Mama, she was confused. But, once he explained how important it was for him, how depressed he had been living with this secret, Mama embraced him, assuring him that she would always support and love him whatever gender he chose.

Papa was not as understanding. Mama decided to wait for Pablo to leave for his various surgeries before sharing the news with his father.

The reaction was just as I expected. Papa was livid with anger. He was so angry that he left the house on a hunting trip for three weeks.

Once he returned, there was enough venison for the entire season.

Everyone was anticipating Pablo's return from his two month transformation. When Mama finally received the call that he would be coming home the next day, everyone was both excited and nervous.

How different would Pablo look?
What are we going to call him now?
What do we tell friends and family?
How is Papa going to accept this?

Mama didn't tell us what time Pablo would be arriving. She just told us that he said early evening. Everyone was sitting at the dinner table, including Papa, trying to act as if it was just a normal meal, when all of us knew that once Pablo walked through that door all our lives would change.

The doorbell rang. Nobody said anything. We all looked at each other, expecting someone else to get up and answer the door.

"Pass the salad," was all Papa said, ignoring the chaos.

"Oh, my gosh," Mama finally said, rising from her chair.

"How much different could he be? I will get the door. I expect all of you to be kind and remember this is your brother returning home," she said, walking toward the door.

When she returned, walking next to her was a magnificent blonde, with slender long legs, perfectly coiffed hair styled in a popular shoulder length flip, gliding into the dining room, wearing a tight-fitting blue sheath dress with matching heels.

Everyone was silent, waiting for Papa to say something first. The tension was so strong that it was like waiting for a tornado to blow through the room, destroying life as we once knew it. Everyone was holding their breath.

Pablo walked directly toward Papa, extended his hand and waited patiently for his reaction.

Papa stood up, placed his napkin on the plate, looked directly at his fourth child, and said, "Had I known that you would look this beautiful, I would have sent all your sisters with you for a makeover."

Everyone started laughing with relief as if we had just welcomed a new member to our family. Papa was hugging his new daughter that he named Jessica, after Jessica Rabbit from the famous cartoon movie, *Who Framed Roger Rabbit?*

"I finally have the privilege to name one of my children without any objection from your mother," Papa said, kissing Jessica on the forehead.

That moment was one that I will always remember with great pleasure. Our family was finally together, united and happy. There were not many good memories like this one.

A few months later, Jessica and I were making plans to move to Miami.

Jessica had connections with the owner of a popular bar that offered her a job as a drag queen entertainer. The salary was excellent, but it was also a way that Jessica could get a work visa while applying for citizenship.

"Marcus really wants me for the show, Alejandra. But I told him that I would not go without you," Jessica said one day.

"That is crazy. This is your opportunity to finally move to Miami, doing something that you want to do. I refuse to be the albatross around your neck preventing you from your dream," I said.

"There is no way I am leaving you here. If it wasn't for you, Alejandra, I would still be Pablo. We are a team. Besides, Marcus will find something for you to do; trust me!" Jessica insisted.

One week before Jessica was to leave Havana, she handed me a plane ticket.

"We did it! Marcus is hiring you as a makeup artist for the show. The pay is good, we can room together, at least until one of us finds a boyfriend, but by then we will both be US citizens and free to pursue any kind of career that we want. The world is calling us, Alejandra, and we are a great team," Jessica said, more excited than I had ever seen her.

This decision to trust Jessica's intuition was only the beginning of my life's journey. Everything that followed once I started working at the *Bam Bam Club*, located in the famous North Beach Miami is a result of fate although according to Emerald it is understanding and practicing *Spiritual Dimension* that truly is responsible for bringing together the *Sisterhood*.

Therefore, exploring the key principles, beliefs, and values that provide us with a purpose in life is what unites us. This may sound fairly straightforward, even elementary, but in fact it requires total dedication until you learn to naturally embrace who you are.

North Shores was where Jessica and I found a lovely, two-bedroom, affordable apartment that was walking distance to the club and the famous bandshell where we could hear music concerts free on a summer evening if we left our windows open.

But it was one very strange Saturday morning when Jessica was spending the evening with a new boyfriend that I woke up early deciding to take a walk to our favorite coffee shop a few blocks away.

There was a slight mist hovering over the tops of some of the houses that I walked past but nobody else was jogging or walking their dog, which just briefly seemed a little odd. But it was still early enough for the streetlights to be on, so maybe everyone was sleeping off their Friday night celebrations.

As I continued to walk through upscale Bal Harbor, 63rd to 87th to be precise, I recognized a few of the paths to secret gardens that I had previously explored, moving past the dog park, now empty, and the uncrowded beaches near the bandshell.

Although everything surrounding me is usually loud, and busy, jumping during the week, it was unusually quiet today.

Jessica would always point out that this neighborhood was a nice blend of chill and lively street life, with some Mama and Papa restaurants among a variety of interesting blends of people and, of course, an amazing beach.

But this morning it was more like an empty Universal set after the movie production had finished shooting their last scene.

Eventually I realized that the coffee shop I was going to was now replaced by a structure totally unfamiliar to me. In its place was a building with a sign that said the *Jungle Inn.*

It was a two-story log structure with steps leading to a front door. Despite my better judgement, I decided to investigate.

Before I could knock on the door, a white rabbit dressed in a black vest with a top hat and holding a pocket watch slightly cracked open the door.

I jumped back rather startled.

"Oh, it's only you! Emerald warned us that you would be coming. Where have you been? We have been waiting days for you," the Rabbit said, obviously annoyed.

I wasn't really sure how to react. I was still trying to figure out why I was here and not enjoying a hot mocha at *Manny's*.

"Well, are you coming in or staying outside like a jabber walk?" the Rabbit said, more irritated than earlier.

Without responding, I stepped hesitantly inside. That is when the Rabbit handed me a scroll tied with a red ribbon.

"You are to read Alice, and I will read the White Rabbit. Do you think that you can follow those instructions?" the White Rabbit asked.

I wasn't sure why I was here or what this encounter meant but instinctively I decided to follow the instructions.

"Do you love me?" Alice asked.

"No, I don't love you," the White Rabbit answered.

Alice frowned her forehead and put her hands together as she always did when she felt hurt.

"See?" The White Rabbit replied noticing.

"Now you'll start wondering what makes you so imperfect and what you did wrong so I can't love you."

Even a little…

You know, this is why I can't love you. You will not always be loved, Alice. There will be days when others will be tired and bored with life, they will have their heads in the clouds and will end up hurting you…

Because people are like this sometimes, Alice. Somehow, they always end up hurting each other's feelings, either by neglect, misunderstandings, or conflicts within themselves…

If you don't love yourself at least a little,… If you don't create an armor of self-love and happiness around your heart…the setbacks caused by others will become lethal and destroy you…

The first time I saw you I made a pact with myself: I will avoid loving you until you love yourself.

Alice in Wonderland

When the White Rabbit had finished his reading, he instructed me to roll up my scroll.

"Emerald has instructed me to advise you that you will never find true happiness or love until you return to your roots in Saint Augustine. The longer that you delay the inevitable the longer there will be a gap in your spirit."

Before I could ask any further questions, the White Rabbit was escorting me from the entrance onto the porch outside.

For a few minutes, I tried to absorb what I had just experienced. That was when I decided that I would have to share this bizarre experience with Jessica as soon as possible.

As I walked down the steps of the log cabin structure and turned away from the street, everything that was once there was gone. Only an empty lot remained. The walk home was as normal as it always had been.

I had no idea how I was going to explain this encounter with the White Rabbit or the need for me to leave Miami for some strange city in Florida called Saint Augustine.

I held my scroll tight, hoping that whatever magical powers it might have would guide me to my new destination safely.

Chapter Eighteen

Wings are of many kinds. Butterfly's wings, vulture's wings, eagle-wings, spread wings of white swans, dragonfly's serene wings, wings of albatross, lovely wings of hummingbirds, tiny wings of a fly, or a bumble-bee wings; and when they fly, they fly their best according to their ability of flying. We should not underestimate the size of those heavenly wings.

Munia Khan
Author

WHISPER

"What do you mean that you are moving? Moving to where? We just got settled down here at North Beach a few months ago?" Jessica said, obviously upset.

"I told you, Jessica, that I was going to be looking for another job. The only reason I agreed to work at the club was because I knew how much it meant to you. But, now that you're settled, it is time for me to find my calling," I said, in a calm voice.

"I never expected you to be working on makeup for drag queens forever, Alejandra, but moving away to a place we have never even heard of before without a job is just plain nuts," Jessica said, beginning to lose patience.

She may be partly right to be concerned. There was no guarantee that I could find a job once I arrived in Saint Augustine. For that matter, I had no idea how far Saint Augustine was from Miami, or even why I was so obsessed with going there. How was I going to convince Jessica that it was my destiny when I wasn't convinced myself?

"Take a seat right here next to me, Alejandra," Jessica said, in her motherly voice.

"Now. Let's look at the realistic, practical aspects of your decision

118

to leave Miami," she continued speaking, taking a seat across from me.

Jessica then calmly began to point out most of the obvious detriments to moving, starting with the obvious legal restrictions associated with my immigration status and concluding by pointing out my introvert personality, suggesting there would be no positive outcome if I were to insist on leaving.

It was that last argument, about being so unsure of myself that I was doomed to fail, that convinced me that I had to leave.

The White Rabbit's message to me was crystal clear, regardless of whether my meeting him was a hallucination or some strange psychological meltdown.

What Jessica was now confirming is how I have felt my entire life. I was at the crossroads, given an opportunity to prove that I am capable of achieving whatever makes me happy without prior approval from anyone.

"Do you remember, Jessica, when you asked me to go with you to Miami after your transformation?" I asked, not sure where my confidence was coming from.

Jessica shook her head affirmatively, but still looking confused as to where this conversation was going.

"At that time, I referred to myself as an albatross, alluding to the negative symbolism in a poem by Samuel Taylor Coleridge, titled *The Rime of the Ancient Mariner*. Do you remember that narrative poem, Jessica? I used to read it to you from a book with colorful illustrations. It was one of your favorite stories," I said, hoping that she could start to understand where I was going with this tale.

"Yes, of course, I remember. There are parts in the tale that are both exciting and frightening, which I suppose is why it was my favorite," Jessica said, listening intently to what I was saying.

"That is correct. Just as in life the albatross can be seen as a connection between the natural and spiritual world that we find ourselves a part of when the young mariner kills the innocent bird and is forced to wear the carcass around his neck as a symbol of disgrace. You see, Jessica, the mariners regarded the albatross as good luck without truly appreciating all of its accomplishments. Did you know that an albatross is the largest known bird alive that can fly for years without ever landing? For the first six years of their lives, they soar in the air, only searching to land on earth when it is time to mate. They are capable of traveling over 10,000 miles in a single journey while circumnavigating the entire globe in 46 days. And we consider the human race superior?" I said, waiting for Jessica's response.

"I had no idea that you were such an expert on the life of the albatross," Jessica said, laughing as she stood up to embrace me.

"I have no idea where this Saint Augustine place is, but if it is where you want to soar off to be my brilliant sister, I have a little money saved to help get you there. Let me talk to my new boyfriend, Daniel, he also might know some people in Saint Augustine. He is an advertising agent that is always traveling for his company. Whatever it is that makes you happy, Alejandra, we will make it happen for you."

It was the first time in my life that I could feel a slight spark of confidence. It was only for a few seconds but now that I knew what it felt like I was hungry for more.

Jessica and I agreed that to ensure this move would be successful we would need to be sure that I had a safe place to stay while searching for a job.

Thankfully, Daniel, Jessica's boyfriend, knew Saint Augustine well. He assured us both that not only was it a popular vacation destination but also a great location to live.

"You may not realize this, but Saint Augustine is the oldest city in the United States. It was founded in 1565. Many people claim that throughout the city free spirits roam the streets. I actually have experienced that feeling walking through the ancient cobblestone streets," Daniel shared with us one evening.

"Are you suggesting that the town is haunted," I asked, rather surprised.

"Oh, yes, absolutely it is haunted. Most people regard St. Augustine, New Orleans, and Savannah, Georgia as the mojo haunted triangle of the United States," Daniel replied, quite matter of factly.

Most of us in my country are familiar with *Santeria,* also sometimes known as Regla de Ocho, an African diasporic religion originated in Cuba during the late 19th century. The belief revolves around deities that derive their names and attributes from traditional Yoruba divinities. It is believed that every human has a personal *oricha,* a West African spirit, that influences their personality.

Healing rituals, as well as offerings given to the spirits of the dead, were a common practice. Although Havana was not a popular place for those who believed in *Santeria,* most of us were aware of the initiators.

That served as diviners and healers in our community.

Would those spirits that Daniel mentioned be followed by a group in Saint Augustine? And, if so, are they groups that I should be aware of?

Suddenly my self-doubts began to surface once again, questioning my ability to deal with these issues.

I decided that the best solution was to take some personal time by myself weighing all the options available.

One of my favorite places to reflect was at the bandstand when there was nobody playing. Tonight, as I approached my familiar spot with a view of the Atlantic Ocean from the cement ledge, I could see a group of ladies dressed in full long skirts gathering on the stage.

There was nobody seated in the stands, but me. Someone had brought with the group a boombox. As soon as the reggae music started, the ladies began to dance.

They were all following the steps of a tall, slender, blonde woman who appeared to be the leader.

As I watched them from my perch, each one floating in perfect unison, adding their own unique flair to the arrangement, I stood up reluctantly allowing the music to flow freely through my veins.

From nowhere, someone nearby took my hand leading me to the stage to join the other dancers.

Soon I was following the others with an inner desire to dance all night. Where this energy came from, I had no idea. But, when the music stopped, everyone formed a circle, walking toward me smiling.

"Hola, Señorita! Where did you learn to dance? You are quite good. Would you like to join our Gypsy dancers ensemble? My name is Margarita. And who are you, my darling?" she asked quite pleasantly.

"Oh, I'm not a dancer. I have no idea where those moves came from. But all of you are so talented. I hope I can see you perform again someday. I will be leaving for Saint Augustine soon, but I will never forget this evening. Thank you for letting me participate with you," I said, excited, turning toward the exit.

"Our Krew travels to Saint Augustine several times a year. Hopefully we will meet again." Namaste was the last word I heard as I turned away to return home.

Walking home in the autumn balmy evening, I continued to

remember my bizarre visit with the white rabbit that led me to decide to leave Miami.

Although there were many reservations still in my mind, none was serious enough to prevent me from leaving.

Returning home, I found a note from Jessica saying that she was with Daniel. She would not be coming home for a few days but would meet up with me at the club on Monday.

Obviously, their relationship was becoming more intense. This was another reason why going forward with my own future plans was essential.

Once I decided on a date to leave, there would be no turning back. After dancing with my new Gypsy friends, I couldn't even imagine anything that would prevent me from moving forward to a new life, one where I would finally learn to love myself.

It was impossible for me to ever imagine how difficult this choice would be.

Chapter Nineteen

So I love you because the entire universe conspired to help me find you.
The Alchemist
Pablo Corlho

WHISPER

It took me nine months to finally board a Greyhound bus to Jacksonville, Florida, with one backpack and a medium sized suitcase that Jessica bought me for my birthday. Everything that I owned was in one of those bags.

Daniel was able to help me apply for a student visa once I registered for classes at Saint John's Community College, which made my leaving much easier.

He also assisted in finding me a place to live close to the campus with a group of other students from a variety of different backgrounds.

The networking community successfully provided me with two jobs at locations where my roommates worked. This made it possible to commute without a vehicle.

There was also little recreational time. My dream of dancing with the Gypsies that I had briefly met at the bandstand was fading away, yet the image of my White Rabbit continued to inspire me to fulfill my dream regardless how distorted it was by this time.

Four years later, I was graduating from Florida State University with a BA in English. What I was to do with this Bachelor of Arts degree was still not clear. Teaching was never an option that I could consider.

Even after completing all of my classes, I still had low self-esteem. The very thought of standing for hours in front of a group of young students just to earn a living seemed like torture.

More education! That was the answer. I truly enjoyed college. I was able to navigate at my own pace, choosing with whom and when I wanted to communicate; it was the most comfortable place that I found for many years.

By the time I was contemplating applying for law school, Jessica had retired from the club, moved in with Daniel permanently, and was seriously considering marriage.

Life for both of us in America was full of opportunities.

Every year we were also able to reunite with our siblings who had all left Cuba a few years after us and were spread across various states. Only Mama and Papa remained in Cuba, although we all tried to get them to leave many times.

My dreams of dancing with the Gypsies never materialized. Life has a way of taking many detours before we arrive at our final destination.

It was not until many years later, once I retired from my legal practice in Washington DC as a patent attorney, that I made the decision to return once again to Saint Augustine.

By this time, I was financially independent, able to purchase a small house downtown, and begin to pursue the original dream that I was seeking many years earlier.

The only problem was locating that White Rabbit who introduced me to a local magical Gypsy named Emerald twenty years ago.

Now that I finally knew who I was, what I wanted, and what I was capable of achieving, the only obstacle that I could think of was that it might be too late.

Was it possible that my time had run out? Maybe, but I was not yet ready to give up.

Where to start was my first dilemma. Now that I had so much free time, I made the decision to learn all that I could about my inner self.

I began to research Yoga, which seemed to be the best place to start. What I learned was that there was an entire certification program that allows you to not only teach but to understand the philosophical benefits associated with this program.

I was fascinated! It was what I had been searching for without even knowing.

Over 5,000 years ago, Yoga originated in ancient India as a philosophical and spiritual practice. There are so many places of obscurity as well as uncertainty of sacred texts directly related to the secretive texts throughout the year that there are many varieties in the modern practice.

What I found most interesting was the metaphysical understanding of yoga. This dualism occurs when the universe is identified as two realities. The first, known as *Purusas, witness consciousness.* It occurs when the abstract essence of the self, spirit, and the universal principle that is eternal.

The second, Praktrti (nature), is bonded with *Jiva,* a living being, where various elements of the senses and activities create a state of imbalance that can only be overcome when *moksa* is achieved with Yoga and Hinduism.

The more I read, the more I was convinced that this was what my life was missing. Once I achieved a definite balance, everything that I was searching for would finally create the unity in my life that was missing.

Every morning I would wake up early, often before sunrise, put on my walking shoes and head downtown.

It was my favorite time of the day. I am a loner, always have been. But walking on St. George Street when only the homeless are still sleeping in the alleys made me feel like I still had some control over my life.

When I wasn't taking Yoga classes, I was mingling among people in masses, trying not to look alone.

Sometimes during the week, I would drive to Saint Augustine Beach, walk on the sandy dunes, and stop by the local art shop.

It was during one of these early evenings that I walked past the covered stage across from the volleyball courts and noticed a group of musicians playing a variety of drums. There were bongos to steel drums.

As I moved closer, there were five ladies dressed in circle skirts. They looked very similar to the ladies that I danced with years ago at South Beach Miami.

The music was once again inviting me to join the group. As if I was young and back in Miami, I started swaying naturally, not caring what anyone else thought.

When the music stopped, it was I this time who approached the group. I was hoping that someone would notice my natural rhythm and enthusiasm. But, no, most of the ladies were only focused on each other.

At last, just as I was about to leave, one of the ladies noticed me.

"Hi there. My name is Sunflower. Our Gypsy Krew is looking for new members. Here is where we meet during the week to plan our events. If you are interested, show up next Wednesday at this address," she said, handing me a card running back to the group before

I could say anything. It was an odd encounter, to say the least.

Was I finally going to fulfill that dream of finding my true passion? And what was that true passion now twenty years later?

I had achieved so much more than anyone expected me to, especially myself, yet it was not enough. Beneath all the glory of my degrees, being a successful attorney, and even feeling proud that I did it all independently, never led me to anyone who could assure me that I was now worthy of being loved.

Oh, there had been several relationships during this discovery journey that included both men and women, but none satisfied either one of us enough to make a permanent commitment.

Perhaps that is the real reason why Saint Augustine continued to appeal to me. This is where it all started.

This is where I found my courage to follow the voices in my head. Were those voices speaking to me once again now? Were they telling me it was finally my time to shine? Maybe.

The address in my hand just might be the final destination that I have been waiting for. If not, it would just be another disappointment that I could add to many others that I have survived.

One of the interesting things that Sunflower mentioned about her dancing group is that she identified it as part of a Krew. That distinction was also used with the dancers I met at North Shore many years ago.

It never meant much to me at that time, but now since I heard it used again, I was curious what it meant.

Why not just say group, or club, or even company? No, there must be some specific significance with the term Krew. I decided to do a little research before my Wednesday meeting.

Thankful to be living in the modern age of technology, the next morning after my morning walk past *Castillo de San Marcos,* on the bay front, I returned home for a quick shower and drove to one of my favorite coffeehouses, *Dos Coffee and Wine,* located on San Marcos, close enough to home and the perfect distance from all the tourist attractions downtown.

As usual it was busy with many regular clients, students from Flagler College with their laptops, and even a few community groups that used this venue to have their monthly meetings.

As I waited in line to place my regular order, I saw an open table that I decided to grab before the morning rush would make it impossible to find anything.

Carmella at the register, who amazingly knows nearly everyone by their first name, as well as remembers what their favorite order is, waved to me as I headed toward the table.

"I got you, Alejandra, no problem," she said as I took my seat.

Within a few minutes, my iced mocha latte with raspberry was delivered to the table with an order of my favorite toast, melted Swiss cheese over tomatoes.

I now had everything needed to begin researching what "Krews" meant.

Finding my favorite *Google* page, where naively I imagined the answer would immediately appear, I instead found pages and pages of Krews, Gypsy Krews from Gaspsrilla Pirate Parade, the Krews of Romany, A Gypsy Krew list, and tons of Gypsy tattoos, along with a variety of Gypsy Krew fashions.

What was not listed is the meaning of a Krew, or the origin. Obviously, my research needed to be streamlined.

Once I located the specific site, I was overwhelmed. Although modern Krews are in every major city around the country, Florida alone has at least one hundred and thirty Krews that are very established with officers that organize social events and fundraisers.

Those Gypsies and Pirates that join a Krew are dedicated to everything that the group desires to accomplish.

These are certainly not the traditional stereotypes of wandering Gypsies that most communities warned citizens to beware of. These were a group of fascinating people that I wanted to explore in more detail.

For my entire life, especially surrounded by eight siblings, I always felt inadequate. This is why Jessica and I bonded naturally.

We were both outcasts. But Jessica overcame that stigma. She learned how to gain respect, even when Papa threatened to disown her. I wasn't yet at that level, but I did know that I was close. Very close.

When I returned home, there was a scroll tied with a lovely rainbow ribbon hanging from my front door. Although I had been living here for a few months, there had never been any neighbors welcoming me to the community or even advertisements attached to my door. This scroll was definitely a surprise.

Once inside I removed the ribbon from the parchment paper, sat down, and began to read the message that began with, Dearest Alejandra:

Never allow anyone to have a bad opinion of you! It will make you become defensive when it is unnecessary. Those hands that point at you are fickle. Although you will not have control over gossip, Peace is letting go. People perhaps are allowed to have their own opinions. It is your reaction that you have complete control over. The most important part of your life is the control over your own reputation. It is your character that nobody is able to manipulate. It belongs only to you. Your word, written or spoken, defines who you are. Your actions are only yours. Others may decide to judge you on their terms, but it has nothing to do with who you have honestly demonstrated you are. Interpretation is left to the artist's discretion.

Emerald

There was no other clue to what I was to do with this revelation, nor why I was receiving this message just at the same moment that I was being invited to join a Gypsy Dancing Krew.

When I was in law school, I discovered Khalil Gibran. He is best known for *The Prophet,* published in the United States in 1923.

His philosophy inspired me whenever I was convinced that I was not smart enough to pursue a law degree. These are the words that I always turn to when I struggle to decide what direction I should go when in doubt.

Do not live half a life,
*And do not die half death (Is "a" missing before "death"?)**
If you choose silence, be silent
When you speak, do so until you are finished
If you accept, then express it bluntly,
Don't mask it
If you refuse be clear about it
For an ambiguous refusal is but a weak
Acceptance
Do not accept half a solution
Do not dream half a dream
Do not fantasize about half hopes
Half the way will get you nowhere
You are a whole that deserves to live a life
Not half a life.

The time has finally come for me to live the words that I have preached to so many!

Chapter Twenty

To be nobody but
Yourself in a world
Which is doing its best day and night
To make you like
Everybody else
Means to fight the hardest battle
Which any human being can fight
And never stop fighting.

EE Cummings

Mandana Morrison

Learning about the Sisterhood evolution and the ladies that were somehow all drawn to Saint Augustine without truly understanding the complete story is a mystery, a mystery that I was not sure was worth solving.

What is essential to know is how the Sisterhood's energy inspires others to understand that life does not revolve around their needs but rather life itself.

How all of this extends positive energy when we are united in a community that exemplifies love is the most powerful discovery.

What Aunt Caroline, Dante, Sunflower, and even I in some enigmatic form contribute to the Sisterhood legacy is what I am dedicated to discovering.

Supporting this legacy, one that I somehow inherited, and learning what the original Gypsies had to overcome to achieve respect in the modern world is essential. I may even be enlightened as to Aunt Caroline's connection to Brigid, Marie and Liam.

There are definitely many discrepancies when it comes to the stories of when and where Gypsies originated. Certainly, there is no lack of documentation.

To avoid spending the next ten years researching what is a fascinating topic, I chose to sift through the material focusing on how the Gypsy culture progressed and more so how Gypsies in the modern era have redefined who they are.

There are parts of Europe today where Gypsies are still shunned as disrespectful, disruptive outsiders. Some are patronized as little more than the source of exotic music and dance. In America the Gypsy reputation is not much different.

Many people still regard Gypsies as nomads that have no permanent roots, with their main source of income being swindling or begging.

Because of this reputation, I was curious to find out why so many successful people in the Augustine community would choose to be associated with such a motley Krew.

That question led me to research the origin of Krews in Florida. It was an interesting discovery.

It was in New Orleans that the term Krews originated in 1857. These were clubs that organized the Mardi Gras festivals for the city of New Orleans.

All year these Krews worked towards planning the gala parties and parades. It is also interesting to note that many of the most exclusive Krews are secret societies.

The *Mystic Krews of Comus* was the oldest secretive group that participated in Mardi Gras from its conception in 1856 to 1991. Prior to Comus, the Carnival celebrations were confined nearly entirely to the Catholic Creole community.

Bernard de Marigny was a French Creole American nobleman playboy that in 1833 streamlined the Mardi Gras Parade into an organized event. In addition, he included the exclusive tableau ball.

Marigny's event included a "living" picture on stage of actors and models stationary and silent, many nude, in erotica poses. The intent was to combine theatre and visual arts. Later this would continue in a slightly different form.

Although *Comus* is given credit for all its contributions to Mardi Gras, there was much controversy over the sharp racial, ethnic, and class tensions that were occurring.

When in 1991 the New Orleans City Council passed a resolution requiring all social organizations to sign a statement that assures there is no discrimination on the basis of race, religion, gender, disability, or sexual orientation in order to obtain parade permits, *Comus* withdrew from the parade never to return.

Learning this story is quite revealing. I was now curious to learn if any of the Krews in Florida, particularly Saint Augustine, would refuse to discriminate?

How advanced are we now in comparison to that original *Comus* Krew in New Orleans?

The first article I found was a webpage for *Ye Mysic Krew of Gasparilla*. I was particularly impressed with the historical accuracy as well as the statement included describing the purpose of the group, which is named after Pirate Jose Gaspar.

Now I was curious to know why this Pirate was being honored. Although the websites state that José Gaspar was an aristocrat at birth and officer of the Spanish Navy, apparently, he is remembered here for terrorizing the coastal waters of Florida while leaving an untold fortune that has never been discovered.

Undoubtedly there must be more about this notorious pirate. If not, what is the purpose in raising money for a foundation named after someone known for pillaging?

Like many heroes that we admire, Jose has a complex tale, with many odd details that cannot be verified. One source states that José Gaspar never existed. He is nothing but a legend that has grown in popularity after being named by the Tampa pirate Krew who celebrates a yearly invasion event, inviting pirates throughout the state of Florida and beyond.

One interpretation that is interesting focuses on the possibility that Gaspar was wrongfully accused by several jilted ladies in the court of Spain, where unjustly facing arrest, he was left no choice but to commandeer a ship illegally, living the life of a pirate.

Since there truly is no other accurate information that disputes these claims, I have chosen to accept this version.

While I was in the library, one article caught my attention just at the moment that I was about to leave. It was almost noon, and I was meeting with Sunflower at 1:00 pm at *Nonna's* for lunch. But this article had me curious since there was nothing that I read similar to it.

The Pirate Empire revealed how captured slaves were offered an alternative to slavery. Ship captains in the 1700's who transported slaves from Africa to the West Indies, now known as the Caribbean, were much worse than many pirates.

Beginning as early as the 1600's when slave ships were captured, pirates would give the slaves the opportunity to join their crew. Human cargo in the beginning was limited to maybe six or seven slaves. However, by the 1700's, specific slave ships were built to carry hundreds from Africa.

Pirate captain Sam Bellamy and Blackbeard had an estimated crew of 50% African. This strongly increased the Pirate captain's power at sea. There have been claims that Blackbeard himself was the offspring of an English nobleman and a half African servant. Unfortunately, without DNA available, this is only speculation.

However, there are historical documents that support another Black pirate known as Black Caesar who is often depicted with Blackbeard. At the time Blackbeard fought his final battle against Lieutenant Maynard of the Royal Navy, Caesar was instructed to destroy the ship if the Pirates were defeated.

As interesting as all of this Gypsy and Pirate history is, my watch alarm was alerting me it was time to leave for lunch. Thankfully, *Nonna's Trattoria* on Aviles is only a few minutes from the historical library.

It was a lovely fall afternoon. Sunflower was sitting in the patio with a glass of wine.

"Greetings, girlfriend! You are exactly on time. Can I order you some wine?" Sunflower said, waving to the server before I could respond.

"You are the only person that I know that always arrives earlier than I do. Were you waiting for very long?" I asked, glancing at the menu.

"No, not at all. I was checking out the thrift store around the corner. Sometimes there are great Gypsy skirts that can add a little pizzazz to make a perfect costume. By the time I am finished with it, you will think that I had a magic wand," Sunflower said, adjusting her sunglasses.

"I wish that I was as talented as you are. The costume designs are amazing," I said.

"Well, thank you, but my talent is a gift that I have no idea how I attained. You, my dearest friend, have talent that we haven't even touched the surface of yet," Sunflower said, reaching across the table, touching my hand and adding, "What is it that is worrying you, sweet Mandana?"

I turned away for a brief moment. The server's timing was perfect.

"Are you ladies ready to order?" the waiter asked.

"I think that we will share a ricotta and roasted tomato bruschetta. What do you think, Mandana?" Sunflower asked.

"Yes, of course. That sounds great," I replied.

Once the server left, I finally asked the question that had been haunting me for weeks.

"Have you heard anything from Brendon? I keep expecting him to simply appear like he did the first time. It has been months since I saw him. I mean, who kisses a complete stranger and then ghosts her? And I still don't know why I am still here?"

Sunflower could sense the frustration in my voice. The more that I keep searching for answers about Aunt Caroline, the more questions appear. There doesn't seem to be any end to this mystery.

"The process is complicated, Mandana. It does require you to have faith, trust, and a lot of patience. I can share with you that what Caroline left you is much more than her beloved Lancelot, a cottage, and financial independence. When you are ready, when you are prepared to take over your heritage, everything will make sense. This I promise you," Sunflower said, smiling.

Although my encounter with Brendon a few months ago was both exciting and confusing, he is only one missing piece to my abstract collection.

"What does the rest of your day look like today?" Sunflower asked, leaving the last bruschetta for me.

"No plans really. But I have been gone most of the morning. I don't like leaving Lancelot locked up for very long," I said, curious as to what Sunflower had in mind.

"I will give Kiara a call and ask her to take Lance on a short walk. There is something that I want you to see. It won't take long but, once you witness for yourself the Gypsies' interaction it will be easier for you to understand why Caroline devoted her extended life here in Saint Augustine," Sunflower said, taking the check before I could insist on paying.

It would be the first time that I was invited to a Gypsy dance rehearsal. Unless you have been fortunate enough to see a full dance production, it is difficult for me to express how much dedication goes into this performance.

"I do want to make you aware that the Gypsies' rehearsals are always private. There are no visitors, no distractions. What you will be witnessing is raw, authentic, natural performance that creates the magic on stage."

"I assure you that I will respect whatever your rules are," I said.

Sunflower smiled, "I have no doubt you will, Mandana. Being a stage performer, you will appreciate all the special effects that are used to enhance our performance, but lately there have been some additions that we have no control over."

That was the last and only clue I was given as we walked across the street to the Lewis Theatre, owned and operated by Flagler College. It was the first time that I had ever visited this auditorium.

"Typically, we rehearse wherever we are lucky to find an empty venue. But, a few days ago, I received a call from the scheduling department offering us the stage for today. The girls are truly excited about having the lighting, music, and especially a real stage to practice on," Sunshine said, opening the front door, allowing me to enter first.

In keeping with the traditional Spanish Renaissance style, it felt as if I was entering another era. Everything from the carpet to the wallpaper was decorated in red and gold.

"I know. It all feels a little dated. But by now you should realize that everything surrounding us is ancient. It is a city that has learned to freeze time while still maintaining modern technology. Everything from the lighting to the sound system has been upgraded to the most advanced available. Henry Flagler's great nephew, Lawrence Lewis Jr., left specific instructions in his will that the auditorium would always have available millions of dollars to upgrade the technology when needed. This is why all of us are excited to at least being allowed to rehearse here," Sunshine said, leading me into the auditorium.

"I am going to leave you here in the upper tier. You will be able to see everything without the dancers being able to see you," she said, blowing me kisses.

Sitting in the darkness, I was beginning to reflect on why Sunflower might warn me about the rehearsal. What did she mean about unexpected surprises?

The only time that I ever saw any of the Gypsies perform was that shadow dancing at the fort and occasionally gliding through Saint George Street late in the evening. I was looking forward to finally watching them on stage.

Suddenly the stage lights were on, the music started, but the curtain was still down. Although I am not an expert in Gypsy music, it was always my impression that it is in the same category as Flamenco.

In my music appreciation class in college, there was a unit that taught the musical heritage of the Romani people. It included a style that showcased the diversity and adaptability of Gypsy music.

What I was listening to at the moment did not resemble anything familiar. What it did remind me of was a popular Russian Klezmer band that could be heard throughout coffee houses in Eastern Europe.

Klezmer bands originated in the eighteenth-century, gaining popularity throughout the nineteenth century, primarily because they were small, ranging from only three to five musicians playing windward or string instruments.

What I was enjoying at this moment was a blend of that passionate tone with a gentle melancholy melody that was almost mesmerizing. The recognizable instruments that created this intoxicating musical blend were revealed once the curtain rose.

There were four band members that included a bassist, a singing violinist, a guitarist, and a mandolinist wearing a vibrant purple gypsy circle skirt.

It was at this time that I began to realize the distinction that the choreographer and the musical director were focused on achieving.

Most people, including myself until I arrived here in Saint Augustine, are not aware that there are various Gypsy dancing styles and techniques that have evolved from the three most prominent types, Russian, Balkan, and Spanish.

In this production the objective is to highlight each of the founding traditions. I am only presuming that what will be presented is the branching off with original interpretations.

Certainly, a challenging project that could lead towards insightful discussions, but would the general public understand or at least appreciate this innovative concept?

Just as I was beginning to identify the Russian language being sung by the violinist, five Gypsy dancers dressed authentically in their Slavic ethnic costumes began to perform in perfect unison.

The vibrant expressive movement, intricate footwork that includes precise tapping to the best of the music, synchronized wide skirts swinging in tempo, artistically balanced with shoulder shimmies and floor work begins with a slow, smooth introduction that gradually increases as the music momentum accelerates.

Something inside of me was awakening, something that seemed

natural yet foreign at the same time.

Why did it feel like I should be on stage sharing every stomp, every accent, every clap that was making my heart beat faster? It was as if for the very first time my dormant blood cells were revived, reminding me that this was what living truly feels like.

The traditional Gypsy flavor that everyone expects is indeed experiencing an innovative Renaissance revival. The folkloric expectations do not disappoint, but they can now be perceived differently by the modern viewer.

The form has now been adapted into a fashionable, beautifully attractive fusion, reminding the audience of a high level nouveau art object, one that is unfamiliar but worth remembering.

As the stage lights began to dim once again, and the Klezmer group was fading into silence, it was evident that the theatrical crew was preparing for a transition, one that I was now quite anxious to see how it could surpass what had just been performed.

As in any dress rehearsal, many of which I recall personally, the smooth transformation from one scene to the next is much more critical than any audience appreciates.

When it is done well, it goes unnoticed, but if it takes too long, or it is too messy, the audience is the first to notice, often using that to criticize an entire production.

I patiently waited a few minutes, surprised how efficient the production was moving. Within less than two minutes, the stage lights were once again dimly illuminated to create a starry evening. The background mural even resembled Van Gogh's quite famous *Starry Night.*

To the right of the stage, visible but not a distraction, was a new small band. The five musicians, this time all male, were dressed in Irish attire. Certainly totally unexpected.

Whatever did the Irish band have in common with the Gypsy dancers? I was about to find out shortly.

Apparently, Sunflower realized, as I did, that those attending this Gypsy Extravaganza performance would also be confused at seeing the Celts included in the Gypsy dance repertoire.

As the band started to perform some music from one of the most celebrated modern Irish groups, known as *Celtic Crossroads,* I was beginning to appreciate how this production was blending the ancient with the contemporary, not only visually but musically as well.

Celtic Crossroads are critically acclaimed for their efforts to create an explosion of youthful energy that incorporates traditional Irish music, bluegrass, Gypsy, and jazz into a melting pot of memorable sounds.

The Gypsy director, who I personally have never met, brilliantly demonstrates her desire to include, expand, and incorporate multi generations in appreciating a new order of Gypsy performers.

"Welcome everyone to our newest production of *Gypsy Extravaganza.* Tonight, through music, dance, and art, we intend to introduce you to a new world of Gypsy Pirate Players that will entertain you throughout the evening. The performance that you will be watching next celebrates and honors our Irish Gypsy heritage. These Irish Travelers were referred to as *'White Gypsies,'* primarily because they were members of a nomadic ethnic group. What you will be witnessing is the authentic step dancing, Celli, and of course the very popular River-dance, which is characterized by a stiff upper body, quick foot movements, and a special tap shoe. We are pleased to bring to you our interpretation of *White Gypsy Dancers!"*

Sunflower faded away as the night mural once again darkened the stage. What was about to happen can only be described as surrealistically phenomenal.

As my eyes were adjusting to a moonlit haze, a light mist began to appear. The robust music that was earlier playing now changed to the familiar new age Celtic pop music contributed by *Enya.*

Her ephemeral spiritual sensuality almost feels sacred, especially at this moment as the Gypsy dancers take the stage, entering from opposite sides in almost perfect time, all wearing full skirts with different Irish print patterns.

The Enya tune is one I recognize as *A Day Without Rain,* from her 2000 album of the same name. Although the words are worth knowing, and I do as a fan of Enya, it is the ambiance at this moment, watching how the dancers gracefully move their arms, swaying back and forth as if a gentle breeze is providing them with the perfect balance needed to move throughout the stage with Van Gogh's vanishing starry night image that is enchanted in a forest atmosphere.

Just as the spellbinding music transforms me into being more than spectator, I notice a couple dancing with their arms wrapped around one another—hers on his neck, his on her waist, while their feet are tapping in perfect unison, first slowly, then faster and faster and faster until it is nearly impossible to separate the man's movements from the woman's.

By this time, I am nearly in a frenzy, stretching my body closer to the front of the row as if I am somehow becoming a part of this couple's embrace.

How can they possibly be moving that quickly, that closely, and still breathe?

And then it becomes clear when the strobe lights start moving about highlighting all of the performers that the couple is nothing but a shadow.

Yes, I can see through them. There is no substance. It is like watching a ghost dancing in Disneyland's Haunted Mansion.

Is this merely an illusion? Why? What is this supposed to represent?

Before I can make any sense out of what I have just witnessed, the music ceases. The performers take their bows, including the Irish Gypsy couple. As they look out into the audience where I am sitting, I notice their faces. It is my Aunt Caroline and her lover Liam just as they appear in the photo on her bed stand. Yet, at this moment, their bodies are empty. They are nothing more than beautiful ghosts.

Caroline blows me a kiss, just as Sunflower did earlier today. Liam, who resembles Brendon, winks directly at me. The stage lights go out, and I wait patiently, although my first instinct is to exit immediately and wait for Sunflower to explain what I just experienced in the comfort of my own home.

But I remain seated, stunned but seated. I gave my word to not make a scene, and I will keep that word!

Chapter Twenty-One

Don't be pushed away by the fears in your mind,
Be led by the dreams
In your Heart.

Roy T Bennett
Author of *The Light in the Heart*

Mandana and Sunflower

"Wow! I mean, super Wow!"

Those were the only words Sunflower said when I told her what I witnessed when the rehearsal finally ended.

"I am not sure that I understand your reaction. Was I the only one to see Aunt Caroline and Liam?" I said, truly awe-stricken still.

"No, of course not. We have all seen Aunt Caroline. Your aunt is the founder of Saint Augustine Sisterhood. It is just…well… it is just that she is very particular who she chooses to appear to. You know, not everyone can accept the afterlife as part of their own life. Frankly, we have all been worried about you, Mandana. I mean…you have been with us nearly a year and still no real mention of seeing Caroline. We were beginning to worry that you might not have been one of the chosen," Sunflower said, finally taking a seat next to me.

"So, now that I have passed any test that Caroline must have thought appropriate, what is next? And how does Brendon fit into this equation? Are Liam and Brendon the same? I mean, they look exactly like each other, but of course Brendon isn't transparent like Liam is. Oh, my God! I am so confused," I concluded.

"Listen to me carefully, Mandana. What happened today is crucial. It may appear that we all know more than you do, but the truth is we know very little. What we do have is the advantage of knowing Caroline for many more years. When she passed it was totally unexpected until Dante explained to us the whole longevity playbook.

We were warned not to reveal everything without understanding what the consequences could be. This is the reason you are learning everything at a slower pace," Sunflower said, speaking softly to avoid attracting attention.

"Most of what you are now sharing is still does not make sense to me. But I definitely believe that I am finally making progress. Can you at least tell me what I should do next with all of this information?" I asked, feeling overwhelmed.

"My suggestion is that you continue to study the modern influence of Gypsy dancing and its powerful effect in reducing the bias hostilities throughout the centuries. Caroline dedicated her life to improving relationships within our community through dance, music, literature, theatre, and art. It was her dream to eventually assimilate all of these qualities with the intent to finally abolish the discrimination that leads to stereotypes and create a loving, peaceful environment. I believe she wanted you to be here today. It was her way to introduce you to the passion in her life. The second piece of advice that I can offer you is to meet with Dr. Dante sooner than later. Share with him everything that you have learned. Ask him directly what your role is in this longevity playbook that he seems to have exclusive access to," Sunflower said.

"All of this sounds like a *Mission Impossible* assignment. At the moment, what I am looking forward to now is simply taking a hot bath, having a cold glass of wine, and jumping into bed with Lancelot," I said, beginning to stand up for the first time in two hours.

"That sounds like a perfect idea. I have shared with you Calypso's and Alejandra's story. When you are ready, let me know and we will continue with the final three. Each of us Gypsies has truly contributed our souls to the Saint Augustine Sisterhood. We were all hand chosen by Emerald. All of us are dedicated to preserving Caroline's dream, and we all have the ability to accomplish what she has left unfinished. Get some rest and have faith in the power of who you are," Sunflower said, handing me a scroll tied with a bouquet of tulips, iris, and mini sunflowers.

It was such an unexpected gift that by the time I realized what it was Sunflower was gone. I decided to leave it intact until I arrived home mostly, because it was such a lovely presentation.

Once I turned the corner leading to Caroline's house (after 9 months I still referred to it as Caroline's home), the streetlights were just turning on, although Kiara must have left the lights on in the kitchen for Lancelot because it looked like a lit Birthday cake with twinkling candles.

Inside I noticed that Lance was sleeping peacefully on his leather couch, strategically placed in the dining nook where he could see wherever I was without ever leaving the comfort that he was used to.

As soon as the door opened, Lance was at my side sniffing logistically trying to determine where I had been all day. I would have to bring Kiara a thank you gift for keeping him occupied while I was gone.

Once I reached for the dog treats, Lance was ready to forgive me, returning once again to the couch.

Although the hot tub was extremely inviting, the lovely floral scroll grabbed my immediate attention. Carefully, I removed the flowers, placed them in a lovely crystal glass and unrolled the parchment paper revealing the following message:

And if you listen closely enough
You may hear your ancestors
Whispering,
"Thank you for fighting.
The battles we were too afraid to fight
Thank you for Healing
The wounds we were too frightened to heal
Thank you for walking
The paths we were too scared to walk
And thank you for pursuing
The dreams we were to (too?) hesitant to
Pursue,
We are proud to call you one of us
And we are always watching over you
Protecting you and guiding you
For our blood runs through your veins
And our legacy lives on through you,
Tahlia Hunter

But who are my ancestors? What legacy have I been called to preserve? And what battles have led me to any dreams that have been left unfulfilled?

As anxious as I am to discover the many possible answers to these questions, there is also a fear that once those answers are revealed my obligations to achieve the expectations bestowed on me may be overwhelming, even impossible to fulfill.

Learning about Calypso and Alejandra's journey to Saint Augustine is definitely moving my self-discovery journey in a positive direction.

Once the remaining three have shared their experiences, it should shed light in many of the darker obscure corners that are difficult to recognize at this moment.

Connecting those dots somehow to Dante's longevity institute I am convinced is related to what I just witnessed tonight at the Gypsy dress rehearsal.

Discovering specifically what that missing link might be is probably not any easier than finding the transitional evolutionary line of modern humans to their ancestors.

The following morning, I reluctantly awakened to darkness. Being mid-October, prior to the yearly shift from daylight savings, it is always still dark at 7:00 AM.

Lancelot had already moved to the living room, knowing the routine we had by now that included morning walks with Jocelyn and Flo most days.

Honestly, if it wasn't for Lancelot's determination to stick to a biologically set schedule, I would probably sleep the entire morning away.

"Okay, buddy, give me five minutes, and we'll be on our way," I said, seeing Lance pop his head through the bedroom door, anxious to see me moving about.

As promised, leash in hand, we were out the door just as the morning sun began to show its warm rays to the east.

"Hey, you two, Flo and I were hoping to see you this morning," Jocelyn said, while Flo greeted me with her typical 'pet me first, please' enthusiastic grin.

I reached out my hand, bending down for her affectionate kisses, while Jocelyn gave Lancelot his favorite beef sticks.

"There have been some really weird events lately that I am trying to sort out," I said, ready to get moving now that the furry friends were satisfied.

"Well, it is October, and we live in Saint Augustine, where weirdness is a way of life. Can you be more specific, or is this a guessing game?" Jocelyn asked.

"If it is a game, I would really like to know the rules so that I have at least a chance at competing," I responded, not sure how much I should be revealing to Jocelyn.

"All I can advise is follow anything and everything that Sunflower has told you. She is your Aunt Caroline's closest confidant. Whatever you need to know she has the answers. Oh, and Yoga! You can never go wrong signing up for a Yoga class. I would suggest early morning at the beach. You will be amazed how exhilarated it will make you feel."

My alarm watch alerted me that I needed to head home. My first stop was back to the library. This time downtown, since it was only going to be a light research project on the interpretation of modern Gypsy dancing. Then back home to read the biographies of the last three Gypsy dancers.

Aunt Caroline had requested that each Gypsy that joined the Sisterhood share her passion either in a written form or record their journey in a video. Most of these submissions were transcribed from live interviews, making the ones I have read thus far not only interesting but authentic.

Sunflower directed me to the specific five that she wanted me to read in a specific order. At the end of the assignment, she assured me that the most rewarding experience would be meeting the ladies, celebrating, and finally understanding what my role is in the Sisterhood community. It is this last obligation of 'my role' that makes me the most nervous.

Once back home, Lance enjoyed lapping the chilled ice water, even on a fall morning. Almost as if he knew that I was on my way out again, this time without him, he found his spot on the oversized doggy bed in the living room. This was the way he communicated to me that he knew that he was being left behind, and that it was my obligation to make certain that the television is set on the *Paw Patrol* station that also includes *Sponge Bob* and *Peppa Pig* if I was going to be away for several hours.

Aunt Caroline and Lancelot had a very special relationship, one that I was still learning to appreciate. What I already knew was that the extensive notes that she left me revealed much more than how to care for her loving companion; they are specific instructions to make her passing less painful for him.

"Okay, Lance. Have I covered all the basics needed to leave you here for a few hours?" I asked, waiting for a positive response.

Lancelot raised his head, looked directly at me with those penetrating green eyes, and somehow, like a bolt of lightning, I realized that I had forgotten to leave his milk bone in one of the several 'hiding' locations.

Caroline had several places that she suggested Lancelot liked to search for his treat. It was a familiar game that he enjoyed playing while she was gone. When she returned, Caroline always praised Lance for finding the hidden treat.

"Okay! Okay! I got it," I said, feeling a little foolish for talking to a dog that could not respond.

Once all my bases were covered, I was finally out the door, this time driving to the local library.

Most of the time I choose to walk or ride my bike wherever I go since parking downtown can be a horrendous problem. But today's visit to the Saint Augustine Library would not be a problem. There was a small but adequate parking lot that during the week always has empty spaces.

Once inside, I found an empty cubicle that I claimed near the research section. A personal peeve of mine is that many libraries have chosen to go totally digital with all their research data. Being maybe an "old soul," I prefer flipping the pages of a book in my hands at times. This is one of those times.

As I walked through the book aisles that references various forms of dancing, I was almost instantly drawn to a particular obscure book placed upside down on an empty shelf beneath the other resource books. This may have been exactly what drew my attention, or maybe it was one of those poltergeist pesky spirits that wants to draw attention to themselves.

Whatever it is that led me to that particular shelf, I was quite pleased. The article that drew my immediate attention was one about "Evolution and Methodology in the 21st Century." Bingo! This was exactly what I was searching for.

Immediately I was hooked when the writer expressed how the Gypsy dancers, she was watching created a desire inside of her to join the group on stage. That was exactly what I had experienced the previous afternoon.

In this scenario, the writer was watching the choreography of a talented Russian artist identified as *Peter Urchenko*. His style is based on the Russian Gypsy dance style with an essential element never used previously. Urchenko systematically collected a wide range of movements and incorporated them into some rich pallets of colors in moods.

The dances have now become an intricate storytelling experience that is not merely an accessory to dramatic art or song, but an essential high art form that can be critiqued independently. What I was now reading was exactly what I witnessed first-hand at the Lewis. Sunflower and her Gypsy dancers had captured a moment that reflected the past, present, and future eloquently.

The real question is could they do that same performance again. The Ghost Sonata dance with Aunt Caroline and Liam could never be duplicated with "living" dancers. Or could it?

Was it ever even meant to be witnessed by an audience? Or was I invading a private moment shared by two passionate lovers?

Chapter Twenty-Two

The sun descending in the west. The morning star does shine; the birds are silent in their nest. And I must seek for mine. The moon like a flower in heavens high bower with silent delight, sits and smiles on the night.

William Blake

RAIN

My mother was an Osage Indian from a very controversial tribe. My father was Irish. When I was born, there was much discussion of the importance of an appropriate name.

After much debate and often heated discussions, three days after my birth the chief suggested that my family compromise by giving me two names. It was suggested that once I was old enough I could make my own decision as to which one would be the best.

My father chose *Rhiannon* of Welsh origin, meaning Queen or goddess. Rigantona was a mythological queen born to a Celtic goddess of fertility. The legendary depiction of Rigantona always shows her wearing a flowing, shining gold dress.

I can still remember today my father showing me these artistic images, attempting to convince me that the name he chose was the most appropriate.

My mother's name for me was always *Aponi,* the Native American word meaning "butterfly." It is chosen to represent a graceful expression of comfort, hope, and transition into a joyful life after moving from the mother's womb or "cocoon" into the natural pursuit of happiness.

Combining my two names I am Queen of the Butterflies.

Because I am the first born and only daughter, my father relinquished his rights to select my brother's names. Perhaps he simply no longer found it worth his time disputing name choices, especially as an outsider in this Indian community.

Prior to my birth, and when my mother was a young child, her family was forced to move from her home in Kansas to Indian Territory in Oklahoma by the United States government. In 1830 there was an explosion of American settlers moving into Indian held territory, resulting in the Indian Removal Act being passed.

What happened next is a double-edge sword scenario. The Osage tribe, now dependent on the government and restricted from living the lifestyle they were used to, were forced to accept conditions foreign to their heritage.

Everything begins with their pantheistic beliefs that all life forms and universal changes are a result of a single, mysterious life-giving force known as *Wa Kon tah*. Humans play only a minor role in this manifestation.

My Osage relatives never claimed that they fully understood how all of this controls their lives, but they acknowledged that there were spiritual visions that would appear to humans with the intent to lead them through life harmoniously with nature. There were some members of the tribe that even claimed they were given the gift to transform themselves into spirit animals.

The Peyote religion was introduced to my ancestors in the 1890's. Although the Osage Peyote church was based on Christianity it also totally rejected all the earlier traditional beliefs. So, by the early twentieth century, 1910, all ceremonies were gone.

Many elders believed that this lack of respect for our nation and culture is what led to the near destruction that followed once they were sent to Oklahoma.

My grandmother was a member of the new Osage Nation settlers that went from extreme poverty to enormous wealth.

"My dearest Aponi, never allow abundance of money to rule your life. It enters through the pores in your skin when you are sleeping, eating away at your heart and brain without understanding the effect until it destroys all that you love," I was told by my grandmother many times.

My grandmother was one of the elderly women during the Osage "Reign of Terror," when murdered bodies were being found fairly regularly throughout the town.

Although at the time there was no direct connection being made between the killings, as the victims began to multiply more frequently, there was suspicion within the community. The Crones, as my grandmother and her small group were called, would sit in their rocking chair observing the chaos surrounding them.

Many years later, long after my grandmother had passed, I came across a book by a Japanese author named Jean Shinoda Bolen. The title of the book immediately caught my attention, *"Crones Don't Whine."* It was the same words that my grandmother would express whenever I became frustrated.

As I flipped through the pages, it was as if my grandmother was leading me to a very specific page. I stopped almost instinctively, first noticing the image titled "Raven Crone," by Beth Wildwood, an artist that I was familiar with because many of her paintings in *Wild Spirit Weaver* are reminiscent of my childhood recollections.

This one in particular has the face of an elderly woman surrounded by a raven's head with ebony black feathers. It resembles an Indian headpiece; one you might see at a tribunal ceremony.

As fascinating as the painting was, capturing my attention even more were the following words that expressed what I always knew my grandmother wanted me to understand.

"A crone is a woman who has found her voice. She knows that silence is consent. This is a quality that makes older women feared. It is not the innocent voice of a child who says, 'the emperor has no clothes,' but the fierce truthfulness of the crone that is the voice of reality. Both the innocent child and the crone are seeing through the illusions, denials, or 'spin' the truth. But the crone knows about the deception, and its consequences, and it angers her. Her fierceness springs from the heart, gives her courage, makes her a force to be reckoned with."
Jean Shinoda Bolen

Although I was reading these words from a book, it was my grandmother's voice speaking to me.

I can only imagine how different life may have been for my Osage relatives had they listened to the Crones. Ironically, had they listened to the Crones, my life would have also been altered, and I would have never left Oklahoma. Perhaps, I would never have even been born.

My grandparents were among the original members of the Osage tribe to buy their own property after using the proceeds from their Kansas land. When their land in Oklahoma gushed with oil in 1923, like all their neighbors, they earned a portion of the $30 million in royalties. Unfortunately, most of those in the tribe were so overwhelmed with the abundance of wealth that they lost all their common sense.

The 2,229 members, including my family, were entitled to equal shares of the oil royalties. For many this extravagant new lifestyle resulted in serious consequences.

By 1921, the United States government decided that the Osage tribe needed assistance in managing their wealth. A group of white lawyers and businessmen deemed many of the tribe incompetent based on their irrational spending behavior. It was determined that to "protect" their investments a guardian should be appointed to manage their finances.

In many situations this resulted in white outsiders proposing marriage to many of the single Osage women. It did not take long before men, including immigrants, learned that this arrangement was the perfect opportunity to guarantee their future wealth without ever working.

Enter my father, Finn Sullivan, only two weeks in America traveling to Oklahoma with a small knapsack and cheap cardboard suitcase. What he did have to offer was a strong impressive lineage, a dignified, drop-dead gorgeous appearance, and a great voice.

It was love at first sight for both my parents. My mother was a few years older than Dad, but he never seemed to care.

Maria, my mother's chosen, not given name, first noticed my father when he passed by with a group of his friends on the way to a barnyard dance. This was a popular event used to introduce the newcomers to the community.

Later, she would share that moment with me when I was older, always taking pride that from all the young girls available that night Finn chose her to dance every dance with. Three weeks later, Finn proposed.

After all the details were revealed about the mysterious deaths of the young women in our community, and with the FBI investigations that followed, the stress was too much. My mother, although never having any evidence or even any reliable information, suddenly became paranoid whenever my father was present. There was nothing that any of us could say or do to convince her that he was not planning on killing her as soon as the investigation concluded.

Although my father constantly attempted to assure her that he was totally committed to both her and me, my mother pointed to all of the miscarriages that she experienced as signs that her death was imminent.

Finally, my father could no longer take the toxic atmosphere. He made arrangements to leave the reservation, taking me with him. I was twelve years old.

Prior to that day, there were weeks of loud, nasty arguments, until finally my grandmother intervened. She arranged for my father to take me without any further arguments. It was never clear how she managed this, but once we were on the train taking us to Boston, Massachusetts, I felt for the first time a sense of relief. It was to be the beginning of a new life that would eventually lead me to Saint Augustine, although at that moment I had no idea where Florida was.

What I do distinctly remember is my grandparents driving us to the train station. By this time my mother had been admitted to a mental facility that nobody wanted to discuss.

"It is the season for the flower moon, my Aponi. Remember what I taught you?" Grandmother asked.

I shook my head, yes, although I was not sure how accurate my answer would be if I needed to prove that I remembered. Sitting next to me in the depot waiting for the train to arrive, Grandmother took both my hands in hers.

"The flower moon is in May. We celebrate the flowers blooming in abundance across North America after a cold, harsh winter. Wherever you are always remember that my love for you will forever keep you safe like the flower moon. We may never see one another again in this world, but you will always hold my heart in yours," she said, placing in my hand a golden heart locket engraved with sunflowers on the front and on the back a full moon.

I could not hold back my tears. For the first time I was realizing that once my father and I boarded that train my life would change forever. Grandfather held me in his arms until he saw the train approaching. He then released me to my father, not able to say anything.

He didn't need to. I could feel the love penetrating through my soul, like the shadows that will always follow me at night, the moon flowers open my mind.

Chapter Twenty-Three

Do not mistake the current chapter you are in
For the completed story of your life
Do not mistake temporary periods of
Transitions
For your final destination.
Do not mistake the current challenges
You are wrestling with
For the whole of your experience.
And do not mistake the limited
Perspective you hold
For the ultimate truth of the universe.

Tahlia Hunter

Rain

When we arrived in Boston, I was not expecting anyone to meet us at the train depot. My world in Fairfield was so limited that anything beyond the pond was an adventure. Whatever my father planned for us now was beyond my imagination.

The train ride was three days. Dad bought us the best accommodations with a sleeping berth and all meals served in the elegant dining car.

Thankfully since resemble my father more than I do any of my Indian relatives we did not experience any segregation. That Irish DNA was definitely flowing in my blood. As long as I kept my mouth shut, nobody would ever suspect that I was half Indian.

"You know, Rain, once we get settled in our own house, I will make sure that you will have everything that you need. You are my princess! Nobody will ever disrespect you. But, for now, it will be much better to let me do all the talking. Do you understand, my beauty?" Dad said at dinner the evening before our train was to arrive.

I shook my head in agreement. The truth was I really had nothing to say to anyone anyhow.

Being silent would be easy. Later in life, it may have been the reason why speaking to people always was difficult. But then that is something that a therapist is better able to evaluate.

As the train approached our final stop, Father instructed me to stay close by him. He didn't want to come this far only to lose me. Stepping off the train platform, we had a porter gather the few suitcases that we brought with us, and we walked toward the exit.

Before we walked through the final door to the outside, a robust woman with strawberry red hair rushed toward Father and lifted him up like a rag doll.

"Finn…oh, my Finn… I cannot believe it is you! I am so excited that you have come here to Boston to live with your dear auntie," the strange lady said.

I stood behind my father, hoping not to be noticed by the fluffy boisterous, flamboyant older lady that reminded me of the Mrs. Santa Claus character in a book my grandmother gave me one Christmas Eve.

"And who is this lovely little lady hiding behind your back, Finn? She looks like a porcelain doll version of your sister Annie back home in Cork," the mysterious lady said, approaching me with her arms wide open.

"Come closer, my child. I am your Great Auntie Maggie. We have all been excited for your arrival," she said before I could move further behind Father.

Auntie Maggie's arms cradled me like a huge swan with soft feathers. I could also smell cinnamon and vanilla as she pressed me close to her bosom.

What did she mean by, "we" have all…? We're "we" like the "who" in Horton Hears the Who? By Dr. Seuss.

I was beginning to feel like Horton the Elephant a character created by the author Dr. Seuss. Grandmother brought this book home from a visit to the local library once when I was feeling very "small" and useless.

She explained to me, that one day I will be an important leader just as Horton the Elephant is in this story to the people of Whoville.

Unfortunately, at the moment I felt more like a "speck of dust" than a hero.

Maybe Grandmother will eventually be right. This strange new world known as Boston was offering me new chapters to explore, ones that might be challenging but also exciting.

Immediately, Maggie made me feel less self-conscious about my Indian identity. Her Irish accent, much different from the typical New England accent, where the "ar" sounds become "ah," made everyone that heard her know she was an immigrant. But at least the ones that were Maggie's friends found her accent a refreshing change to the norm.

Once I felt comfortable enough to start expressing myself verbally, I found that my voice was mimicking Maggie's Irish brogue at times.

There was a weekend several months after I arrived in Boston when Maggie and I were in the kitchen making loaves of fresh Irish wheaten brown bread. Every month she would bake all day and then on Sunday deliver the loaves to the homeless shelters.

Whatever was leftover Maggie kept for her neighbors when they visited during the mornings with a hot cup of Irish breakfast tea.

Everyone who visited came for the special blend of several black teas combined with Assam and Ceylon.

The neighbors always waited anxiously for the monthly shipment from Ireland to arrive with more authentic Irish food and tea.

Not only was I learning about my Irish heritage, but I was also acquiring the same Irish accent as Maggie.

"These are my care packages from the old country. They keep me grounded to the homeland. America is where dreams become reality, but Ireland is where my heart remains," Maggie would share.

It was the very first time since leaving my mother, and the only home that I ever knew that I understood a sense of belonging.

After Father and I moved into our own small bungalow a few blocks from Maggie, I would stay with her after school, doing my homework on her kitchen table while Maggie worked on designing the latest fashions for her clients all from her own home.

Ladies from as far as Salem would travel to Boston for Maggie's designer clothes. She was well known throughout the New England region as an elite couture. Many high society young ladies ordered their original cotillion gowns a year in advance to ensure that they would be available.

When Maggie's seamstress business could no longer remain in her small cottage, one of her loyal clients was able to secure for her a lovely shop downtown, located in the center of many larger well known department stores, like *Raymond's* and, *Filene's Sons Department Store.* In addition to owning one of the only places in town that offered original custom ladies' gowns, Maggie was able to hire exceptional seamstresses, all immigrants eager to find a reliable job.

With the construction of the Boston Elevated Railroad to Forest Hills, the entire commercial center for local residents as well as commuters was now easily accessible. It did not take long for *Shamrocks to Stardust Designer Fashions* to become a successful brand company. True to her word, Maggie continued to respect her Irish roots by offering her traditional teas, sweets, brown bread to all her clients that visited. *Shamrocks* was soon known as not only the best designer shop in Boston, but it was also where everyone wanted to be seen.

By this time father was a well-established realtor. After five years of raising a child on his own, he was ready to remarry and restart his life. But it would always be Maggie that I felt the closest to.

It was my senior year in high school when Maggie, decided that it was finally time to understand much more of my Irish origin.

"How much has Finn shared with you about our heritage?"

Maggie had started referring to my dad by his first name when speaking with me.

"Not much. I know very little about anything in my past, including my Osage traditions, my mother, or even what my life was like prior to arriving here in Boston seven years ago. It is as if an eclipse occurred wiping away all my memories. The only recollection that I barely have is of an elderly woman handing me this sunflower locket that I have never removed from my neck," I said, curious as to what prompted this discussion.

Maggie walked over to a bookcase located in the drawing room of her office, pointed to the leather sofa in the middle of the room, and instructed me to get comfortable.

"This may take a few hours for you to understand. If it becomes too tedious, we will stop and resume at another time. But this information needs to be shared with you now. Soon you will be moving on to college or trade school. Finn and Shannon will be planning their wedding, and there will be no other convenient time for you to learn this critical information."

The tone of Maggie's voice was now serious. I couldn't begin to imagine what this book would reveal that was life altering, but one thing that I have learned in my short life is that I have limited control over anything and everything.

Rather than reaching for a family photo album with pictures of my ancestors, Maggie opened a large leather-bound antique tome, placed it on her desk, and turned it to a specific page that was marked with a peacock feather.

"Rain, meet Ann Glover, an Irish Catholic laundress and seamstress that was deported to Barbados in the 1650's during Oliver Cromwell's occupation of Ireland. When her husband died in Barbados, Ann and her only child, a daughter, moved to Boston where she hoped it would be safer. But, as a widow with a child, she could secure only a job as a housekeeper for John Goodman, who had five children." Maggie paused to watch my reaction as she pointed to Ann's daughter.

"Quite a stunning resemblance between the two of you, don't you think? Molly would have been the same age as you are today," Maggie added.

She was correct. The young girl that I was looking at could have been me! It was an eerie feeling. Mysterious, yes, but life changing? Not so much, yet.

"This is only the first of many other discoveries that I thought might interest you," Maggie said, as if she could read my thoughts.

"Whatever happened to Molly and Anna, and how does all of this relate to us?" I asked.

"Anna is Finn's sister. Before her marriage, she was part of an exclusive group of Gypsy druids that practiced mysticism. These beliefs and practices were deeply rooted in spiritual practices intricately weaved into their reverence for nature. The Druids were well respected keepers of our oral traditions. They were the philosopher/scientist scholars that shaped Irish culture, leaving behind a legacy that continues to explore our myths and legends," Maggie added.

Now mathematics has always been my weakest subject, but I do have extraordinary critical thinking skills, and something was not adding up correctly. This is 1967. Although I never asked when Finn was born, logically, he must be at least in his late thirties or early forties. Regardless how carefully I calculated the numbers, Finn could not be alive today and have a sister who lived in the seventeenth century.

When I pointed this out to Maggie, she smiled and said, "You are now beginning to understand the relevance of what your heritage means."

As the afternoon tutorial continued, the details became even more bizarre.

I learned that during the summer of 1698 some of the children that Anna was caring for became Ill.

Martha, the eldest daughter of Mr. Goodman, had been disrespectful to Anna, and she was punished for her bad behavior. Shortly after that incident, the daughter became sickly. The doctor who was called diagnosed the illness as witchcraft related.

Anna was soon arrested and put on trial. She refused to speak anything but Gaelic although she certainly knew English. This stubborn behavior resulted in Anna being found guilty of witchcraft. The fact that she and Molly had previously lived in Barbados, well known for practicing witchcraft, led to Anna's sentencing, death by fire.

There was no evidence of what happened to Molly. It is as if she disappeared from earth entirely. However, many years later, in the late twentieth century there are photographs that appear to show Molly dancing with a group of Gypsies traveling in America.

"What I am about to now share with you, Rain, might be disturbing to you, but it must be known and never shared with anyone outside of our immediate family. Do you understand, my child?" I knew Maggie was asking me to take an oath of secrecy. I agreed to do so.

"Very well, then. There are places on earth that only a very few sacred Druids know that allow them to travel through time. Finn, I, and now you are included in this group. Later, you will meet others. What you must know is that without the proper training it is possible for you to disintegrate into a dark hole never to be found again. None of us know what happens at that moment." Maggie closed the oversized book, returning it to its original place on the shelf.

It was difficult for me to believe that I was being told that my father was a time traveler and that Maggie was suggesting that I had a doppelgänger gypsy who managed to escape the Salem Witch Trials into another dimension.

Was she also implying that maybe, just maybe there is no doppelgänger and that Molly and I are the same person? What is it that I needed to learn the most to accept my next mission?

"Open this scroll, my child, and read the words by a future prophet not yet born. Refer to her advice often. It will guide you to where you must go next. Tomorrow we will be traveling to Salem for *Banquet with the Damned*. It is a Halloween celebration that alludes to Shakespeare's Macbeth. Each year there are people who attend in costume, always wearing masks from many different time locations. It will give you an opportunity to learn everything essentially needed before your departure," Maggie said, without offering any further explanations.

Before I could ask where, why and when I was going to be leaving, she was rushing out of her office for an appointment with an important client. I was left to contemplate everything on my own.

That is when I became aware of the scroll in my hand. It was tied with several lovely orange and green ribbons, the colors associated with the Irish flag. I opened it and began to read the words carefully, hoping for some divine wisdom.

From a stone, I learned the art
Of remaining still.
From the river, I learned the art
Of remaining in flow.
From a falling leaf, I learned the art
Of remaining detached.
From a breeze, I learned the art
Of remaining gentle.
From a mountain, I learned the art
Of remaining strong.
From a gentle raindrop, I learned the art
Of remaining calm.
From a seed, I learned the art
Of remaining patient.
From a seashell, I learned the art
Of remaining open.
From a tree, I learned the art
Of remaining grounded
From a drifting cloud, I learned the art
Of remaining free
From a modest flower, I learned the art
Of remaining humble.
From a forest, I learned the art
Of remaining regenerative.

At the bottom of the page was a sunflower stamped in gold. Immediately it reminded me of my Osage grandmother as I reached for the locket that I never removed from my neck.

Chapter Twenty-Four

She is full of love and stars
And all things dark
She is messy
And, out of place
A perfect example of chaos
Your heart will burn having known
Her
And just as quickly as she storms into
Your world
She is gone
Off on her next adventure
Ready to set more souls on fire

Nicole Carlyon

RAIN

Salem is only twenty-five miles from Boston. Everyone who lives nearby or visits Salem expects that they will experience some form of supernatural activity while visiting. What is not necessarily expected is to be invited during Halloween week to a haunted mansion where the Banquet of the Dead is hosted by the headless horseman and Steampunk witches.

I had never attended any Halloween event other than the traditional trick and treat activities, and that was even a new experience after moving to Boston.

Finn was not a great fan of anything associated with the occult, which now that Maggie shared with me all of the supernatural activity associated with him or with his ancestors seemed out of character. Nevertheless, it was only the two of us attending this dinner and spending the night in one of the most haunted mansions in Salem—*Ropes Mansion.*

Maggie prepped me for what to expect, starting with the historical significance of this estate. It all started with Samuel Bernard and his four marriages and three funerals. His last wife actually outlived her husband. But, after Samuel's passing, Nathanial Ropes, an upcoming attorney, purchased this property.

Unfortunately, Ropes was a loyalist at the wrong time. The colonists were infuriated with his political ideology, and in March 1774 they attacked the Ropes mansion. Although the colonists may have contributed to Ropes' death, it was the smallpox epidemic that ended his life the following day. He was only forty-seven years old.

Sixty years later, Nathaniel's daughter Abigale died in that very same house when her petticoats caught on fire from embers in the hearth.

Many years later, after my first visit, I read that this same home where Maggie and I were invited to celebrate the free spirits surrounding us caught fire in 2009, destroying the ceiling, carpets, and wallpaper. Many attributed this accident to Abigale's ghost seeking revenge.

It was still unknown to me why we were spending the evening with a group of strangers celebrating death.

"It is impossible, Rain, to honor life without respecting death. This banquet for the dead is an example alluding to Shakespeare's Macbeth, an unnecessary tragedy. When Macbeth chooses to take the advice of the Weird Sisters, he makes the choice to follow evil, resulting in his demise. Most of the costumes that you will be seeing tonight are the ones I designed," Maggie said with pride.

"It must have taken you forever to design all of these outfits," I said, genuinely impressed.

The Steampunk theme was elaborately represented throughout the evening. Maggie had to give me a brief historical lesson about the significance of this attire. It was nothing that I was familiar with.

"Fashion design requires you to understand a variety of lifestyles that are often associated at times with retro futuristic technology and sometimes even science fiction literature," Maggie said, pointing to a young couple resembling something from a Jules Vernon novel, combining various art movements with architectural elements.

"Okay! I think I get it. You have layered several different types of styles, colors, steam cannons, or even aircraft pieces to create a totally whimsical outfit," I said as if an epiphany had just happened.

"Exactly! There are times when I also enjoy experimenting like I did with your costume. There is a little bit of fantasy, horror, and romanticism in every stitch," Maggie said, handing me a folded hand fan.

Once the fan was open, I saw there were skulls, witch brooms, and black cats outlined in silver and gold metallic paint.

"Ooh! The perfect accessory to my total collection," I said, searching for a mirror to admire my completed look.

I had to resort to looking at a reflection from a window on the way into the castle banquet hall. Within a few moments there was a procession led by regal sentries that looked as if they had just stepped out of the pages of a historical document illustrating Henry VIII's soldiers.

"I am beginning to feel like we are extras in some elaborate Hollywood movie setting for a new movie production," I said, as we were directed to our seats.

"This is much more spectacular than anything that a movie director could ever imagine, my dear. This is science fiction, fantasy, quantum physics, and surrealism coming all together for one evening."

Nothing really made any sense to me yet. Although for some very odd reason, the entire atmosphere was quite comfortable. It almost made me feel as if I had been here before.

"You, have," Maggie said, placing the linen napkin on her lap.

"I have what?" I said, surprised.

"You have been here before, just in another dimension that you are not yet able to recall. That is why you are here now. It is the final stage that you must complete before you can safely move forward."

"How did you know what I was thinking? Have you always been able to read my mind?" I asked, not sure if I liked Maggie delving into my private thoughts.

"Not really. I may have been more tuned into your mind when you were much younger, but that was only done to protect you. As you grew more independent, I tried to allow you to mature naturally. Well, as naturally as possible when you have moved about as much as we have."

Before I could ask any more questions, guests were being seated nearby, and the music was getting louder, with jesters, jugglers, Minotaurs, Centaurs, Mermaids, and Harpies bringing platters filled with exotic appetizers and steaming beverages as well as, plenty of intoxicating bubbles that appeared to float everywhere in various hypnotic indescribable colors.

Maggie finally caught my attention, which by this time was wandering throughout the hall, fascinated with all of this incredible pageantry that seemed endless.

"Although it is tempting to become absorbed in all of this pomp, tonight your eyes and mind need to focus on what you are seeing with some of the images that are stored in your memory. Let's begin with *Beowulf*," Maggie said, as if she was testing my understanding of its significance to where we were tonight.

There are actually many similarities to the setting described by the unknown *Beowulf* poet who is credited with the most important English literary work in history.

Although when I read the translation a few years ago the emphasis was on the heroes and monsters, sitting here at this moment I recall how essential to understanding Herot, the mead hall is. This is what creates the juxtaposition throughout the entire tale.

It is also here where Grendel continues to attack the Danish people, turning a celebration hall into a death chamber. The name of the hall itself is significant, meaning "hart" or "stag," often combined to be known as the "Hall of the Hart" or symbolically representing the first signs of humanity. It is where the people gather to plan how to conquer the wilds and control its central station for power.

It is noteworthy that these celebratory feasts were much more vital than a gathering place. In *Beowulf* it is where life begins, where it ends, and most importantly where resolutions are realized, resolved, and repeated.

"Bravo, Rain! This is exactly why we chose this castle. It is authentically *Herot Hall*. The perfect location for our yearly meeting (I'm confused here. Even the décor is genuine." Maggie sounded pleased.

And now I understand the advantage of her being able to read my mind. It saves me from repeating myself.

The similarities to *Herot Hall* are much more than coincidental. It is as if we have been transported back to this specific location for a few hours to experience the glory of *Beowulf's* victory.

On the walls are antlers of Hart's replicas, I am assuming similar to the ones that the Danes hunted and brought back as their victory trophies.

Is there also perhaps an interesting parallel to Grendel choosing the very same location to seek revenge on Beowulf for destroying her son?

I waited a few minutes, expecting Maggie to comment on my thoughts but there was no response. Maybe there was no reason to analyze the obvious?

"Now that is an observation worth responding to. Lesson number one, Rain…nothing that you presume is ever obvious. Let's take a moment to survey what we see now. You are able to relate it to another time and place that leads you to some interesting but distracting conclusions. This setting is merely a setting. The fact that it resembles *Herot Hall* means nothing to those who have actually experienced the original. We are gathered here to share our annual activities with one another, learn from our mutual travels, and introduce our guests to those that will be their future mentors."

Is Maggie referring to me? Am I about to meet a mentor? Why? How do I fit into this very odd group of guests that I would never recognize in the future since everyone is in costume and wearing masks.

"Costumes and masks my dear is common attire everywhere you travel throughout the universe and time. It is learning how to see beyond those masks that will make the journeys you take much more rewarding."

Since we arrived at this banquet, it has been Maggie speaking the entire time in response to my thoughts. However, the situation was about to change when the chair next to me became occupied by an enchanting maiden dressed all in white, with the most translucent gems floating harmoniously throughout her gown.

The images on the gown all resembled love and peace birds. Some were doves, others were blue birds and sacred ibis. Then there were Agapornis, a small group of parrots in the Old-World parrot family known as Psittacosaurus. All monogamous, devoted eternally to their mates. I was able to recognize all of these species thanks to my Osage grandmother who taught me many years ago to respect and understand my natural habitat.

"Sunflower, I am pleased to introduce you to my beautiful grandniece, Rhiannon," Maggie said, with pride.

When the magnificent fairy princess, which is the only way I can describe her, took my hand in hers, a surge of joyful energy filled my veins.

It is impossible to recreate how for the first time in my life I felt boundless; eternal love surrounds me like the sunshine nourishing the earth.

Could this be my Mother Nature claiming me, saving me from my own Grendel monster?

"Sunflower is your past and future, Rain. She will be the one to guide you into a new world where everything, and everyone you meet is a life lesson," Maggie shared with me.

"I have brought you a gift, Rhiannon. It is a mirror that reveals a message that will help you in the transition that we are about to move towards. Listen to its wise advice; keep it close to you until we move into the future," Sunflower said, waiting for me to accept the gift.

The mirror did not reflect my face as I assumed it would. There was no image visible. Then suddenly the banquet hall became totally dark, and in the mirror was a lovely lady wearing a loose bright skirt that changed colors like a rainbow as she twirled through an unknown street, laughing, smiling, extending happiness everywhere.

The background music stops suddenly, and I hear someone talking directly to me now:

Thank you, Rain, for the mistakes you made so that I could discover what it means to be wise…and the moments of doubt that you faced, which helped me discover what it means to have faith. Without taking those wrong roads that lead you to some unpleasant places I would have never discovered where I am supposed to be. Those masks that you sometimes had to wear made me a more authentic me, and when you took life for granted, it taught me to be grateful. I would never be who I am today without your learning curve. We will always share what we can with others to prevent them from failing.

It wasn't until the end of the dialogue when the lights came on once again that I realized that this Gypsy lady is me.

Chapter Twenty-Five

Sewing is a way to mark our existence on cloth, patterning our place on this world, voicing our identity, sharing something of ourselves with others and leaving the indelible evidence in our presence in stitches held fast by our hand.

Clare Hunter,
Threads of Life: A History of the World Through the Eye of a Needle

RAIN and SUNFLOWER

After my evening at *Banquet of the Damned,* I never saw Maggie or Finn again. The specifics on how I arrived at Saint Augustine are impossible to recollect.

One moment I was sitting at the Medieval banquet hall with my great-aunt and a sparkling fairy princess, and the next moment I found myself waking up to the sounds of ocean waves outside my window.

For some strange reason, I am not surprised, although I do realize there is no logical reason why I am here.

"Good morning, sweet Rain. It is okay that I refer to you as Rain, yes?"

Sunflower asks, carrying into the bedroom a fluffy white bathrobe that she places at the end of the bed.

I look around, trying to put together some of the missing pieces to my life. Nothing looks familiar.

"How did I get here, and where is here?" I ask reluctantly.

"How you arrived is not as important as why you are here. At this moment you are at Vilano Beach, more specifically Porpoise Point. We are a few miles north of downtown Saint Augustine, Florida. Now, the reason you have been selected to join the Sisterhood is that your heritage is rich with talent. More important is that you will be sharing all the spiritual teachings that enhance our mission. Much of this may seem overwhelming considering that you have been transported ahead in time to the twenty-first century, but I assure you that many of us have traveled a much longer distance and are thriving nicely," Sunflower said.

Next to the nightstand on the bed was the mirror that I remember gazing into just before everything changed in my life.

But here in my new environment everything appears to be much more natural. Even Sunflower is no longer the glowing, sparkling fairy princess that I remember being enchanted with.

This morning she is wearing cutoff jeans, a T-shirt with the words *Peace* and *Woodstock Forever,* her long chestnut brown hair pulled back in a ponytail with a blue bandana across her forehead. When she is dressed like this, it is impossible to guess how old Sunflower is.

"But what can I possibly contribute to your *Sisterhood?* I have no real skills. When I attended the banquet with Maggie, I was completing my senior year at Boston High School, not knowing what direction my life would take me next. And now here I am suddenly waking up at a beach house in a strange location that I had no idea existed," I said, definitely needing some logical answers to a bizarre situation.

"Every one of the Sisters that have arrived to Saint Augustine have experienced this initial anxiety. Some adapted easier than others, but it is our common thread, our bond, that ties us together. That is your contribution, Rain. Maggie is an extraordinarily talented designer. You have inherited that gift, although at this moment you may not even recognize it."

Is Sunflower suggesting that I become a seamstress? If she needed a seamstress, why not simply bring Maggie to Saint Augustine? And that magic mirror that started all this shows me dressed as a dancing Gypsy, not sitting at a sewing machine creating costumes.

"But, Sunflower, I really do not even know how to sew very well. I would occasionally assist Maggie with her designs, but certainly I am far from being an expert seamstress," I said, beginning to wonder if maybe Sunflower had chosen the wrong person to become one of her special "Sisters."

"You are confusing the technical details of sewing with the creative process of designing. Let me give you a lesson on what sewing can accomplish when it is properly employed," Sunflower said.

I listened attentively to the following explanation, learning most importantly that sewing is an activity that joins a community in a variety of ways.

"In many cultures sewing is an art that requires precision and skill. More so, the practice of sewing symbolizes healing, hope, and communication. These are all ideals that the Sisterhood strives to preserve. As a metaphor, sewing not only creates something new, but it often takes older items and repairs them, making them functional once again. Doing this recycles items that were once thought to be useless. The Gypsy Dancers are committed to making everyone understand their worthiness," Sunflower emphasized.

I nodded my head, but was still not confident that I had any of these skills. The teenage Rain from Boston had a lot of catching up to do with the 21st century Rain.

"Are you beginning to now understand why we are seeking to have our fashion designer create costumes that the world recognizes for their beauty stitched with compassion?" Sunflower asked, hoping to inspire her newest protégé.

"Yes. It is becoming clear now that you have provided me with some definite examples. But I am still not confident that I have the skill you are searching for," I added, reluctantly.

"Have no fears, my dearest Rain. What I am about to share with you is a story that will assure you of your destiny," Sunflower said, reaching for the mirror on the nightstand.

When she handed me the mirror, I gazed once again into the glass. This time an Indian maiden appeared, wearing an unusual garment.

In the 1920's, Mille Lacs Band the granddaughter of the Ojibwa Wisconsin Tribe medicine man became deathly ill. Just as it appeared the child could not be saved, another medicine man, in a dream, was approached by his Indian Spirit guide, instructing him to have the Indian squaws design a *Jingle Dress* for the little girl.

Once the dress was completed, the child was instructed to dance. However, by this time she was too weak. The entire tribe lifted the child up into the air in her *Jingle Dress* until miraculously the young girl was able to be lowered to the ground and dance on her own.

From that time on, many other tribes have adopted the *Jingle Dress,* often referring to as a *Prayer Dress.*

The garment has rows of ziibaaska'iganan (metal cones) sewn on it. Rolled snuff cone lids are usually hung from the dress with colorful ribbons close to one another so that they can make a melodic sound when they hit each other, resembling a wind chime.

It is tradition to have 365 cones attached to a dress, representing every day of the year. These dresses also come in a bright, vibrant range of colors, from a mellow yellow to a vibrant blue, to a deep red with shiny and sparkly materials attached, and often also include metallic fabrics with fringes, embroidery, and lace.

Most of these dresses have three quarter length to full length sleeves and are at least mid-calf to ankle in length. At the waist it is secured by a thick leather belt. Even the moccasins worn by the dancers are embellished to match their gowns.

It is because of these specific details that the dance moves need to be also very precise. The main objective is to create a specific "Jingle" sound that recreates the sound of rain. This requires the dancers to be light on their feet, moving in time with the drum precisely, stopping when the drums stop.

The dancers are taught to keep their feet low to the ground while dancing, kicking their heels in unison while tapping their toes to the beat. The dance is performed in a zigzag pattern representing one's journey through life.

Modern versions of the original choreography also include dancers keeping their hands on their hips, occasionally removing them to open their colorful fans made from eagle feathers.

"Are you beginning to notice the similarities between the Indian dancers and the Gypsies?" Sunflower asked.

"It is an interesting parallel, but I still have no idea how this applies to me," I said, bewildered.

"The person who initiated the Jingle Dress design was you, Rain. It was in a different place and time, but it is a talent that Emerald, our Sister leader, recognized. She has been following your many different accomplishments throughout her travels. In fact, while in Ireland, before selecting Saint Augustine as the site for the Sisterhood, the two of you met. You, of course, will not recall that moment now, but perhaps later once you are introduced to the other Gypsy dancers, you will," Sunflower said.

"Presuming that all of this is accurate, and it must be since nothing else makes any sense, then what exactly is my contribution?" I asked, feeling that I must be expected to somehow earn respect from this group that summoned me here.

"You will never be expected to offer more than you are capable of giving. This beach house is where you will reside and design our costumes. Once we all gather informally to discuss our projects, you will take our ideas and make them a reality. Each garment will be a work of art reflecting the specific Gypsy it has been designed for. The actual sewing will be done by another group of talented seamstresses."

Everything was finally making sense. Throughout my lifetime, wherever I was and whatever I attempted I failed. My lack of self-confidence prevented me from achieving anything that I wanted to accomplish. Finally, it seems that I may become recognized, and contribute to this mysterious group.

During my time with the Saint Augustine Sisterhood, what I have appreciated most is learning that there are no dead ends that prevent us from moving forward once we understand that every path chosen is an opportunity for redirection. The mistakes that cause us the most pain are only lessons that teach that nothing is a failure. Everything is a chance to improve what we originally intended.

My unanswered prayers are guiding me toward better choices, allowing me the freedom from self-doubt that revives dreams that were once thought to be lost.

Yes! I am now ready for this journey to begin.

Chapter Twenty-Six

I don't know, but I've been told that if you keep on dancing you will never grow old.

Steve Miller

Mandana

"Now that you know three of the Gypsy dancers' stories, read your aunt's letters, and have seen the dancers perform on stage, are you starting to understand why The Sisterhood is such an amazing group of women in Saint Augustine?" Sunflower asked.

I glanced down at Kiara, who was working in her garden while Sunflower and I visited on her porch. It took me a few minutes to know how to honestly respond to Sunflower's question.

In some ways learning about Calypso, Rain, and Whisper did make it easier for me to understand that we were all drawn here without any real logical. And yet it seems that Caroline and Emerald both knew exactly who they wanted to be included in this Sisterhood family that they were forming.

What is still unknown is how Dante's longevity research program is an important factor. And what does Brendon know about the Sisterhood? At our first meeting there was a definite romantic connection that drew us both together as if we had always known each other. But then nothing.

The entire recollection of that evening is bizarre, at times even disturbing.

"Mandana, have you zoned out on me? Did you hear anything that I just asked you?" Sunflower asked once again.

"Oh, I am so sorry, Sunflower. Yes, each of the gypsies' stories is fascinating. Watching them perform together the other evening certainly made me realize how talented each of them is. What is still disturbing is Brendon's reaction after our first meeting. It is as if he disappeared. I have no idea how to find him. And how does the *ELI* Project fit in with the Sisterhood?"

"It may seem that there are many unanswered questions, when in fact the answers have always been available when you allow yourself to see and hear beyond all of the distractions. The *ELI* Project has always existed. Most people live in a narrow space of perception that prevents them from seeing and appreciating the esthetic beauty that surrounds us. Once we are able to break away from our normal, but distorted perception we are free to experience what the real world offers," Sunflower said, rising from her wicker rocker and walking down to the garden where Kiara was now planting seeds in a newly cleared area.

"Just as this flower bed has been cleared for new growth, your Aunt Caroline came to Saint Augustine with the vision that she could plant a new garden of women who have been living in many different universes while sharing the same desire to enlighten their new world with the experiences and knowledge they brought with them. Caroline knew that Dante had been experimenting for many years with the longevity project. When she approached him with her ideas about the Sisterhood, he was impressed by what she shared with him. Together they began to form an alliance that would assure that the Gypsy dancers had a fulfilling future."

When Sunflower had finished planting the seeds with Kiara, they both joined me once again on the porch.

"Are you suggesting that the ladies Caroline and Emerald selected have somehow traveled from their original location in other time eras, and now are part of Dante's Extended Life Project?" I asked, finally understanding this phenomenon.

"Well, yes, and no. First, ELI is no longer a thesis, it has been proven for many years. Using DNA from Caroline, Dante was able to produce a vaccine that allows each of the five original Sisters an extended lifespan." Sunflower finally confirmed what was earlier suggested.

"Does this mean that they will all live forever? And how is it that Caroline passed away if she had the original genetic code?" I asked.

"That is really all the information that I can share with you now, Mandana. I hope this is enough. Everything can be very complicated and confusing if you don't have some time to reflect on how this directly affects you. Once you complete your meeting with Dante, the remaining two gypsies' stories will reveal many of the missing details you are searching for," Sunflower said, handing me the final two folders.

"When will I be meeting with Dante?" I asked, eager to finally learn more.

"Tomorrow at 11:00 AM. Would you like me to join you?" Sunflower asked.

"Not really. I think this is a visit I need to confront myself. I do appreciate everything that you have shared with me, however. It will take me time to put all of this into some logical order, if that is even possible," I said, deciding to return next door to spend some time with Lancelot.

"If you have any other questions after your visit with Dante, call my cellphone. I will be at the beach house most of the day with Rain designing costumes for our December extravaganza downtown," Sunflower said, embracing me on my way out.

It was still fairly early when I got home, but because of the time change it was already dark inside.

As I walked through the house with the flashlight that I always kept near the back door, Lancelot approached me from the front room appearing rather disoriented.

"It's okay, boy. I'm home now. I forgot to set the light timer for you. Forgive me, sweet boy," I said, kneeling down to let him know that he was safe now.

Immediately I could tell that something was happening. Something with Lancelot was not normal. It was more than anxiety, although he was breathing heavily. After carefully examining him for any injuries, I wrapped my arms around his chest. We both sank to the floor.

With Lance's head cradled near my chest, I began to sing an Enya song that we listened to every night, hoping to ease any fear he was having.

Wait for the sun,
Watching the sky
Black as a crow
Night passes by

His heart started beating normally once again, but I continued the tune for several minutes, until finally it seemed safe to release his head from my bosom.

"What was all that about?" I said, looking directly into the dog's green eyes.

Lancelot stood up once again, appearing normal but refusing to let me out of his sight as I moved toward the guest room where my computer was.

"That's okay. You can stay with me as long as you need to," I said, still worried that I may have overlooked something.

Tomorrow morning, I would definitely need to call the vet. There was no need to take any chances that something may be wrong that I had not noticed.

As I was checking my emails for the day, I realized there was one from Brendon a few days ago. How I could have missed it I had no idea. When I clicked to open it, I saw the message was only a few lines:

If you are not busy Saturday night send me a text message. Maybe we can meet at Meehans for drinks?

Brendon

What? Just when I thought that he had disappeared forever, I am being invited for drinks? Maybe Sunflower is right about being patient.

Not really sure how long this message had been floating in cyberspace, I took a chance and responded that Saturday at 8:00 PM I would be there. Then it occurred to me that we never exchanged phone numbers. How did Brendon know mine? It would be something that I added to my collection of inquiries, although I didn't want to bombard him with a bunch of random questions that might appear as an inquisition after waiting a month to hear from him.

After a restless evening with many episodes of interrupted sleep, my alarm alerted me that it was time to start a new day. Lancelot was lying at the foot of my bed, appearing back to normal, curled up next to me, totally ignoring the alarm. I moved closer to him. He raised his head toward the window as if checking to see some sunlight.

"It's coming, Lance. Trust me the sun will be out by the time we are ready for our early morning walk," I said, as we both stretched in the same direction at the same time.

It was earlier than usual when we left since my appointment with Dante was at 9:00 AM so we didn't see Flo or Jocelyn as usual. Also,

I decided to take a shorter route, still concerned that Lancelot might be suffering from some type of infection. I was happy to notice that at least for the moment he was back to his usual self, sniffing every few yards, stopping at the pond to watch the local ducks take their early morning swim.

Once we arrived back home, I took a quick shower, left Lancelot his treats in the normal places, turned on *Paw Patrol,* and somehow managed to arrive at the *ELI* location fifteen minutes prior to my appointment.

"Good morning, Ms. Morrison, Dr. Griffith will be with you shortly. May I offer you a cup of coffee or perhaps tea?" the receptionist greeted me as I took a seat in the lobby.

"No, thank you," I answered politely.

Taking the opportunity to scan my messages and let Sunflower know that Brendon had contacted me, I noticed a text alert.

Meehan's at 8:00 PM is perfect. Looking forward to seeing you again. Brendon

I was tempted to reply but decided to leave everything safely as it was.

Sunflower suggested that I share with Dante what happened last night with Lancelot rather than take him to the veterinary. It seemed like an odd suggestion, but I added it to the other questions that I was going to ask.

"Dr. Griffith will see you now, Ms. Morrison," announced a nurse that opened the door leading to the back room.

As I entered Dante's office, he was sitting behind a large desk that faces a glass window with a spectacular view of the Matanzas nlet.

"Welcome, Mandy! May I call you Mandy? It was how your Aunt Caroline always referred to you," Dante said, stepping out from behind his desk to greet me.

I was rather taken aback at the request because it had been years since anyone called me Mandy, although when I was younger it was my nickname. And, all the letters from Caroline addressed me as Mandana.

"Yes, of course. I am grateful that you have agreed to meet with me. There are just so many questions that I have related to my Aunt Caroline's passing, her life here in St. Augustine, and her devotion to the Sisterhood," I said, not wanting to delay my objective for being here.

"Well, then, I am certainly glad to give you as much information as possible, but I must warn you that everything associated with Caroline is extraordinary. What I will share with you may even seem impossible to believe. But I assure you it is all very real."

Dante's tone was now much more serious and direct. What was about to be revealed sounded much like a science fiction novel.

Apparently, Caroline first appeared in Saint Augustine during the turn of the nineteenth century. Nobody has any evidence as to where she came from, although her Irish accent made most people assume she immigrated from Ireland. By the time that Dante was introduced to her in the 1960's, Caroline would have been nearly one hundred years old. But the photograph that he shared with me is a beautiful redhead lady, perhaps in her late forties, wearing a flapper dress. They were attending a Roaring Twenties fundraiser at the Lightner Museum.

Dante had just started the ELI Institute. Once he learned more about Caroline's mysterious youthful appearance, he knew that he must arrange for some extensive testing.

What Dante discovered through those tests and conversations with Caroline is that she had a rare genetic mutation that prevented her from aging. This, however, was not enough to extend her lifespan eternally. Caroline was still prone to accidents, illnesses, and catastrophic injuries, but, as long as she was in a stable environment, her survival could continue for an unknown number of years.

Knowing this information, Dante and Caroline worked together to create a vaccine that would provide women with similar genetic mutations, the benefit from this treatment extending their lives beyond any preconceived expectations.

"So, if I am understanding you correctly, with the aid of my aunt's DNA you have been able to create a vaccination that increases the life expectancy in this community?" I asked, almost speechless.

"Yes, and no. It is still in an experimental first stage. The vaccine does not work on everyone. The additional benefit is that your aunt was also a time traveler, another reason why she had an extended lifespan. Once Caroline decided to establish a Sisterhood in Saint Augustine, she began to research who she wanted to include and what their mission would be. Gypsies and Pirates historically have had many difficult obstacles to overcome. Places like Florida, New Orleans, and the Caribbean began to initiate a new movement of Krews that were dedicated to contributing positively to their community. A new generation of Pirates and Gypsies were born."

Dante paused, allowing me to absorb all of this information, before continuing.

"If everything that you have just revealed to me is valid, I still do not understand why Aunt Caroline left me as the executor of her estate. I am not even a blood relative. Until I received the letter from Caroline's attorney, I wasn't even sure who she was," I said, still confused.

"What I have shared with you, Mandy, is only a very brief explanation of a very complex situation. But what I can assure you is that you are definitely the right person to be continuing Caroline's legacy. And you are also a direct descendant, which qualifies you for the longevity vaccine. Any further details Sunflower and Emerald will share with you. I believe that they have provided you with the dossier for each of the Sisterhood Gypsies. Once you have completed reading their stories, the final details will make more sense," Dante said, standing once again, suggesting that our meeting had ended.

Accepting that Caroline was a time traveler, even from a respected medical professional, is still difficult for me. But what truly surprised me is that Dante insisted that Aunt Caroline and I are relatives, close enough for me to benefit from the genetic vaccine, if I want it.

There are two more Gypsy bios that I need to read first. My date with Brendon, if I can call it a date, must somehow also be related to this triangle of events.

Darn it! I forgot to ask Dante about Lancelot. I will put it on my list to call tomorrow and ask his advice.

At least for the remainder of the day there are no further outings. I plan to complete studying the two remaining documents before tomorrow's date with Brendon.

As I am driving home, I see the leftover Full Blood Moon from last night peeking through the clouds.

That reminds me that it is the last night of October, Halloween! We are at that threshold of crossing the line, an imaginary line where the course and direction of our lives will be recognized, bringing messages from the spiritual realm.

This was Caroline's favorite night when a thin space exists between the veil of earth and the mask of reality.

Chapter Twenty-Seven

I know the dark delight of being strange. The penalty of difference in a crowd. The loneliness of wisdom among fools.

Claude McKay,
Harlem Renaissance Poet

JADA

Bob Marley and I were conceived in the same countryside village, known as Nine Mile, Saint Ann Parish, later referred to as the slum of Trench Town, near Kingston, Jamaica.

By the time I was born, Marley was already a legend. The story of how he was able to become that legend, in spite of all his misfortunes, beginning with his birth, was what kept most of us from giving up on life.

Like Marley, I am the product of a biracial relationship. My mother was Jamaican, and my father was from Portugal. Unlike Marley, whose mother, a nineteen-year-old village girl, was seduced by a sixty-year-old British naval officer who was working as a plantation supervisor, my father was a merchant marine who fell madly in love with my mother.

While working on the ship docks, Dad would stop at the local pub where my mother was a barmaid at my grandfather's tavern.

In 1972 when the song *Brandy* was released by Looking Glass, my dad would sing the lyrics to my mom, especially when she was in a rotten mood.

There's a port on the western bay
And it serves a hundred ships a day
Lonely sailers pass the time away
And talk about their homes.
And there's a girl in this harbor town
And she works laying whiskey down
They say, Brandy fetch another round
She serves them whiskey and wine...

Every time that Dad sang this song, my mom's eyes would light up, as if whatever he or we had done was no longer important. Not having any money was never a problem. Sometimes it may have been inconvenient, but, as long as there was music and laughter in the house, and we were together, nothing else seemed to matter.

Until Dad had to return to Portugal.

It had been eight years. When he informed mother that his first wife was pressing charges against him for bigamy, there were no other options available. Since he was a Portuguese citizen, Jamaica would be forced to extradite him if the charges were not dropped.

In 1976, after Mom realized that Dad was not coming home, she packed us all up, and we moved to Kingston. Grandfather objected, of course, but my mother was convinced that the only way that my brother and I would have any chance for a better future was if we left the Jamaica "ghetto" as she called it.

By this time, Bob Marley was being recognized as a legitimate singer and writer. His son, Stephen Marley, was born the same year as my brother.

Our mother was convinced that once Bob Marley knew that they were both from Nine Mile he would embrace their friendship and include mother in his band as a drummer. The only problem was how to get close enough to Marley for her to see him.

When we arrived at Kingston by train, none of us had any idea where we were going to stay or even if we would have enough money to eat. My brother and I were prepared to panhandle if necessary, at least for a short time, to have food.

You can just imagine how surprised we all were when we saw someone holding a sign at the train depot with our last name: *Welcome Armstrong Family.*

"Momma, who is that holding the sign with our name?" I asked as the train pulled up.

Mother said nothing, but she made sure that we had all our belongings in our possession once we stepped off the train and approached the man holding the sign.

"We are the Armstrong family. Have you been sent by Bob Marley?" Mother asked, as if she was as always expecting to be met at the train depot by someone from Marley's entourage.

"Yes. I am here to take you to Mrs. Rita. She will explain to you what your duties will be," the elderly gentleman said.

None of us dared to question who Rita was and what our duties were to be. I know that mother was simply relieved that wherever we were going it meant that we would all have a place to sleep for at least one night, and most likely food.

After that, nothing was guaranteed.

That was the first day of what would be ten years with Bob Marley. Mom never played drums for Marley, but she did teach his children, all eleven of them, although at different times, how to dance, sing, and play a variety of musical instruments.

We never discovered if the fateful sign with our name at the train depot was really meant for us.

Once Rita, Bob Marley's wife, learned that we were from his birth town, she insisted that it was God who sent us, and that we belonged with the Marley family.

The next ten years we spent traveling with the Marley's. They provided us with the most wonderful experiences and memories that anyone from the ghetto could imagine. Meeting people from so many different parts of the world changed our entire expectations of what we were capable of accomplishing, as well as what our limits were, based on racial diversity.

Prior to this, all we knew was a small island, 142 miles long, surrounded by water. Suddenly, now we had the opportunity to travel to places that once were only strange shapes on a map. The greatest lesson that we all learned is always be prepared for the unexpected.

Even Bob Marley, whom everyone seemed to admire, was surrounded by bodyguards protecting him from those who were determined to kill him because of his political activism.

On December 3, 1976, armed gunmen attempted to assassin Marley on Hope Road, shooting him in the arm and chest. We were not with him at the time, but just knowing that anyone could get that close to Marley made my mother reluctant to travel any longer with him. We almost always arrived a few days later.

While I became obsessed with the philosophical theories that surrounded me, many introduced by Bob Marley himself, my brother began illustrating everything he learned in his sketchbook. Later those artistic contributions would be invaluable impressions illustrated in various artistic mediums.

There were also many people who admired Bob Marley's musical talent that never understood his dedication to mysticism. At the early age of seven, Marley was accurately reading the palms of many neighbors who later affirmed that his predictions became reality.

It was after returning from Kingston once on a visit that Marley announced that he was going to be a famous singer, and no longer could read anyone else's future. He kept that promise with the exception of close family and friends. It was because of what Marley revealed to me later that I made the decision to move permanently to Saint Augustine, despite having many other offers after his early death at the age of thirty-six in 1981.

There is no doubt that Bob Marley's contribution to Reggae, a slowed down version of Ska, eventually transformed to Rastafarian, inspiring ideas of personal and spiritual freedom as well as peace, love, and community unity.

Whereas Ska features punk rock with a horns section, Marley added the traditional music of Nyabing, consisting of chanting and drumming to heighten the ideas of black redemption and reparations.

Many critics of reggae labeled the Jamaican music as that of the oppressed, but, in fact, it is that exact defining characteristic that enlightens people everywhere in the world.

While we were in London once visiting a friend that Marley knew only through letters, he revealed to me how reggae is a life-altering form when people accept it as a spiritual consequence.

He then shared with me the story of a black schoolboy, Benjamin Zephaniah, whose letter complained that "I'm a poet from Birmingham, but nobody is listening to me in England. What do you think of my poems?"

Only because Marley encouraged Benjamin to continue writing, was the young man able to become famous for "dub poetry," a form that was thought to be nonexistent when he first met the singer. Later he attributed Marley's support for his success.

In reality, dub poetry originated in Kingston, Jamaica, in the 1970's combining reggae rhythms with socio-politically conscious lyrics.

It was because of these specific experiences that Marley suggested that I learn more about the Yoga philosophy. He suggested that once I was able to understand how to balance the internal structure with the external environment anything in my life would be possible. What Marley always encouraged his followers to do is find ways to spread love and peace to others.

Those of us who admired Bob Marley regarded him as a prophet, a title that he did not embrace himself. Rather, he would say that his mission in life was to be a mystic messenger.

Knowing that the mystic music is meant to be profound, reaching emotional intensity, Marley always strived to leave his followers in a hypnotic, intoxicated state of mind.

During one of our discussions about the significance of music as an art form, Marley quoted one of his favorite sources,

*In fact, music excels religion, for music raises the soul of man even higher than the so called external *(no hyphen? –so-called) form of religion...*

Hazrat Inayat Khan
Indian Sufi Master

"Whatever you choose to pursue in life, Jada, always include music. That has been my saving grace."

This is one of the final lessons that I remember before Bob Marley's untimely death.

I did exactly what he suggested without ever truly understanding how my life would change until I met Emerald on the island of Barbados many years later at my exclusive Yoga studio. The moment that she greeted me I knew that everything that Bob Marley taught me was about to come true.

"You must be Jada?" I heard someone ask.

"Yes, I am Jada. May I help you? We are closed for the afternoon, but I would be glad to review with you what my studio offers. Can I get you a refreshing glass of tea or juice?" I asked, moving toward the front of the studio.

As I approached the sunlit vestibule, the shadow from a distance now appeared much clearer. The young woman, dressed in a gray peasant blouse with a green leather corset that perfectly accentuated her Caledonian colored circle skirt, extended her arm toward me, saying, "I am very glad to meet you, Jada. My name is Emerald."

Immediately, the various shades of green appeared to be much more than a coincidence.

In yoga, heart chakra, where your divine self and your human self-meet, is represented by the color green for health and growth.

"Have we ever met previously?" I asked, feeling a sense of belonging in this stranger's presence.

"The answer to that question, my dear, depends entirely on your perspective on parallel universe theory. Perhaps one day, we might engage in an enlightened discussion on the topic, but for the moment I am here to invite you to join our dancing troupe known as The Saint Augustine Sisterhood," Emerald said, taking a seat on one of the chairs I added for prospective clients who wish to observe prior to joining the studio.

I was rather taken aback by the request to join a group in a city that I had never heard of before.

And dancing? What type of dancing? I am a Yoga instructor, not a dancer.

Before I had the opportunity to ask more questions, it was as if the mysterious Emerald had vanished somehow right before my eyes, leaving only a parchment scroll with a green ribbon tied around it on the chair where she had been seated.

I walked outside to see if somehow I could catch a glimpse of where the lady had gone, but there was not a trace. Once back inside the studio, I removed the ribbon and opened the scroll.

Written was the following message:

Trusting your inner guidance will lead you toward the direction where dreams become reality, and reality aligns with the special gifts provided to you by the universe. It is your responsibility to share those gifts of compassion by living a life that bears witness to injustice and act strongly to protect those who are suffering from this state of mind.

The Saint Augustine Sisterhood embraces you, without prejudice or exception.

That was it. Nothing more. No address. No date. And yet it was all that I needed.

Somehow Emerald was the one I was waiting for without even knowing that she was coming.

After Marley passed away, everyone who was touched by his music and even more so by his message felt abandoned, lost.

Every day in my studio before my sessions would start, I listened to the lyrics from Marley's song *War*.

Until the philosophy
Which hold
One race superior
And another
Inferior

Is finally
And permanently
Discreditive
And Abandoned
Until the color of a man's skin
Is of no significance
Than the color of his eyes
Me say war

And then I would turn around everything that I had just pumped into my soul, close my eyes, and imagine the peaceful, spiritual teachings of Buddha, taking deep breaths, uniting my spiritual self with the universal Divine.

It was my daily ritual. But I always knew that there was something more, and it was coming. I just had no idea that its name was Emerald.

Chapter Twenty-Eight

"There are women who make things better…simply by showing up.
There are women who make things
Happen
There are women who make their way
There are women who make a
Difference,
And, women who make us smile
There are women of wit and wisdom
Who through strength and courage
Make it through,
There are women who change the world
Everyday,
Women like you."

Ashley Rice

Jada

Ten days later I was on a plane from Barbados to Jacksonville, Florida. 2,989km, 8 hours and 20 minutes is what it took for my life to finally come to a complete point of understanding.

Many of us are in a perpetual state of confusion without even understanding why. I was one of the lucky ones.

My time with Bob Marley prepared me for knowing the difference between living and existing. What did Marley specifically teach me? Whatever it was Emerald thought it important enough to include me in the *Sisterhood?*

Nevertheless, it was a question that I had to answer before I made the decision to leave Barbados. If I could not answer that question, all I was doing was moving aimlessly with no purpose.

Before making the decision to leave Barbados, I decided to visit my personal Yoga guru, she was not only the most knowledgeable person on the island, I trusted her advice above anyone I had ever known, including my own mother. Marley introduced me to Arias once he convinced me to study Yoga.

"There is no one that I have ever met that will provide you with the opportunity to learn the most essential techniques of yoga while enlightening you," Marley said. He was right as usual.

Arias' Barbados retreat specialized in a private six week session that required a total immersion experience. It explored the history, philosophy, anatomy, physiology, and principles of Yin Yoga, as well as Gentle Yin. What I never expected was how Arias would teach me to be a spiritual leader. The course was intense. It began with tracing Yoga back 5,000 years ago to northern India.

"Do you realize that the very word *yoga* was first mentioned in ancient sacred texts called the *Rig Veda?*" Arias shared with the six of us one early morning.

The other five students were from Barcelona, Spain, attending to complete their Yoga certification. I was the only one attending for personal enrichment. All of us listened attentively, although the historical lessons were obviously the least favorite, especially before the crack of dawn.

Sensing our difficulty focusing fully on the facts that were being shared, Arias instructed us to do the child's pose. Although very basic and often used in a beginner's class, it is also the perfect move towards calming and relaxing when feeling overwhelmed. And it was a position that we all were familiar with.

From a kneeling position, with widened knees and pointed toes toward the mat, arms and hands extended toward the front of the mat, you let your bottom come back to rest on your knees and hips.

With your chest forward, keeping a tall spine, your forehead and chest should relax on the mat.

After a few minutes in this pose, Arias instructed us to sit up naturally.

"As you all now realize the very basic yoga pose is as essential as the most complex. As is everything in life that we experience and share with others. The reason why we are here this morning watching the sun rise together, strangers, yet united, is not coincidence. But each of you will discover that in the following weeks we are together on this journey."

Arias continued explaining to us that the *Rig Veda* is a collection of over one thousand hymns and mantras in ten chapters known as *mandalas. Yoga* was defined from this spiritual practice and is amongst the six schools of philosophy in Hinduism.

Although this session included many historical facts that I was not sure I would ever need, Arias was wiser than I could ever imagine being. Knowing this made me absorb everything like a sponge in need of water.

One of the most important aspects of the early morning rituals was learning the language of yoga, which is actually Sanskrit, the root of many Indian languages, and the oldest in the world.

Pranayama is used to describe breathing exercises associated with yoga. But in Sanskrit it is the life force within everyone. When instructed properly, it is the yoga method to clear physical and emotional obstacles to free breath in our body.

Ujjayi, commonly translated to mean victorious breath, is performed by restricting the air flow at the back of your throat, while breathing in and out of the nose. The sound of exhalation has been compared to the ocean.

By the third week of our session, spending every waking moment together, our group began to unite.

The five Barcelona ladies were lifelong friends that ranged in age from twenty-five years old to sixty.

Marcella was the youngest of the group and the organizer.

"We are all like sisters. In Barcelona, although our ages range from twenties to sixties, this doesn't matter! We learn from each other. Each day that we can share laughter, happiness, and joy is a blessing. And you? What brings you here all alone?" Marcella asked.

It took me a few moments to answer.

Why was I here? I wanted to learn more about Yoga, but it was so much more than that. I wanted the type of friendship that Marcella had with her sisters, but that wasn't why I was here.

"I am not really sure. A close friend referred me to Arias. Living in Barbados, owning my own Yoga studio, this opportunity just seemed like the perfect fit," I said, not even convincing myself that this was the truth.

By the end of the six weeks, we were all family. Marcella invited me to visit Barcelona anytime.

"You know Jada, I have a very handsome brother that would go crazy if he met you. Then we could be real sisters," Marcella said, smiling.

"If I wasn't planning on moving to Saint Augustine in a few weeks,

I just might have taken your offer seriously," I said, embracing Marcella as she was preparing to leave.

It was now only Arias and I.

Was I ready at last to now take that leap of faith and join Emerald in St. Augustine? How would I know if I was ever ready?

"I hope that these past six weeks have prepared you for your next adventure. It has been a great opportunity for us to bond. I have enjoyed your contribution to that bonding experience," Arias said.

"I certainly do not feel that I have contributed much during my stay, but certainly I am leaving with so much more insight than I arrived with. Thank you for sharing so much with all of us," I said, hoping to sound sincere, since I truly was.

"May I add just a little more advice specifically to your situation?" Arias asked, waiting patiently for me to agree.

"Absolutely. I am about to travel to a new world, a foreign world to me. I am insecure and fear that those who expect me to contribute will be disappointed. I have no idea even what the expectations are. It is all such a mystery. And, yet, it is something that I feel I am being summoned to by a spiritual force beyond my control," I said, nearly in tears.

Arias took my hand and led me to the lovely grotto facing the Atlantic Ocean.

We sat down, silently absorbing our surroundings, listening to the waves in harmony with our breath.

"Every journey in our life, Jada, is different. Are you familiar with the term Gypsy Atman?" Arias asked.

I was still unable to speak but shook my head no.

"Gypsy Atman is the belief that we are all travelers through life seeking our spiritual journeys through different worlds. The word 'Gypsy' means traveler, and the word 'atman' means soul. Love and compassion are what will guide you to those who will nurture your soul. There is a common thread that unites us. This is what you are now experiencing, Jada. There is nothing to fear. You will soon be among your Sisters who will each share with you as you will share with them your gifts," Arias said, standing and taking the goddess Yoga pose.

In Hindu the Goddess Kali is posed in a victorious stance with her arms extended out and her feet planted firmly in a squat. It is a powerful pose that strengthens the feminine power and helps to connect the space just beneath and behind your navel that is described as your energetic core.

I stood up facing Arias, taking the same exact pose. I was now ready to meet my Saint Augustine Sisters.

Chapter Twenty-Nine

Blessed are the Gypsies, the makers of music, the artists, writers, dreamers of dreams, wanderers, and vagabonds, children, and misfits—for they teach us to see the world through beautiful eyes.

Anonymous

Sunflower

There was only one more biography left to read. *Sunflower's!* Although each of the others was fascinating, it was only Sunflower that I personally knew.

The others were all like characters from an interesting novel, but Sunflower was real. What was her story? As much as I really wanted to meet up with Brendon, I was so close to the end of this Gypsy mystery that I could not put it off any longer. Besides, my desire to finally unravel who Emerald was, and Lancelot still continuing to be lethargic was just too much for me to ignore. Lancelot didn't seem to want to go anywhere, even on his daily walk.

Dr. Dante sent over some medication by courier, which I thought odd at first, but later Kiara told me that Caroline never really trusted any of the veterinary doctors. She claimed that they never cared about extending the lives of animals but rather were more interested in making money when the animals were already ill.

Apparently, Dr. Dante cared for Lancelot as if he was a human patient. If there was no improvement from the medication, I was instructed to bring him into the office immediately. As of the past few hours I could not detect any significant improvement. Under these circumstances, I really had no choice but to stay home.

"Brendon, it's Mandana. I am so sorry, but I am going to have to cancel tonight," I said, already regretting my decision.

"Is everything alright? I don't mind meeting you at your place if that is more convenient. I can pick up anything you would like for

189

dinner," Brendon said, sounding disappointed.

"That is very sweet of you, but Lancelot hasn't felt well the past few days, and I really don't want to leave him alone. Besides, I also have one more Gypsy bio to read. It is Sunflower's. I am really anxious to learn how all these dots are somehow connected to my life and why Caroline has left me with this mystery," I said, hoping that Brendon would understand.

"Well, if you change your mind, give me a call. I will probably be here in the studio most of the evening. You do have to eat eventually," he said, waiting for me to respond.

"I do have one question. How long have you known all of the dancing Gypsies? And do you know their life stories?" I asked.

There was a brief moment of silence.

"Are you still there, Brendon?" I asked, waiting for an answer.

"Yes, I am. I just really don't know how to exactly answer that question on the phone. It requires a more detailed explanation," he said, sounding hesitant.

I wanted to pursue those questions but decided that it would be better to address them in person.

"Okay. I am sorry if I may be moving in uncharted waters. I just thought if you had some personal insights that you would like to share it might be helpful," I said, sounding disappointed.

Brendon must have picked up on the tone of my voice.

"Mandy, I can assure you that once you have finished Sunshine's bio and met all Five Gypsy dancers brought here by Emerald all of your doubts will disappear. And, if you think that I am hesitating because I was ever romantically involved with any of the Sisterhood, I can assure you that never happened. They are all like my sisters as well," Brendon said, emphasizing the word *Sisters.*

I was not sure how we arrived at this awkward personal situation in our conversation, but I was determined to reroute to a normal tone.

"When I have finished this bio, I owe you a homemade dinner at my place. Although it might be homemade elsewhere and delivered here, the invitation is still open," I said, hoping that we were now back to a normal conversation.

"That sounds more like a truce, but I will hold you to that invitation," Brendon said.

I decided not to push back any further, letting the "truce" arrangement suffice, turning my attention to the dossier titled:

I was born a flower child in the *Age of Aquarius.* It was to be a time when humanity takes control of its own destiny on earth, revealing the truth and expansion of consciousness where people will experience enlightenment. Astrologers suggest that an astrological age is a time period that causes major changes in those that live on earth, including shifts in culture, society, and politics.

My parents were far ahead of their time. When my father inherited ten acres in the New York Catskills, it was nothing but an isolated oasis. Exactly what he wanted. Away from what he saw as an arrogant society that only wanted people to follow a conservative lifestyle.

The Byrdcliff Art Colony near Woodstock was one of those early utopian communities that included 1500 acres and seven farms. It was established in 1903 and included thirty buildings nearby. Artists like my mom and dad would practice every imaginable trade from metalwork like daddy to pottery and painting like my mom.

When they weren't busy creating artsy items to sell to the tourists, there was the farm to tend to. Mom and Dad decided that the best way to get reliable help must be to have ten children. I was number ten in that group. There were four girls and six boys, and I believe they would have continued on procreating if it hadn't been for my illness.

For several years I suffered with high fevers and seizures before it was diagnosed that my (why pelvic, *aren't the kidneys left and right?) kidney was only functioning at 12%. By that time when I was four, my parents took me to Chicago where the doctors concluded that I needed reconstructive kidney and urethra surgery.

Although this surgery helped, the pain remains even today. Thankfully, the antibiotics have kept the infection under control. You might think that having your youngest sibling suffering with such a traumatic condition would bring the family together. I mean, you know, hippies are all about peace and love!

Not my family. Stormy, Autumn, and Meadow, the oldest sisters, still today complain how they were responsible for caring for me during my recovery. Until one day they all seemed to disappear.

My grandmother, who moved in with us after Grandpa passed away, became my new caregiver. One afternoon, when the boys were in the fields working, and we were sitting on the porch, I asked my grandmother how old she was.

She was always complaining about her aches and pains after returning from waitressing at the local café where Mom also worked for extra money.

"Today, my little Sunflower, I feel like I am two hundred years old. But sitting here with you reminds me why I am still here on this earth," she said, sipping a cup of tea.

"And are you still here because of me?" I asked, suddenly happy to imagine that anyone in this house was actually happy that I was still here.

Grandma bent down as far as she could, scooped me up to her lap, and gave me a huge hug.

"What I want you to always remember my Sunshine is that whenever things in your life seem too difficult always keep doing what is expected, but do it slowly, little by little. Never let the future dictate what you are doing today. Live for the moment the best that you can. The French call this *Carpe Diem*," Grandma said.

"What is the French?" I recall asking, confused.

"France is a beautiful country very far away. Someday I am quite certain that you will visit France, and when you do, *Carpe Diem* will all make sense to you," Grandma answered.

"You are a very wise lady, Grandma. I am glad you are here for me," I said, sincerely.

Grandma kissed my forehead and continued her advice.

"What I share with you today may not seem important now. But each time that you remember it your life will be made much easier. Next time you are in the forest, watch how nature surrounds you with advice. It is the same advice that I share with you only in a different language.

"Each day you are advancing without even knowing. Notice each step that you take, never go faster than you feel comfortable with, and before you know it, you will have arrived at your destination.

"Everyone will praise and admire you for all of your accomplishments." Grandma waited to hear my reaction.

There wasn't any. It would be many years and many tears before I could understand what my Grandma was teaching me that afternoon. But I did exactly what she said.

Each afternoon in the forest, I would study the birds, the trees, and the ants. Watching the wildlife and insects working together offered me a sanctuary, a place where I felt welcomed without prejudice. This was my safe place.

It was where I learned:
From a stone, to remain still
From a river, the art of motion.
A falling leaf taught me the art of detachment.
The mountain was me strength. (my strength?)*
Raindrops offered serenity.
A caterpillar taught me resilience.
A seashell the possibility of opportunity
Remaining free was visible in every floating cloud,
A modest flower taught me to be humble,
From my butterfly friends the art of graceful movement was learned,
Snowflakes are each unique,
And every flame is passionate.

I was never able to share what I learned with my grandmother, who passed away five days after the lesson she taught me.

But, several years later, on the top of the Eiffel Tower, I shouted loudly, *Carpe Diem* and left a bouquet of sunflowers on the outside railing in honor of Grandma.

Chapter Thirty

There is a sacredness in tears. They are the messengers of overwhelming grief, of deep contritions and unspeakable love.

Washington Irving
Author

SUNFLOWER

It is often argued among astrologists when the age of Aquarius is to technically begin. Some argue that since the Age of Pisces began in 68 B.C.E., the Age of Aquarius will not start until 2597.

Others argue that the Age of Aquarius will begin in the 22nd century around 2160. However, in 2021, the seven planet stellium in Aquarius have led theorists to now believe that we have already arrived.

Astrologer Ruby McCollister observed that since the arrival of Uranus there has been a "flourishing of science, technology, philosophy, literature, music, social opportunities, in virtually every aspect of human life, which exploded Western civilization toward liberation, freedom, and choice."

What does all this mean and how does it affect the Sisterhood?

To begin with, as explained to me by Emerald, the elements required to raise the level of conscious comprehension of the earth and its inhabitants require the proper physical, mental, and spiritual guidance provided by a long evolutionary process. This process has been developed throughout several generations to the extent that it is now possible to achieve the first stages of humanitarian fulfillment of human needs and potential. This new Age will offer a new human picture that challenges the old-world ideology of blood relationally.

Emerald is my mentor, my guru, my spiritual leader. It is as if my grandmother is living through her words of wisdom.

At a recent Sisterhood fellowship after hours of dance rehearsal, Calypso asked a question that we have all wanted answered.

"With all the abundance of new possibilities that the Age of Aquarius offers, what is our role as Saint Augustine Sisters. More importantly, why were we selected by you?"

The entire room went silent. How was Emerald finally going to address this topic?

"In this new age, each individual has the ability to find their own light and bring it forth to illuminate those who have not yet found their calling.

We express our light through dance and music. Each one of you has a unique talent that blended together provides a necessary element to the whole experience.

Vincent Van Gogh identified himself as a *Painter of Music.*

Hear his words, and then create your own vision:

The Crow Mother

The saddest song is the one you have not sung!
It has never been heard, no words, no notes, or feelings to inspire
Many are holding their songs deep
Within themselves
There will never be a "perfect" time or
Moment to sing
Singing just happens!
*It is a reflex of the soul's desire to speak! * (I'm not sure why these asterisks are here. Did you do it?)*
Like laughing
Like crying
Do you have a song?
Have you sat alone and quieted your mind long enough to hear?
If you started to sing your song what
*Would the words be, what would its **
Story say...
This is your healing power!
Find your song
Sing it out into the universe
Let its reverberations call the healing.
You so deeply long for
Let the emotions that are hidden away
Arise and take flight
Your song is your healing
Don't leave this place without singing

Your song,
The Crow Mother…Caw
I can hear you!

From that day forward, Emerald was our Crow Mother.

To me she is so much more. Not only did Emerald provide me with the opportunity to find myself during the darkest moments of my life, but she has also never left my side.

At sixteen years old, I left home. Grandmother was gone. Mom and Dad were trying to do the best they could. Everyone, except the boys, whom I barely knew, were all gone. Childhood was rough, but the teenage years were even worse. I never fit in at school, or at home. My sanctuary was the forest, but even there I knew (the peace?) was only temporary. *

One afternoon, after deciding to leave home, I went to my private grotto. A place that no one knew existed but me. I sat down on a weathered stump and cried out to God!

"My Lord! Forgive me for not knowing how to address you. I have never been to church, but I do believe. I believe in You! Please teach me to believe in me," I said, falling on my knees with my eyes closed, not knowing what to expect next.

There was a silence that I have never experienced before or since. It was impossible to know how much time had passed, but suddenly, I felt a surge inside my body. It was nothing like I had ever experienced before, nor was it anything that I could ever describe.

Once I was able to open my eyes, the light was everywhere. It was not necessary for any words. Whatever was happening was happening inside of me.

The entire experience lasted only a few moments, enough time to know that God had just promised me to never leave my side. This is where I found God, and I knew from that time forward that I would never walk alone.

My sister Storm, who had her own apartment, was always my safe port. She was my first role model of what Sisterhood truly meant.

But it wasn't enough. I needed to get away from all the negativity that was strangling me.

Now that I reflect on those years, I realize it was when I decided to join a group of happy, outgoing, eccentric friends that were preparing to hitchhike across the East Coast to follow *The Grateful Dead* that my life was saved.

These hippies and Rainbow families gave me a fresh start. It is when my life changed. No one knew me. Sunflower could finally be anyone that she wanted to be. I watched, I learned, I gravitated to others that were always smiling and happy. I trained myself to smile even when I was depressed.

Even today I consider myself a lone wolf; a survivor, a warrior who knew even at an early age that I had to take control of my thoughts and emotions, or I would never exist long in this world. Learning that the simple act of smiling allows you to control the world around you most of the time is priceless.

Without giving the *Grateful Dead* too much credit for my transformation, and in some ways my survival, I would be remiss to not acknowledge the influence that being a *Dead Head* had on my life.

The Deadhead subculture originated when people like me and the Rainbow Family began traveling around the country to follow their concerts in the 1970's. A definite prequel to my later Gypsy life.

Very similar to the original Gypsy communities, Dead Heads created slang and idioms unique to their music. This included the Grateful Dead's improvisation during their performances which made each concert unique. Over the course of their thirty-year career, this band performed over 2200 live shows.

During all these months that I was traveling throughout the country with all these lovely people, I never knew that my mother was determined that at least one of her girls would go to college. That girl was me.

I have no idea how she found me, but one afternoon at the hippie commune in Cornell on May 8, 1977, Mother appeared from nowhere. This was the date of the most famous and well-regarded Grateful Dead Concert of all time. Of course, there was no way for me to know this at the time.

Later it was documented that it was that three-hour concert that contained music from across the first decade with such precision and originality that everyone remembers. Everyone but me!

My mother made sure that I would be returning home immediately, where I was now enrolled in a college that I had never heard of. It was such a different perspective of my mother, one that I never expected but am definitely grateful for now.

As difficult as it was for her to let me go on my journey, I realized later that she had lived vicariously through me. You see, my mother always had the Gypsy spirit, but never the opportunity to live the dream.

College was another place to learn my boundaries. Whereas my hippie lifestyle had no boundaries, here I soon realized to not be so trusting of everyone. I wanted to believe that everyone is honest, but realistically I knew this belief was naïve.

What was not clear was how all that I was learning would contribute to my life. Completing college was a challenge that provided me with a sense of accomplishment, but it was not enough.

What was missing? I had no idea until Emerald found me.

After college all I wanted to do was move as far away from Oregon as possible. When the offer to work for a chemical company in Tennessee came through, I immediately accepted. Nobody in my family, except my mother, could understand why I wanted to live in Tennessee.

My previous life never included music or the arts. Even the radio and television in our house were always tuned to the news. It was not until I moved to Nashville that I realized I had a natural ability to dance to any beat that I would hear, even country music, which was not necessarily my favorite.

For the first two years in Nashville, I struggled. It was much different now than it was when I was with my hippie and Rainbow family on the road. I had acquaintances here but still felt alone. What I wanted was to find people who wanted to share their artistic talents, or at the very least attend events that offered concerts.

Then one evening when I was driving home from work, someone invited me to a backyard party called *Haunted Flying Circus.* It didn't sound like my type of activity, but I was desperate to do something beyond watching "Wheel of Fortune" every night.

I took out the paper with the directions, entered them into my GPS, and away I went. The moment I arrived and saw all the cars lined up on the streets, my nerves began to surface.

Quickly, I pulled my hair back into two ponytails, tied my button-down purple blouse, slightly revealing some skin, threw off my boots, and slipped on some spiked heels I keep in the back seat for who knows what. It was time to do some exploring.

The moment I opened the gate to the backyard, I felt that I had walked into another time dimension.

There were four low-flying aerialists, women dancing in big skirts, classy artistic pole dancing, a belly dancer, pirates, and a variety of different imaginary characters.

But the best part is that everyone was welcoming, friendly, and made me feel as if I belonged.

Immediately I knew that this is where I was meant to be. Not just for the evening but for my life.

But, before I could speak to the choreographer of this event, I was handed a parchment scroll tied with lovely yellow ribbons and sunflowers. The creature that handed me the scroll resembled a lovely forest imp but disappeared before I could ask any questions.

"Aha! I see that Emerald has been here," a lovely lady dressed in purple tights with a lovely matching headscarf said. I recognized her as one of the amazing aerialists.

"And who might Emerald be?" I asked, still examining the scroll.

"Oh, I will need to allow Emerald to be the one to reveal that to you. However, I strongly suggest you open the scroll. It is a life changing resource," the lovely aerialist said.

I took a seat near one of the fire pits and unraveled the ribbon, placing the sunflowers in my hair. This is the message that I read:

My dear, the voice in your head that

Is not truly you, You mistake it for being you, But that voice is a collection of all of the beliefs, opinions, and messages,

That you have ever heard

From the outside world,

That your mind has received

And, is narrating back to you

The you that you are

Is the one who is aware of these

Thoughts,

The observer of the thoughts

The voice that tells you that you

Aren't good enough

That you aren't pretty enough,

Only comes from the voices of other

Minds,

That have been told those things

That they have then told you

None of this has to become your story

Or be true for you
This is why a young child often sees the
World as a beautiful magical place
And believes themselves to be capable of anything
Because they have not yet heard the voices in their head that have
learned
To mistake for being themselves
This is the true path to peace
Remembering that you are not your thoughts
And learning to silence the mind
And not mistaking it for being you.
Tahalia Hunter

*You are hereby requested to join the Saint Augustine Sisterhood. Your
presence will be appreciated as soon as possible.*
Emerald

"Welcome, Sunflower. Your invitation to the Sisterhood is a transformation that cannot be ignored.

My name is Arias. I can assure you that once you arrive at Saint Augustine a new world will be yours to explore. A world unlike any other that you may previously experience."

I was soon to learn that Sisterhood is a relationship built upon trust, respect, and honesty. Something that I had been searching for and longing for my entire life.

What I never expected to discover is that the human soul only wants to be united with its mate.

Chapter Thirty-One

Claim your place in the sun and go forward into the light. The tools are there; the path is known; you simply have to turn your back on a future that has gone sterile and dead and get with the program of a living world and a re-empowerment of the imagination.

Terrence McKenna
American Ethnobotanist and Mystic

Mandana and Emerald

Well, there it was. A definitive blueprint for The Saint Augustine Sisterhood.

Yet everything that I now know about the five Gypsies has still left me with no specific answers as to why I was summoned to this town by a deceased aunt that I have no recollection of ever meeting.

My first reaction is to call Brendon. There is a missing link that I may have overlooked that he knows. Too many oddities are left without a resolution.

For example, what is Brendon's connection to the mysterious Sisterhood? Why were these women summoned from various locations to join the Sisterhood, and maybe just as important why did they all agree to drastically alter their lives to become Gypsy dancers?

Before I even had the opportunity to decide what to do next, my cellphone started ringing. It was 2:00 AM. Who would be calling me at this time of the morning?

The number was Brendon's.

"Hello? Is everything alright?" I asked immediately.

"Funny that you should ask. That was why I was calling. When I was driving home from the studio, I noticed that your lights were still on," Brendon said, sounding concerned.

"You are driving past my house? Like right now?" I asked, rather surprised.

"Well, no. Actually, at this very moment I am parked right outside your front door," he said.

I moved over toward the bedroom window, pulled back the drapes, and there he was waving to me, parked under the streetlight.

"Some people might call that stalking. Are you stalking me, Brendon?" I asked, tongue in cheek.

"Never! Well, maybe a little. Are you going to ask me in, or do I have to stay out here in the forty degree freezing cold?" Brendon said, sounding desperate.

"Alright, I will heat up the Keurig machine. You can come in for a short time, but I need to get to bed soon. I have a morning breakfast date that I can't miss," I said walking toward the front door.

As soon as I opened it, there was Brendon bundled up like he lived somewhere in Ohio instead of sunny Florida.

"Should I be jealous about this morning date you have? I mean, you cancelled our date last night but this morning it seems Lancelot is well enough to abandon him for a few hours," Brendon said, unwrapping his neck scarf, and removing his heavy coat.

I had forgotten how attractive he was. And that Irish accent was so pleasant to my ears.

Maybe I just didn't want to remember since it had been so long since we had seen each other. Then I suddenly realized that here I was standing in my hallway with no makeup, my hair in a messy bun, wearing yellow duckling flannel pajamas.

At least my duck slippers matched!

Great! After tonight Brendon will think twice before he ever calls me again.

"Actually, I have been so engrossed with the Gypsy dossier that I have neglected Lance for a few hours. Thanks for reminding me to check on him," I said, moving into the living room.

There he was. Sleeping peacefully on the recliner near the floor heater that he has claimed as his own domain. I bent over to check on his breathing. All seemed quite normal.

For just a brief moment, he opened his eyes, realized it was me, and went right back to sleep.

"It seems whatever Dante gave him is working. Maybe I need to ask him for some of that miracle drug," I said walking back into the kitchen.

"Dante has been said to be the Miracle Worker by all the Gypsy

Sisters," Brendon said, taking a seat at the breakfast nook.

This gave me the opportunity to ask him about his relationship with the Sisterhood.

"Now that I have finished the final biography, I was wondering if you could enlighten me on your association with this group?" I said, handing Brendon a cup of coffee.

"I'm not sure what you are referring to exactly? As an artist, the Gypsies offer me a great variety of challenging expressions to capture on canvas. Just like many other abstract objects in this city. But, other than that, we have no bonding relationship."

I was trying to determine if the tone in his voice was sincere or defensive. I determined it was a little of both.

"I certainly was not implying that I wanted you to reveal any personal admiration for any of the Gypsies, although you must agree that they are all uniquely beautiful.

*I was simply hoping that you could share with me how Emerald persuaded them to be (in?) this Sisterhood. I am not even certain that I know what the *Sisterhood* is. I certainly have no idea why my Aunt Caroline wanted me to be part of this mysterious group," I said, hoping to clarify my point.

"Perhaps you should ask Caroline that question," Brendon said, sipping his coffee.

"Oh, that is a brilliant idea, except Aunt Caroline is no longer with us. That is why I am here in the first place," I said, trying not to sound annoyed with Brendon's response.

"Saint Augustine is well known for its spiritual and paranormal activities. Many times, the answers to the questions that people have are right in front of them, but they are too busy looking at the landscape to recognize the garden. I suggest that you ask Sunflower at your breakfast meeting," Brendon said, standing up, reaching for his jacket and scarf.

"I didn't tell you about my meeting with Sunflower this morning. How did you know about it?" I said, surprised.

Brendon bent down to where I was sitting, looked directly at me with his crystal blue eyes that reminded me for some reason of Van Gogh's *Starry Night,* and kissed me.

"This is a small town, Princess, not much is a secret around here," Brendon said, leaving from the back door that he entered by.

I am not sure if it was the kiss or the idea that Brendon knew about my meeting that surprised me more. Both were totally unexpected and a bit odd. Nevertheless, I had to admit the kiss was perfection.

It was 3:00 AM before I closed my eyes. When the alarm went off at 10:00 AM, my first reaction was to text Sunflower that I was not going to be able to make it. But then I felt this wet nose on my cheek and realized that it was Lancelot. He was letting me know that it was long past his time for food and a walk.

I managed to drag my body out of the bed, strolled to the kitchen, served Lancelot his daily meal, and texted Kiara, hoping that she could do the walking this morning.

Thankfully, she immediately texted back: *Sure. No problem. I have the key. Will be there at eleven! K*

"Are you satisfied now, Lancelot? Everything is good. Whatever it is that Dante is giving you is making my life much easier too," I said, bending down to give him neck hugs.

Sunflower also texted me, confirming that we were meeting at DOS, a local coffee and wine shop on San Marco at 11:00 AM. Since it was too far for me to walk, and too cold for the bike, driving was my only option. Not a favorite option in St. Augustine with its lack of parking.

I can only imagine that Sunflower chose DOS because from November to the end of January downtown Saint Augustine is inundated with tourists from everywhere, visiting this ancient city during the *Nights of Lights Celebration.* Anyway, as I recall, DOS has its own parking lot and serves the best mocha in town.

When I arrived, there was one table near the window that I immediately claimed. Most of the other ones were taken by Flagler students with laptops out and headphones on. A few minutes later, I saw Sunflower in line at the counter. She texted me that she would get my hot mocha with oat milk and meet me at the table shortly.

I wonder how people like my Aunt Caroline ever survived before cellphones.

"Hey! Good morning, Mandy! How do you feel now that you have completed all the bios? Any interesting insights? I mean, mine was probably quite tame compared to the other girls, I expect," Sunflower said, handing me my hot mocha.

"You haven't read the bios? I just assumed that everyone in the *Sisterhood* had read all the bios," I said, rather surprised.

"Oh, no. Emerald is the only one that knows our past lives. She has always said that she never wants us to forget where we came from, but to always use what we have learned to make a better tomorrow. Emerald has provided each of us with so much knowledge that without her I really am not sure the *Sisterhood* could survive," Sunflower said seriously.

"There are just so many gaps still between my purpose here, Aunt Caroline's role, her friendship with Emerald, and now Brendon," I said, sounding overwhelmed.

"Brendon? What is going on with Brendon? The last time we spoke you were disappointed that he hadn't called. Is there something new that you haven't shared?" Sunflower asked.

I wasn't sure how much I really wanted to share. I definitely was not going to mention the kiss. I was still processing what that might mean.

"Last night, or I suppose early this morning, Brendon stopped by the house after I finished reading your bio. He said that he was driving home from the studio and noticed my lights on. Anyway, more importantly, when we started talking about what was still missing in this scenario that I somehow find myself a part of, I mentioned my Aunt Caroline. He suggested that I ask her directly why I have been included with the Gypsy *Sisterhood*. When I reminded him that Caroline is dead, he suggested that it shouldn't matter and left it at that. His response confused me even further," I said, waiting for Sunflower's reaction.

"What I am about to share with you, Mandy, is not going to be much. Emerald is having a holiday gathering at her home next weekend, before the annual Blackbeard's Gala. It is a tradition to celebrate our blessings, review what we want to accomplish the following year, and naturally rehearse for the Gala. We all expect you to be there at both events. And I can assure you that later everything will begin to make much more sense," Sunflower said.

"Emerald did invite me to both, but I wasn't going since I have nothing to wear. Formal affairs have never been my priority. Besides, I would feel totally out of place," I said.

"Oh, you must go, Mandela. Especially if Emerald has already invited you. Nobody turns down Emerald's invitation. As far as a costume, we have a seamstress that will take care of that for you. You will finally meet our brilliant Rain. She can make a formal gown from a knapsack. You will be absolutely stunning, Mandy. And, of course,

Brendon will be your escort for the evening. That in itself should be all the incentive that you need," Sunflower said, smiling.

It was becoming quite clear that I really had no choice but to ride this perfect storm to its destination, hoping only that no tsunami would be in my path.

Chapter Thirty-Two

There are certain people that will inhabit a small, quiet space inside your heart despite any circumstances, happening or situation. They left a piece of themselves when your souls collided upon impact. And, there they will always subtly remain...

Victoria Erickson
Author, Writing Coach

MANDANA and EMERALD

Somehow everything was finally coming together as Sunflower alluded to that morning that we had breakfast two weeks ago. My 18th century Marie Antoinette gown designed exquisitely by Rain had just the right amount of Pirate Gypsy flair to make it uniquely beautiful. Even the plumed hat reflected a mystique that brought a sense of excellence beyond anything that I was used to. The entire affair resembled a Broadway production, much more elaborate than my traveling *Cats* troupe.

Tonight was Emerald's Holiday Extravaganza. It was much less formal. Everyone was wearing comfortable holiday leggings with fluffy sweaters and bright poinsettia headbands.

Most of the Gypsies had been rehearsing hours earlier for *Blackbeard's Gala and The Enchanted Grove* production. They were all now ready for a relaxing evening with plenty of delicious food catered from some of the best local downtown restaurants, a full bar, and even musical entertainment.

Our first event, however, was in the library movie room. It was located past the dining room and before the outside patio. Everyone was escorted into the massive seating area where every chair was a comfortable recliner. There were exactly fifteen chairs, and once everyone was seated, there were only five chairs remaining vacant.

"I am so very pleased to see you all here tonight at our annual private holiday soirée. As many of you are already familiar with the format, I won't burden you with the details. However, tonight we are also privileged to have with us Mandana Morrison, Caroline's niece. Since Mandy has never attended one of our events, I have prepared a short video that illustrates *Saint Augustine Sisterhood* and why we have dedicated our lives to this movement."

The lights begin to dim, and the screen automatically lowers. There is a black and white photograph of two women. One woman is extremely tall and dark-skinned; she's wearing a brocade elegantly beaded floor length gown. Her arm is extended over a much shorter, simply dressed white woman.

The caption reads: Ella Williams late 1800's.

Everyone in the room is silent, keeping their eyes on the screen, waiting anxiously to hear more. A few more minutes pass before Emerald moves closer to the screen, now holding a small microphone.

"I may not even need to use this silly device to project my voice but what I have to say about Ella Williams and the Saint Augustine Sisterhood needs to resonate in each and every one of you tonight."

This definitely got my attention.

"Ella Williams, who you see pictured here, was born in a small town in the American South to a family of sharecroppers. What made Ella different from others in her similar situation is that she was extraordinarily tall at a very young age for no specific reason. When Ella finally stopped growing, she was over seven feet tall and the tallest woman documented in the African origin community.

Growing up with this stigma was challenging. Sometimes as challenging as the prejudice that she faced as a young black child in the South. But her parents, who were born into slavery and now free, were determined that Ella overcome all the odds against her. They encouraged her to embrace her uniqueness and use it to achieve her dreams.

In a time when prejudice and injustice were rampant, Ella became a diligent student, escaping from all her inhibitions through the pages of books that transported her to new and different worlds.

Mr. Johnson, a traveling showman, heard about Ella's extraordinary stature. He made an offer to her family that he would add Ella to his show in a special program. However, Ella was reluctant to be swayed by this exploitation. Instead she teamed with a charismatic young preacher that suggested the two of them join the circus to promote messages of hope and equality. They formulated a plan to challenge societal norms by promoting understanding.

Ella's act in the circus showcased not only her height, but also her charm and eloquence while Isaiah used his platform beside Ella to deliver powerful speeches on equality and the necessity to embrace diversity. Ella and Isiah's journey with the circus became a powerful force to break down racial barriers.

It was Ella's courage to challenge societal norms that paved the way for you ladies to remind the world that strength comes in all shapes and sizes." Emerald motioned for the theatre lights to be turned on.

Everyone in the room applauded Emerald's speech. A few of the Gypsies came over to personally thank her for choosing them to be a part of her "dream team" as they referred to the *Sisterhood.*

There was no doubt in my mind that Emerald was a phenomenal leader. My only question was: Where was she leading us?

As if she was reading my mind, Emerald announced that after a fifteen-minute beverage intermission the next slide on *The Road to Sisterhood* would begin.

"So, Mandy, are some of your doubts and questions finally being answered?" Sunflower asked, handing me a glass of Chardonnay.

"That was quite a speech. I am beginning to understand that everything that Emerald wants the Gypsy Dancers to do requires authentic passion. Only then will there be any harmony. What I am not sure is where that devotedness comes from," I said, anxious now to hear what will follow next.

"You are on the very edge of a blossoming relationship with the world, Mandana. At any moment thousands of flowers will burst forward from your mind. But it is those insecurities that continue to prevent the blooming process from beginning. Somewhere, for some reason, you stopped believing that anything is possible. We have all been at that wailing wall listening to the negative voices calling out our names. Stop looking for those dreams elsewhere; they are here." Sunflower placed her hand on my heart. And, for one very brief moment, just like that first meeting with Brendon, I knew that the truth I was waiting for was just waiting to be spoken.

The thousands of blossoms that I had been waiting a lifetime for were about to explode into a color, fragrance, and delightful joy never experienced before.

"Alright, lovely Gypsy Sisters, if you will take your seats for one last time, we are going to introduce our newest *Sister* to the *Road to Sisterhood.*"

This was the first time that Emerald or anyone else referred to me as *Sister*. I was hoping that after this film I would understand what *Sister* means.

Each slide presented an interesting exhibition. The first one was titled *Women Masters, By curator Rocio de la villa, Madrid, Spain.*

Although it features women artists from 1500 to the early 1900's, it is the connection and contribution that shows us how effective *Sisterhood* has become from its early conception in 1390 when the term *Sisterhood* was first introduced by British writer John Gower in *The Lover's Confession.*

When Medea, wife of Jason, sends a golden mantle to Jason's new wife Creusa, and she dies after wearing it, Gower writes that the Sisterhood Creusa believed was genuine with Medea is false.

This brings out an important distinction between the rivalry of false Sisterhood that even in our current community we need to understand and always be aware of once a toxic relationship between women surfaces there is no positive outcome in continuing friendships. The entire crux of the *Sisterhood* ideal stems from honesty, respect, and gratitude.

The next slide introduces *Flower Power* in the *Sisterhood* movement. The artistic examples are a testimony to the early gentile role botany played with women who shared delightful afternoons exploring natural wonders that surrounded them.

Our environment certainly encourages us to celebrate in our movements those natural experiences we encounter with nature. Just as we acknowledge that *Sisterhood* is a bond that goes beyond family ties, the connection that we form with one another allows us to build each other up, being together through the light and dark journey.

As Gypsy dancers, this is our goal. To share the validation and affirmation that we have with one another and a community that needs to hear and see our stories.

Our Sisterhood saga is unifying unbroken Circle where each member contributes a unique interlocking chain that connects the past with the present and the future."

Once again, all the Gypsy dancers were on their feet, dancing, laughing. This time everyone encircled Emerald with loving embraces. I was now included in their Circle, and that Circle felt complete.

I felt Emerald take my hand at the same time that my cellphone started vibrating.

"I am so sorry. I have to take this call; it's from Kiara," I said, moving away.

"Mandy, it's Lancelot. I stopped by to feed him, and he was on the kitchen floor lethargic. I called Dante, and he is on his way over, but I think you need to come home also," Kiara said.

"I'm on my way. I should be there in 10 minutes max," I said, suddenly realizing that I had not driven here. Where was Sunflower?

"Is everything okay?" Emerald asked.

"No. It's Lancelot, my dog. I need to get home as soon as possible, and I can't find Sunflower," I said, trying to catch my breath.

"It's going to be okay. I'll take you home," Emerald said, calmly.

"You can't leave your own party, Emerald. I can take an Uber," I said, trying to locate the app.

"Nonsense. Come with me," Emerald said.

Before I knew it, we were turning the corner at Riberia and pulling into my driveway. The car next to the curb must have been Dante's.

Once inside, Emerald went directly to where Lancelot was lying on the kitchen floor. She sat down next to him and cradled his head. After a few moments, his eyes opened.

"What do you think you're doing, you silly goose. I told you when I left to be good and I would bring you home soon, now look at you," Emerald said, trying to maintain her calm composure.

"How is he, Dante?" I asked, standing behind Emerald rather confused at what was happening.

"I gave him an injection that should bring him back to normal for a few days," he said, directing his answer to Emerald rather than me.

Emerald took a deep breath, and asked, "How much time do we have?"

"Maybe a week or ten days. You know what must be done, Caroline," Dante said, walking through the back door.

Caroline? What did Dante mean by calling Emerald Caroline? And what is happening in ten days?

Chapter Thirty-Three

Sometimes in order to see reality illusion needs to be shattered.
Chitra nakshatra

EMERALD

The entire *Sisterhood* project started once Liam and I realized that although we were able to move throughout the multiple layers of time, we really still had no control over how long each era we occupied would last.

There were other logistical challenges as well. For example, Liam and I both had DNA that somehow contributed to our extended longevity, but this did not protect us from any of the other dangers, including murder, fatal accidents, or such minor bodily injury as concussions.

During my time in Boston in the late seventeenth century, there were innocent women being accused of witchcraft while at the same time others were practicing a variety of much more dangerous acts without being noticed.

Liam and I, of course, were both very aware of the severity of these accusations as well as the outcome.

The most difficult part in these situations is always remaining silent when you know that what will happen is tragic. On the other hand, sharing our knowledge that could prevent the deaths of innocent people might change the course of future events or lead to our own demise.

There were also times that Liam and I were separated without ever knowing if we would be reunited again. That made us as vulnerable as the rest of the human race. It was during one of those separations and reunions that Liam suggested that we memorize lines from *Little Gidding,* a poem by TS Eliot, our favorite poet. This would be a way that assured us that wherever we were, in whatever different physical form, we would recognize each other. It was actually quite brilliant and never failed.

It was during one of our last time lapses together that we made the decision to find a city that would offer the least number of changes. A home base that we could return to on a regular basis.

At the time we were in Connemara, Ireland, during the sixteenth century. Ireland was our birth country but neither Liam nor I had any idea how this visit to Connemara would influence the rest of our lives regardless how long that might be.

It was also in Ireland where we originally met as Brigid and Liam, fell in love, and learned to love one another no matter what bodies we would later possesses.

As fate might have it, this time I was on a pirate ship, *The White Seahorse,* whose captain was Grace O'Malley. Liam was also there as her first mate. What I learned from Grace's story led me to Saint Augustine and the determination to establish a *Sisterhood* of Gypsy dancers that would promote a harmonious lifestyle as a model for anyone that they would encounter.

When Grace was a young child, she cut her own hair short enough to be disguised as a boy to join her father's seafaring adventures. From that time on, people would refer to Grace as Granuaile, meaning bald Grace.

From that early age, Grace traveled throughout Europe until the age of sixteen when she married Donal of the O'Flaherty Clan. At this time, inconveniently they were the sworn enemies of the O'Malleys, forcing Grace to move to her husband's home at Bunowen Castle, near Ballyconnely in Galloway.

Once Grace started having children, it eased the tensions between the two clans. Then her father passed away, the children were grown, and Grace took over her father's whole fleet, which controlled most of Ireland's west coast.

It soon became known that Grace's fleets that traveled to many countries selling a variety of goods, were not always legal. Grace soon became known as the *Pirate Queen.*

It was during this time that Liam and I met Grace. After the death of her husband in battle, she remarried another powerful chieftain, Richard Bourke. This marriage meant that Grace was now dividing her time between several castles as well as sea adventures. It often also meant fighting many battles against neighboring tribes, most notably the Joyce's, who proved to be quite challenging.

In 1586, after Grace's enemy Richard Bingham attempted to remove her titles and seize her land, she requested a meeting with Queen Elizabeth. It was granted. When they met, Grace refused to bow to Elizabeth, stating that she was herself a Queen and therefore they were equals.

The communication that took place between the two was entirely in Latin, since Grace spoke no English. Nevertheless, at the conclusion, Queen Elizabeth restored many of Grace's titles and most of her land.

When Grace returned home to share this story with me, I decided it was time to share my story with her as well. During most of our time travels, it is much safer for Liam and I to become familiar with our territory and remain as much under the radar as possible when it comes to details.

This, however, was a different experience. Grace was a powerful, independent Irish woman that I trusted and respected. What I was learning from her I now realized was what I needed to teach others less confident than me.

Grace was not surprised by my story. She had heard of other time travelers from her sea voyages to Europe but had never met any, particularly not an Irish woman time traveler.

It was after I shared Liam's and my story that Grace gave me a map to a location that she called *Stonehenge*.

"If you should sense anything going wrong while you are here, my Sister Emerald, take this map with my permission for you to meet with *Druid Maidens*. They will assist you to leave this century safely," Grace said.

It was the first time anyone had ever referred to me as *Sister*.

Three weeks later, the very first time that I had ever felt the need to be prepared for an exit, I summoned Liam, shared with him Grace's map and we were on the next ship leaving Ireland to England. Locating Stonehenge was an entirely different experience.

Arriving at Liverpool from Dublin Port was much easier than traveling from Liverpool to Stonehenge by carriage, the only practical way to travel during the sixteenth century. To add to this dilemma, in the sixteenth century, Stonehenge was not a tourist attraction as it is today. Nobody understood why anyone would want to travel there unless they were Druids or perhaps witches.

To put this into perspective, it was not until the eighteenth century that scholars noted that there was a relationship between the lunar and solar calendar.

And, to add further confusion to our visit, we were aware that the first known excavation by the Duke of Buckingham in 1620 would not even start for another twenty years. The famous Aubrey Holes, named after the antiquary John Aubrey, who was the first to record the ring of pits in the late seventeenth century were not yet discovered.

Yet none of this mattered much to Liam and me. All that we needed was a passage that would safely transport us to another world; it really did not matter which world as long as we were together. You can, therefore, imagine our surprise and delight when we were greeted at Liverpool by a carriage and two guides that were prepared to take us to our destination.

Although not much was shared with us as to where or how long our journey would last, we trusted our benefactors implicitly. The male was dressed in a traditional Druid white knee length tunic with a bird feathered cloak and his hair plaited in braids. On his head was a bird-speckled headdress that resembled a helmet with fluttering wings.

With this man was a female companion also dressed in an ankle length printed frock. An attractive white apron tied to the shoulders covered her entire outfit. A black cloak or shawl covered her braided head, reminding me of pictures I had seen of the Celtic war goddess Catubodua.

Once we arrived at Stonehenge, we were immediately greeted by the head priestesses who instructed us on what we could expect next.

"We have been informed by a mutual trusted friend that you and your companion are time travelers. If this is accurate, your ability to enter Earth's Chakra should be successful with nothing preventing either of you from entering a new world," said the high priestess.

I then asked permission to move forward. Not familiar with the protocol in regard to this particular circumstance, I waited for a signal. The priestess acknowledged my request by gesturing, nodding her head that she approved it.

"Although we have traveled previously, this will be our first attempt at changing our location at our will. Can you provide us with any further advice once we arrive at our new destination?" I asked, foreseeing that we might need to do this again in the near future, depending on where we were taken.

"What I am able to provide you is knowledge. As you are aware, there is nothing concrete that you are able to transport with you. Even the clothes that you are now wearing will change once you arrive in your new world. However, what is in your mind remains with you. It is your responsibility to be able to filter the necessary components, since as you are aware by now there is much that you accumulate wherever you travel.

"Therefore, what I am going to share with you is essential. Shadows. Always remember that shadows will lead you to new beginnings or past lives. They are the mobile portals wherever you travel.

"The next essential lesson is to create your own home base. This is where you are able to return, refresh, and teach. Teaching others is your mission. Without this knowledge there is no purpose, and your gift begins to fade away into a void. None of us want to be in a void."

"May I ask one more question, worthy priestess?" I asked, while trying to absorb all that I was told.

The priestess once again affirmed my request.

"How do I know where my home base will be?" I asked, confused.

"Only you are able to determine the answer to that question. When the time comes, you will know," the priestess said, leading Liam and me to a secluded waiting area hut that resembled the entrance to a cave.

"You have said nearly nothing about this pending transformation since we left Ireland weeks ago. Why haven't you contributed any thoughts to this venture?" I asked, finally realizing that Liam may be ill, or maybe even worse, just tired of being with me.

"This is the first time in weeks, Brigid, that you have asked for my opinion. Does it even matter at this point? After all, here we are, about to leave for the unknown at any moment," Liam said, sounding more concerned than irritated.

Whenever Liam referred to me as Brigid, it was a warning that he was not happy with my actions. But there was little that I could do to change the situation.

"What is it exactly that you seem to be disturbed about, darling?" I asked, not expecting the response that he was to provide.

"Now that you are finally asking, I am concerned with us attempting to take control of an uncontrollable situation. Have you forgotten that when we first were separated and then reunited it was entirely unexpected? We have no idea why or when transformations are going to occur but somehow, they always benefit us. We have never been separated, and the time travel comes at the most inopportune time. Once we begin to make adjustments to this, I fear that complications will be beyond our control," Liam said, sounding quite stoic.

He was right. I had not thought about the consequences. But now that the priestess had enlightened me about ways to avoid disasters and improve on the experience, I was anxious to get started.

"You may be right, Liam, but sometimes we must take destiny into our own hands. Finding a home base will assure us that if separation does occur there will be a reliable solution. Do you have any suggestions as to where that home base should be?" I asked, hoping that by including Liam in this most important decision he would forgive me for my earlier self-centered actions.

"I do agree that now that we are here, at this time, we must go forward with the priestess' plan. Let's decide before our departure to assure that if complications arise, we will be able to recover," Liam said.

After several hours of reviewing some of our most favorite places, Liam suggested an unknown location that he recalled learning about when we were in Spain during the sixteenth century, ironically the same century we were presently in.

The colony was located in America, one region that we had never heard of. It was founded by a Spanish admiral, Pedro Menendez, in 1565 and named Saint Augustine, honoring St. Augustine of Hippo since his ships landed on shore on the date that the Saint is honored.

I liked the idea that it was a town that offered a spiritual experience. Of course, at this time I had no idea that I would be living during the twenty-first century in the most ancient city of America, or that I was certainly not the only spirit from the outside world to reside there. That epiphany would come much later.

Thankful that Liam and I had resolved our differences, we were now prepared to move forward. What neither of us was prepared for was where we arrived.

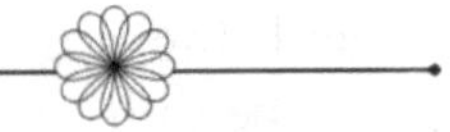

Chapter Thirty-Four

Do not live half a life
And do not die a half death
If you chose silence
Then be silent
When you speak do so until you are
Finished
If you accept then accept it bluntly
Do not mask it
If you refuse than be clear about it
For an ambiguous refusal is but a weak
Acceptance
Do not accept half a solution
Do not believe half truths
Do not dream half a dream
Do not fantasize about half hopes
Half the way will get you nowhere
You are a whole that exists to live a life
Not half a life

Khalil Gibran
(The Prophet)

Emerald and Sunflower

It was not until my trip to Boston in search of Rain that I first met
Khalil. It was only for a brief moment when he stopped in at the
shop where his mother was a seamstress, but it was a moment
worth recalling throughout my travels.

On the way out of the shop, we nearly collided on the front
sidewalk. After mutual apologies were exchanged, Khalīl hesitated for
a few seconds, turned to me, and said,

"What I am about to say right now makes no sense to either one of us, but I have no doubt that there is a divine purpose that I must share it with you. Never live a half life, my dear friend. You have been sent here to live a whole life; now go forward and fulfill that destiny."

We never met again. No other words were ever exchanged. Yet, years later I bought *The Prophet,* by Khalil Gibran where those words appeared once again.

Liam's instincts proved valid. During our departure from Stonehenge, we were separated. I had no idea where he was when I woke up on a bed in a suburban neighborhood in California in the twentieth century.

Later I was told by a charming young woman that they found me passed out on the front steps of her porch, called an emergency rescue team, who revived me and found nothing wrong with my vital signs. That is when the kind lady led me to a bedroom where I must have fallen asleep for several days.

When I awoke, I discovered that she and her husband were undocumented immigrants from Persia.

They had decided that it would be safer for them to keep me in their home, for at least a little while, than risk the authorities learning the truth about their status.

Later I learned that The Morrison's, were sponsored by major corporations that were hiring educated immigrants to work for their companies for far less money, but with the guarantee that they could obtain their citizenship papers expediently while earning a reasonable salary in a safe environment.

Actually, although illegal, it was a win-win situation for everyone.

Although at the time I was unaware of the many political ramifications of this arrangement, it certainly was a convenient solution for me while I tried to determine where Liam was, how to find Saint Augustine, what I was to do for finances, etc. Adding to all of this confusion, during my next follow-up doctor's appointment, it was discovered that I was pregnant.

WHAT? Pregnant! Impossible!

For the past two hundred years Liam and I spent together, not once was there any chance that I would become pregnant. Even after many years of desperately trying before all the time travel started, we were told it would never happen.

So now that I am in the twentieth century, and my husband is missing, fate has determined that it is my time to give birth?

Marissa and John, my benefactors, were as surprised as I was when they were told the news. Then I had to explain to them the complete story and why it would be impossible for me to keep the baby.

That was when Marissa and John proposed that rather than have an abortion, I could give the baby to them to raise. It sounded like a possibility as long as I could remain here long enough to give birth.

Once the decision was made, the Morrison's decided to transfer to the Carmel Valley in Northern California where nobody knew them after the birth of our baby. They also agreed to provide me with the financial stability to move to Saint Augustine, Florida, although I really had no idea where that was.

The following nine months I spent reading, researching, and meditating. I also kept praying to all the Gods in the universe that they would allow me to remain in this century for the birth of our child.

That is how I now referred to this life to be as not mine but Marissa's and John's as well.

After exactly nine months and nine hours from the day I arrived in California, our daughter Mandana Morrison was born. Within seconds of those first breaths, I handed Liam's and my daughter into the living arms of her new parents, Marissa and John Morrison.

It was not until Mandana was about eight years old that I visited the Morrison's again at their request. Marissa had been diagnosed with breast cancer. She wanted to be assured that if it was fatal, I would promise to stay in contact with Mandana as her "Aunt."

John would, of course, be there for her as much as possible, but Marissa reminded me that they had no relatives in this country. If anything were to happen to John, Mandana would be an orphan and possibly deported to Pakistani. A fate that Marissa wanted to assure would never happen.

I tried to assure them both that I would do whatever I could, but not ever knowing what my future would be it was impossible to guarantee Mandana's security.

Then I saw my child. She was the perfect combination of love between Liam and me, held together in this petit flawless body. Her ocean blue eyes were exact replicas of Liam's. And, when she tilted her head to the side with a half-smile, it was as if I was staring in a mirror.

That is the moment I decided to establish the greatest group of women that I could find on this earth to share their talents with each other and my daughter when the time comes. The Saint Augustine Sisterhood was born.

Then the complications started. Once the Sisterhood formed, I had to find a way to bring Mandana to Saint Augustine without revealing who I was until I could locate Liam.

"That is not as difficult as you are making it sound," Sunflower said one day while we were brainstorming.

"What do you have in mind? It can't be anything too crazy, or Mandana will never even respond. I know this because she has my skeptical genes running through her veins," I said in a doubtful tone.

"We'll have your attorney contact Mandana, explaining that you have passed away and as her only living relative she is the executor of the estate.

"We will then arrange for a mock funeral, allow her a few months to read letters left by you and the Gypsies' bios, and finally reveal the truth once she realizes how great Saint Augustine and the Sisterhood are. You can even be part of this façade since she really has no idea what you look like. It is a perfect plan," Sunflower said confidently.

"It may sound perfect now, but I have no idea how she will react once she learns the truth. And she must be told the truth since she is carrying the longevity genes like Liam and me," I said, revealing the real necessity for our reunion.

In addition, I needed enough time to bring Liam back to meet his daughter.

That was the conversation Sunflower and I had six months ago. What I did not foresee was Lancelot's reaction to this façade, nor Brendon surfacing and showing romantic interests in Mandana.

Brendon is a time traveler as well. He has also become best friends with Liam, although I am certain that he has not shared his affections for Mandana with her father. Brendon is also one of the only people that Liam entrusted our secret poem with as a safety measure to identify one of us if our form is altered.

For some odd reason at this very moment my mind is filled with Shakespeare warning me in the words spoken by Puck in *Midsummer's Night Dream:*

If we shadows have offended
Think of this, and all is
Mended
That you have but slumbered

Here
While these visions did appear
And this weak and idle theme
No more yielding than a dream
Gentle do not reprehend. (V.I)

Just as Puck echoes the concerns of being misunderstood, I can only hope that Mandana can understand that our intent as "shadows" is no more than a reflection of the hidden truth.

Chapter Thirty-Five

Integrity is telling myself the truth. And honesty is telling the truth to other people. Truth without love is brutality, and love without truth is hypocrisy. An unbelieved truth can hurt a man much more than a lie.

Spencer Johnson

The Grand Finale

What do you mean you aren't going to Blackbeard's Ball?" Sunflower said, loud enough for some of the guests in the coffee shop to stop talking and turn around to stare at us.

"I can't go! I mean how can I even believe anything that anyone tells me in this town anymore?" I said, disgusted.

"Is this still about Dante the other night calling Emerald Caroline?" Sunflower asked in a much more subtle tone.

"No, not exactly. It is about nobody explaining to me why I am here and what is expected of me. I get half-truths from people or bios of people that I hardly know. What is it that makes everything in this town a mystery?" I asked, frustrated.

"Maybe you are just overreacting to what happened. Emerald and your aunt were very close friends. Almost like sisters I would say. It was just a natural mistake for Dante to refer to Emerald as Caroline," I said, hoping that was enough to mend any broken fences.

Mandana said nothing for a few minutes as if she was mentally processing what was happening. She reminded me of Emerald at that moment. Both were quite meticulous and very stubborn. I was just hoping once Mandana learned the truth it would not result (in a backdraft effect.

At the end of our lunch, I was fairly certain that she had changed her mind about going to the ball.

"Okay? So, we are set for Blackbeard's tomorrow night?" I asked, wanting to confirm our plans before we left.

"Yes, as of now. Of course, a house could land on me on the way home, or the wicked witch from the east might send me poisoned apples when I arrive home. But, barring all catastrophes, I will see you tomorrow night at the Lightner," Mandana said, in a much more playful tone.

"Well, I do think that you are slightly mixing your wicked witch allusions but besides all that I can't wait to celebrate with you tomorrow night," Sunflower said, following Mandana through the exit door. It did seem like the longest twenty-four hours that I had ever experienced.

Even giving birth for nine hours seemed less stressful than this."

What if I cannot convince Mandana why it was necessary for this charade to bring her here?

Will everything that I set out to accomplish the past twenty years finally result in a simply vain attempt to gain control over a life that none of us have control over?

"Are you second guessing yourself again, my darling?" I heard a familiar voice from the back of the bedroom near the window say.

When I was finally able to see beyond the shadows on the wall, I recognized the intimate movement that I have known for several centuries.

"LIAM?" I shouted, knowing it was him before he said another word, but still stunned at how much he resembled the same Liam I remembered losing twenty-five years ago.

Liam said nothing else but swept me immediately off my feet, threw me on the bed, and there was only one intimate thought rushing through his brain, which unfortunately I had to stop before it became more than I could handle myself.

"What are you doing?" Liam said, as I pushed his hard body away from me.

"We can't do this right now! I cannot go into a lengthy diatribe at the moment," I said, breathing heavily.

"But we have a daughter that is waiting for us at Blackbeard's Ball. And, she has been waiting for twenty- five years to meet you without even knowing it," I said, attempting to pull myself back together in a presentable form.

"A daughter? How is that possible? And what is a Blackbeard Ball?" Liam asked, totally confused.

"There is far too much to explain at this moment. I will try to tell you as much as possible on the way to the gala. You do look amazing, Liam. Perfectly dressed. Where did you come from in that formal attire?" I asked, impressed by all the medals.

"I am glad that you approve. I was a general during the Napoleonic era and thankfully transported just before being sent to Siberia in the freezing winter. I do much prefer this climate in this strange place you call Florida?" Liam asked, verifying we were in the correct location.

I nodded, confirming that he was correct. Whatever it was that the priestess did when we were first transported from Stonehenge made it possible for Liam to return to the home base even if it did take him twenty-five years to arrive.

Once we entered the Lightner and all of the Gypsy dancers saw me with Liam, they rushed to greet us. I am not sure who was more overwhelmed, Liam or the Sisterhood. The people I could not see were Brendon and Mandana.

I decided to take the opportunity to greet the Royal Family of Saint Augustine. Sunflower had suggested that I request they make the announcement once Mandana arrives that there is a formal declaration. At that time Liam, who was not originally included since we had no idea where he was, and I will be formally knighted for our service to the community. Then Mandana will be summoned when the announcement is made that she is officially acknowledged as the daughter of Liam and Caroline Marie Bridgid O'Sullivan Callahan bestowed with the same royal rights as her parents.

Sunflower's suggestion is quite brilliant. Although Mandana may be slightly shocked at the news, it is unlikely that she will react improperly. I will then announce that my daughter is the legitimate heir to the Saint Augustine Sisterhood with all of the privileges to continue the mission that our group has dedicated itself to providing for over one hundred and twenty-five years to this community.

At that point there will be champagne flowing and an abundance of toasts with fireworks being set off over the Matanzas Inlet.

What could possibly go wrong?

I really do not even want to imagine.

Five minutes later, Mandana, dressed ironically in a Marie Antoinette inspired ball gown, is escorted into the hall by the dashing and debonair Brendon O'Malley, wearing the exact same uniform as Liam.

Why had I never realized that Brendon's surname was the same as the Pirate Queen, Grace? Could he be her son? Not the time to ask now. Too many other important details to deal with this evening.

"Brendon? Who are those people sitting at the elegant table in the front, dressed as royalty with crowns?" Mandana whispered.

"Those are the Royal Family of Saint Augustine. They only appear at the most regal events.

To be selected as part of the Royal trio, the applicants must have family genealogy that traces back to the Minorcan survivors who settled in Saint Augustine in 1777.

Amazingly, most of this group is able to trace their heritage back to the Spanish who settled here in the 1500's. A committee selects the trio that will represent the same royal family of Spain who was in power in 1672, the same year that construction began on Castillo de San Marcos. Those who are chosen will portray Queen Mariana of Spain, King Juan Carlos, and Princess Margarita Maria. Just as a FYI, if for any reason you or we are called up in front of the Royal Family, remember to curtsy or bow, and most of all show respect," Brendon said quietly as we walked past the bar and Buffett and took a place at a table in the front row of the stage.

"Are we allowed to sit here?" Mandana asked, skeptical.

Brendon picked up the place cards with their names printed in gold, which Mandana totally ignored while listening to his historical commentary.

"You can trust me, babe. I will even keep your head safe during this event," he said, snickering.

Mandana intentionally ignored his bad joke.

Once the lights began to fade, sitting so close to the stage Mandana noticed one of Emerald's Gypsy Dancers dressed as a Shaman enter holding a microphone.

Although her face was painted, and she was wearing an elaborate peacock headpiece, she could tell it was Whisper. She had never heard her speak before but recalled the bio of her life in Miami.

When Whisper began to introduce the story of the Enchanted Grove awakening with the magical creatures, the entire Alcazar dining room was silent. She was capturing over three hundred people's attention. Although the violinist, sword dancers, forest fairies, talking trees, statuesque roses, and drummers were all superb, it was Whisper's narration that everyone was raving over.

During the performance, Mandana never realized that we were

seated by ourselves until she recognized all of the Sisterhood dancers performing, including Sunflower and Emerald.

Once they took their final bows, everyone was back at the table, returning with a standing ovation. Emerald took the seat next to Mandana. Sunflower sat on the other side, near Brendon. Just as Mandana was about to congratulate both of them with bouquets of flowers that Brendon somehow managed to bring with them without her noticing, the Royal Family stood up, and the room was silent once again.

This time it was Mandana's name that was being called. She looked around not knowing what to do, noticing that Emerald was no longer next to her. That was when Brendon stood up, took her arm and led her to the Royal Table before she had a chance to say anything.

Once they were standing in front of the Royal Family who at this time were also standing, Mandana noticed Emerald on her right side with a strange man next to her, dressed in the same uniform as Brendon.

All eyes were on them.

"What am I doing here?" Mandana asked, her voice trembling.

"No need to panic," Brendon was whispering, holding her hand tightly.

Mandana heard nothing after that. All she was doing was following a script that Brendon was repeating in her ear, until he placed her hand into the matching gentleman's hand standing nearby.

That is when Mandana heard Emerald say to her, "I am honored, my dearest only child to introduce you to your father Liam."

My father? And Emerald my mother? Not possible! But wait? Is Emerald also Caroline?

I turned directly to Emerald, and for the very first time I could feel the connection. I did not *know* how or why, but it was there. My mother, father, and me.

"Are you okay?" Brendon asked, holding my other hand now even tighter.

"I think so. I am not sure why, but yes, I am," I said.

Before I could ask any more questions, the Gypsy dancers surrounded me.

"Don't fear anything, Mandana, our spirit is going to lift you to a level that you have never reached before," Sunflower said, and suddenly I was dancing, almost floating.

It was truly a magical evening, but the next morning was when I knew that I had found not only my Sisterhood, but my forever family.

"I am so sorry, Mandy, for all the secrets and charades that were needed to get you here but, because of the complications in your father's and my life, there did not seem to be any other way," Emerald said, as we sat on the porch on her patio enjoying a late breakfast.

"The previous Mandana might have reacted differently, but Mandy is just extremely happy to learn that she has a family that loves her this much to create such a spectacular production," I said.

"Dr. Dante will be meeting with you later to explore and explain to you all of the scientific details surrounding your longevity, which by the way Brendon also has access to, just in case you were curious," Emerald added.

Whatever happens between Brendon and me, I am certain has somehow been played out before in another life. Finding out how we have found each other now will just add to the many chapters in my life.

"I also know that Lancelot must be thrilled you have returned. Dante suggested that there might be a time lapse needed soon?" I said hoping that nothing had expired yet.

"No need to worry, Mandy. Lancelot, Liam, and I will be taking a short, well-deserved retreat soon, but, once we return, life in Saint Augustine will resume as it always has for over six hundred years," Emerald said, handing me the final scroll from the Sisterhood, tied with purple ribbon, violets, and with my name printed in gold.

By the time I opened it to read, Emerald, Liam, and Lancelot had all vanished.

It was only Sunflower and I.

"Let me have the honor to share the Grand Finale with you, Mandy," Sunflower said, taking the scroll from my hand.

Tabula Rasa

Inside yourself you will now find

A preserve which you can claim.

As your own.

Avoid the need for fault finding,

Rather, open up your arms to embrace.

That every seed and weed

Is nourished by the knowledge

That the soul is made richer

By Sunshine, Calypso, Rain, Jada
And loving Whispers
Your Sisters
Your Life Lines
To a world preparing to burst into
Blossom
Your Loving Mother,
Caroline, Marie Brigid, Emerald, O'Sullivan Callahan

It was the perfect ending to a perfect beginning.

Bibliography

Binder, Julie *The Big Fat Truth About Gypsy Life.* The guardian.com. February 25, 2011.

Carmona, Sarah. *New Perspectives of The Genesis of Gypsy History.* European History of Mediterranean.

Eichler, Liz. *Cincy Fringe 2023 Reviee of Thread and Bone.* June 6, 2023.

Explore Yoga, Meditation, and Ayurveda Retreats in India. Gypsyatman.com.

Explore the Ancient Roots of Yoga. Google Arts & Culture.

Exploring Vintage North Beach. thenorthtropic.com.

Golden, Tyler. *Why is 5/8/77 Cornell Thought to be the Greatest Grateful Dead Concert?* Farartmagazine.co. I'm. March 4, 2023.

Glynn, Mary. *Memories of a Green Street in the 1920's.* Jamaica Plain Society.

Haliczer, Jay. *Krews Through Time: 300 Years of Mardi Gras.*whereat.com February 15, 2023

Huxley, Aldous. *The Doors of Perception/ Heaven and Hell.* 1954.

(The) Irish Woman Who was the Last Witch Hanged in Boston. Irish central.com. November 16, 2023.

Johnston, Kathleen. *The 18 Bob Marley Facts You Need to Know.* GW Magazine.com.uk. February 6, 2021.

Lessons from a Gypsy Lifestyle. Yogaonthebeach.com.

Lucey, Candice. *What is a Gypsy? Their Beliefs and Lifestyle Explained.* Christianity.com. October 12, 2023.

Mohammad, Farrah. *The Pirate Creed.* Jstor Daily. Daily.jstor.org. July 31, 2018.

Nicks, Stevie. *On Gypsy. Inherownwords.com.*

(The) Old Religion and the Druids Lifting the Veil on the Mysterious Priests of Early Itey. Brehonscedmu.org. March 26, 2023.

O' Mahony, Olivia. *Folklore Friday: The Six Greatest Love Stories of Irish Myth. Shamrock gift.com.* January 21, 2022.

Pennycooke, Makecha. *The Power of Sisterhood.* November 20, 2023.

Raff, Katherine. *The Roman Banquet.*metmuseum.org. October 2011.

*Religion and Expressive Culture-Osage.*every culture.com.

Rhodes, T.S. *Black Pirates/The Pirate Empire.*

Russian Gypsy Band Munster. Scarlettentertainment.com.

Sunflower Facts Symbolism & History Guide. Bloomandwil.com.

Walker, Malea. *The Osage in Historic Newspapers. Envy, Ridicule, and Racism. Headliners and Heroes.* November 30, 2021.

What to Know About 'Killers of the Moon," A Guide to the Osage Murders. Nytimes.com.

Wington, Patti. *The Magical Legend of Tir na nOg. Learnteligion.org. April 22, 2018.*

Petr, Yurchenko. *Evolution and Methodology of Gypsy Dance in the 21st Century.gypsydance.org.*

Zaru, Deena. *The Jingle Dress: The Story Behind a Native American Dance and its Power of Spiritual Healing. ABC news.go.com.* November 15, 2021.

Gypsy Pirate Players of Saint Augustine

Photo Credit: Stephen Rosché
Facebook: Stephen Rosché

About the Author

Eleanor Tremayne is an award-winning author of six novels, *Destiny Revisited, Destiny Revealed, Seven Days in Lebanon, The Mermaids Grandson, High Tea with Ophelia,* and *The Agape Journey.*

Literary Titan Book Awards writes:
"The Agape Journey is one finely and researched and executed work that can be read as a postmodern female Bildungsroman. The narration by protagonist Imani creates a gripping story from the very beginning till the last words."

Moving to Saint Augustine, Florida in July 2019 with her husband Mark, and her beloved Weimaraner, Enya inspired Eleanor every day to continue with her passion for writing. In June 2023 Eleanor and Mark had to say goodbye to their much-loved Enya who was fifteen years old.

Eleanor has included a tribute to Enya in Sisterhood as Lancelot her